Age of Consent

The Cruel Side of Love

Jiffy Day

Author

This is a work of fiction. Names, characters, businesses, places, events and incidents are either the products of the author's imagination or used in a fictitious manner. Any resemblance to actual persons, living or dead, or actual events is purely coincidental.

-Adult Content-

ISBN #13: 978-0-578-56442-5

Chapter 1

My name is Donna Grant. I was born and raised across the New River in Galax, Virginia. But the town of Fries has meant so much to me that I come here to be alone and sit by the river. The name of the town is pronounced as *freeze*, but spelled as *fries*. When I have the time, I come here to read my diary to bring back a time in my life that was so exciting I had to write it down as I experienced it.

I said my name is Donna, but when I was a very young my father started calling me Princess and it stuck. My father was a well-educated, hard-working man. His father owned a lumber mill and provided building materials for the surrounding towns in Southwest Virginia. My father helped his father manage the lumber yards. He also had his real estate license. He was well known and well-liked by most of the people in the area. Remember the saying about being born with a silver spoon in your mouth? That was me. I had everything I asked my dad for. I was his little girl and what his little girl wanted, Dad got for me. I never thought of myself as pretty because I wasn't. You could say I was that ugly duckling, homely but rich.

I never made many friends in life, mainly because I was told I was better than everybody else. It took me a long time to realize that was just not true. I could tell you all kinds of things about my very young years, but it's the same old story about a spoiled little rich girl. I did have one special friend, Michelle. Her dad was the president of the local bank. Our parents got along and Michelle became my best friend, my only friend.

Dad could have sent me to a private school, but Mom wanted me to get in the real world before I went to college. In a small town like Galax, you could tell the haves and the have-nots, I was told there were certain people I shouldn't be around.

The bad thing about me and Michelle being best friends was that we thought we were above people. We had a bad habit of making fun of them just so we could laugh and think we were superior. I often think about how many people Michelle and I made fun of and how we hurt them. One day we actually had a little girl crying because we were laughing at her dress and how she looked. We gave no thought that other people were not as privileged as we were. Our parents could afford to buy us good clothes. That's only one instance, but there were many that I'm ashamed of now. Quite honestly, I'm ashamed to mention other things we did and the things we said about people, who were less fortunate than we were.

The school year that Michelle and I started tenth grade there was a new boy going to our school named Jeff Gray. The story had it he was supposed to go to Woodlawn High School in Carroll County, but because they had no football program, Galax City Schools and Carroll County got together and paid the tuition for Jeff to go to Galax High School.

Jeff was a loner and stayed to himself. He was quiet and acted like he had a chip on his shoulder. One day a boy said something to him he didn't like and before he knew it, Jeff knocked him in the floor. The word got around quickly that you didn't mess with Jeff Gray.

Jeff had broad shoulders and thick, curly hair. He always looked like he needed a haircut, he wore sunglasses a lot inside and outside. I have to admit he looked cool. When it got cold, he wore a black leather jacket which just gave him that tough-guy look, but I found out later he acted that way because he was hurting so bad inside. It didn't take long to find out Jeff couldn't read or write and that's when Michelle and I started making fun of him behind his back.

One day, we were walking down the hall going to class, Jeff was in front of us, we were making faces and acting silly. Suddenly he turned around and caught me making a face at him. He looked at me as though he could've killed me, but he never said a word. For some reason, I felt sorry for doing that, but Michelle and I didn't care about people's feelings back then. We were having fun and that's all that mattered to us.

During the summer after ninth grade, Jeff had all kinds of problems and stayed in trouble. He liked to fight and had a reputation for being a bully. None of the parents liked Jeff. Everyone knew he had a girlfriend who went to Woodlawn School. They had met in the seventh grade. I knew that was very young, but that was the story I heard. For her age, she was much more mature and academically above Jeff. Jeff failed the third grade so he was a year behind. I didn't give him a thought until we had a civics class together.

Civics was my second class in the morning, only one more class before lunch. The teacher was not in the room, the class hadn't started. I was sitting in the back beside Jeff. I don't know why, but Jeff pushed his desk over beside mine. This surprised me, and I kept thinking he was going to say something to me about making fun of him. Everybody knew Jeff was unpredictable. He could blow up for no reason and the fact he had caught me making a face at him made me nervous. I was scared, but he surprised me. He was nice to me. He asked me about my grandfather and his lumberyard. His voice was soft and mild-mannered. I was surprised. While he was talking, I wanted to put my hand up to protect myself, but I sat there and listened to him nervously. Then Jeff did something which surprised me and changed me all at the same time. He kept leaning into me and before I knew it, he kissed me on my lips.

"Why did you do that?" I asked.

"Did you like it?" he asked.

I stared back at him with a startled look. "I don't know what to say."

Then Mr. Lindsay came in and started class. I found myself looking at Jeff a little bit differently. For some reason, Mr. Lindsay went out of the room again and Jeff turned and looked at me. "Princess, would you like to be kissed again?"

I stuttered and stumbled and said, "Yes, I would."

"When the bell rings, you've got to go down the hall and up the steps for your next class?"

"Yes, I do."

"I thought so. Will you follow me? I'll meet you under the stairwell. I'd like to kiss you again if that's ok?"

I never answered him, but when the bell rang, I followed him right under the stairwell where people couldn't see us.

When we got there, Jeff took me in his arms, held me close and kissed me with a long, wet kiss. It was the first time I had been kissed that way.

"Did you like that?"

"Yes, kiss me again." Jeff pulled me close. I could feel his hard body. He was strong from football practice. We kissed again. I could feel my face flush. Being held and kissed felt so good I could not believe it. I was glad Michelle wasn't in my class or I couldn't have done this.

The bell rang and Jeff said, "Let me go out first so nobody sees you with me. I'd like to do this again. How about you?"

"Yes, I would. Perhaps tomorrow we can do it again?" Jeff looked around the corner, started walking away and left me standing there. I waited for a few minutes and then I came out and went to class. After that, I couldn't focus on my books; all I could think about was Jeff Gray. It was a moment I'd never forget.

The rest of the day was different for me. I passed Jeff one more time in the hallway on the way to classes. I smiled at him and he smiled back. The day finally came to an end and I went home as though I were someone else. I knew Jeff had to go to football practice and I couldn't wait for tomorrow to see him again. After supper, I went to my room and I started my diary.

Dear Diary,

Jeff Gray kissed me today. I don't know what to think about it or how I really feel about it. I just know I like him kissing me and I hope he will kiss me again tomorrow. I can't wait to get to school.

The next day when we got to civics, Jeff sat beside me and asked, "Are you going to follow me after class?"

"Yes, I'm looking forward to it."

"So am I," Jeff said. The class came to an end and he got up. I followed him out the door. We walked at a faster pace on the way to the stairwell. I was right behind him, but I stopped for a moment to make sure nobody saw me. When Jeff turned the corner to go under the stairs, I saw my chance. Nobody was really looking and I slipped under the stairs behind him. He wasted no time and grabbed me in his arms. When he did, I dropped my books on the floor. The kiss was long and sweet. I didn't want to stop.

"I've been waiting all morning for this," I said.

"Me too," he held me so tight. The warmth of his body on mine made my nipples get hard. I'd never experienced that before. The second kiss was even better than the first.

And then we just stood there as he held me close, he kissed me on the side of my neck and tingling went through my body. “You’re making me feel so good.” I told him whispering in his ear. “How am I making you feel?” I asked him.

“What do you mean?”

“Please tell me.”

“Ok,” he paused. “You’re making my dick hard.”

I didn’t tell Jeff I really didn’t know what he was talking about. I was so new at this.

Jeff pulled me tighter and I loved it. “Listen, Princess, you’re too young for this. I know I’m just a year older, but have you ever had a boy in your life like this?”

“No never. Why are you doing this to me?”

“Because…” before Jeff could finish what he was going to tell me, the bell rang and he peered around the corner and slipped away. I picked my books up off the floor and I was almost late for my next class. I had a feeling in my body that I couldn’t explain. Jeff was changing me and I wanted more of him.

Every day we met under the stairwell. Each time it was more intense and each time I was more entranced. I had something to really look forward to. You could say I was getting my education in more than one way. An education about life, Jeff was my teacher.

On Thursday, Michelle and I were standing in the hallway talking when Jeff came walking by. I looked at him and he looked back at me. That’s when Michelle started laughing. Jeff looked down at the floor and looked back as he walked by.

Michelle asked, "Did you see him look at you? Do you know what Brennan told me about him? He was in class and they asked him to read and he couldn't. The whole class laughed at him. It made him mad. People said Jeff just put his sunglasses on and sat there without moving. Just his body language scared everybody and they could tell they better stop laughing. Everybody said the mood changed in the room and everyone slowly stopped laughing and the teacher calmed everybody down. Jeff was different. You could tell when you pushed him too far.

I looked down at the floor. It hurt me that they made fun of Jeff.

"What's wrong? Do you think that's funny? He's so big and dumb."

I didn't laugh. I really didn't respond. I found myself trying to make excuses to get away from her. The good thing was she wasn't in civics with me so I didn't have to lie to her to go to my special place.

The end of the week came, which meant Friday night football. My dad always took me to football games. Michelle would go with us, I got to watch Jeff play. I was mesmerized by him. I watched him, knowing I wouldn't be able to see him until Monday. I had to come up with a plan. That night I wrote in my diary about watching Jeff play football and all I could think about was that first kiss. I wrote I was changing and I didn't know why.

Fall came, the colors of the leaves were beautiful, the crisp smell of fall hung in the air. It was my favorite time of the year. I found it romantic just thinking about it. Saturday morning, Mom took me to the barn so I could tend to my horse. We kept a horse up behind the Star Drive-in. It's not that far out of town, but while I was there Saturday, I came up with an idea. I wondered if I could get Jeff to meet me there on Saturday mornings. We could be alone and not worry about being seen together. I couldn't wait to get back to school Monday to tell him about my idea and maybe after school he could meet me there and spend a few hours with me at the barn.

Sunday morning, during church, my mind wandered. My imagination was out of control like a lovesick girl. I was having fantasies about Jeff and how far I would go with this. All I could think about was how strong his body was. He would hold me just for that short moment in school under the stairwell. I thought about the changes in me and how my body was changing.

On Monday morning, Michelle and I got to school at the same time. I looked down the hallway and Jeff was talking to some of the football boys. I couldn't wait for civics class. I had to make it through the morning.

I walked in the classroom and Jeff was sitting in the back. As I walked to the back of the room, he smiled at me. When I sat down, I looked over and asked, "Do you know where Goodson stables are?"

"Yes, why are you asking?"

"I board my horse there. I go there after school and on Saturday mornings. How would you like to meet me at the stables?"

"I don't know. Won't there be a lot of people there?"

"Sometimes, but they're in and out. I may go out today after school. The weather's nice. Could you come out and see me?"

"What time?"

"I have to go home and change clothes and get my mom to take me. She'll drop me off and come back and pick me up. How about 4:30?"

"You're sure nobody will say anything if I'm seen out there before you get there?"

"I don't know, but that's what time I'll be there and I'll be there for over two hours before Mom comes to pick me up. We'll have a few minutes together if you'd like to be with me."

"Are you sure you want to be with me in a place like that, just me and you? I mean, of course, I want to be with you."

I was glad to hear him say that. "Ok then, when you get there, just come inside. There may not be anyone else there but me." We sat through the class and I couldn't wait until it was over.

When the bell rang, I followed him under the stairwell. This time I laid my books on the floor. Jeff thrilled me. I felt like I was. I couldn't explain what I felt like but it was so much different, it was so exciting to have his big, strong arms wrapped around me holding me so tight and close. He was kissing my neck that made my body react in a way I liked.

Right before the bell rang, he whispered in my ear. “When I see you at the barn, I don’t know how I’m going to control myself.”

I wasn’t sure what he meant by that, but I liked hearing it. He wanted to be with me, that’s all that mattered. Later I wrote that in my diary.

GOODSON STABLES

Chapter 2

When I got home from school, I told Mom I wanted to go to the barn and tend to my horse, and she agreed to take me. My mom and I had always been very close. I trusted her enough to tell her everything. Michelle told me she would never tell her mother the things I've told mine. I knew I was young, but Mom has taught me things and was always honest with me. We had a good relationship. We've talked about boys and yes, we've talked about sex, but there was no way I could tell her about Jeff Gray and that he kissed me. I was afraid she wouldn't understand. I just started seeing him and I didn't want to stop.

I didn't know what time Jeff would be at the barn, I just hoped he would come. When we got there, Mom walked in with me and watched me brush my horse. I was afraid Jeff would show up while Mom was still there, but after a few moments, she told me she was going to town and would be back in a couple of hours. I was glad she left. I thought she would mess up everything and I didn't know how I was going to explain it if Jeff showed up.

Once she left, I heard a voice up in the hayloft. "Is the coast clear?" asked Jeff. "Can I come down now?"

"Yes, Mom's gone. Come down, you scared me. I didn't know you were up there."

"I've been here for about fifteen minutes. I didn't know I was going to beat you here." He came down and walked up to me. "I've been waiting all day since we were under the stairwell, I can't get enough of this."

"I'm so glad you're here," I whispered in his ear.

"Are you sure you're glad I'm here? You know what I want to do to you?"

"I hope you want to hold me and kiss me and tell me how much you enjoy it."

"Yes, I enjoy it too much." While he kissed me, I was having such a good time and enjoyed every minute of it. "Let's go up in the hayloft," he suggested.

"Ok." I followed him up the ladder and when we got up there, he took a horse blanket, laid it down and we both lay on it. Now when he kissed me, his hands were roaming. "Jeff, you've got to slow down."

"Ok, do you want me to slow down?"

"I don't know. You're scaring me, but I like it all at the same time."

Jeff stood up and looked back at me. "Maybe I better go before this goes too far."

"Don't go."

"Are you sure?" he asked.

I extended my hand up for him to take, I pulled him back down beside me. We started kissing again. I couldn't keep his hands from roaming. "Stop! Maybe you shouldn't do this."

He never answered me, and I let him continue. He didn't try to get inside my blouse or in my panties, but I didn't stop his hands rubbing all over my body. I couldn't resist it. I know we were kissing pretty heavy ever since that first day at school under the stairwell, but it was getting more intense and I was reacting to his touch. I rolled over on top of him and I was straddling one of his legs. He put his hand on my butt and pushed forward and before I knew it, I was rubbing myself against his leg.

"Do you like that?"

"Yes, I do."

"Then do it harder. Push yourself on my leg. I like it." I did and then he rolled me over and put his hand between my legs. I knew deep down I was going too far, but I couldn't stop. Before I knew it, he brought his hand up to my waist and forced his hand down into my pants on top of my panties. He was rubbing me between my legs while we kissed. I grabbed his hand and pushed it harder on me.

Then he stopped and sat up. "I better stop doing this."

I was breathing hard. "Don't stop. Just come back and do some more." He laid me back again, but this time he put his hands under my panties and rubbed me and I could feel his fingers go through the hair. I was breathing very heavily. We were both sweating and then all of a sudden, he put a finger in me. I went limp. I just lay back with my eyes shut. He reached up and he kissed me on the lips again with his hand between my legs.

"Do you want me to stop?"

"Yes...No." That's all I could say. For a few minutes, he just played with me and I lay there. He kept moving his finger in me and he hit a certain spot and I took a deep breath. I didn't know what to do. I just lay there.

Then he whispered in my ear. "Will you jack me off or let me stick it in you?"

"No, Jeff, I don't want to get pregnant. I don't know how to jack you off either. You have to show me."

Jeff rolled on his back and unzipped his pants and pulled them down. He took my hand and put it on his penis and told me to squeeze and go up and down.

"No, I don't want to do that. Please, Jeff, don't make me do this."

"Yes," he said in a mean voice. He lay there and the more I pleased him, the more I liked it. Finally, Jeff got so excited that he got off. I'd never seen that before and I didn't know what to expect.

"Here's my handkerchief, Princess. Wipe your hand off." Jeff cleaned himself and told me to pull my pants down. He crawled over on top of me and we laid there and I could feel him. I told him not to put it in me. I was afraid I'd get pregnant so he didn't. But he rolled off and put his finger in me again.

He asked me to jack him off, and finally, we both got off. I had never felt that before. "I told you what I want to do. I didn't think you would do it. Are you sorry you let me do this to you?" he asked.

I grabbed Jeff around his neck, kissed him and whispered in his ear. "No, Jeff, I'm not sorry, but I don't know what to say to you. This is my first time."

We lay back down on the horse blanket and Jeff continued to kiss me. I didn't know what to do. I was excited and scared at the same time. We stood back up, threw the horse blanket down and climbed down the ladder.

He turned around and said. "I better go before your mom comes back. Do you want to do this again?"

"Yes, I'm coming back Saturday morning, about nine o'clock."

"I'll come back then. We've got a football game Friday night and it's an away game. Are you going to be there?"

"Yes, I'll be there with my parents and Michelle. I can't wait to see you tomorrow. Jeff, I've got to ask you something."

"What?"

I didn't want to make him mad, "Nothing, see you tomorrow under the stairwell. I can't wait. I won't sleep at all tonight."

He kissed me one more time and before he walked out the door I said, "Give me your telephone number."

"Why?"

"So I can call you."

"Why would you want to call me?"

"I just thought," I paused. "If you don't want to give it to me it's ok."

"Why can't I call you?" He asked.

"You know if you called me my parents will want to know who I'm talking to. I don't want to do anything that may stop me from seeing you again."

"Ok, you just answered my question. I'm not good enough for your parents."

"It's not that. I don't have boys calling my house to talk to me. They would question anybody, not just you."

"Princess, you know better. If they knew you were seeing me and what we were doing, you know what would happen."

"Yes, I know. They would stop me from seeing you and I'm sorry about that, but I'm telling you I don't want to stop seeing you. Jeff, you are good enough for me."

He gave me his telephone number and left me standing there, shaking.

Finally, Mom came and got me. She asked me why was I so quiet? I told her I felt bad.

"You feel bad? What's wrong Princess?"

"I don't know, Mom. Maybe my time of the month is getting close."

"I know how that can be. It's just a curse we women have."

When I got home, I got in the shower and then finished my homework. I couldn't help myself. I was going to call Jeff. In my room when I was sure nobody was listening, I dialed Jeff's number. His mother answered the phone. Her voice was sharp and rough. She startled me and it took me a moment before I asked to speak to Jeff. I could hear her yell for him and he came to the phone.

"Hello," he answered.

"It's me. I just wanted to talk to you."

"I was thinking about you."

"You were? I'm glad to hear it." I couldn't let him know I was thrilled he was thinking about me.

"Yes, I was hoping I didn't go too far with you today. I couldn't help myself."

I didn't know what to say. "I'm fifteen. I know a few things about this. You're only a year older than I am, but you seem to know everything about it. I know I'm not the first with you. I had no idea. Never in a thousand years would I believe you'd be my first, and I'm glad."

"Listen to me. You know this isn't going anywhere. Your future is going to be with somebody with a good education somebody much better than me. You know it's never going to be me in the end."

"Right now, I don't care. I just know you're so exciting. You're one of the popular football players and you're seeing me. I never thought – I don't know. I can't explain it. You are thrilling to me. And what makes you think it won't be you?"

"You know damn well if your parents knew you were seeing me – forget about what we're doing together, just hearing my name would stop it and you know it."

I tried to make a joke with Jeff. "Well, I'm not going to tell them if you're not. Let's see what happens and just let it go day by day. I'm just saying let me live. You've got me, a loss for words."

"I better go, Princess. See you tomorrow."

"I can't wait. You know how much excitement you've brought into my life?"

"It was only a kiss. Don't you dare start having feelings for me! It's not going to end up well. As young as I am, I know what it is to have a broken heart. And my parents are constantly fighting. I went too far with a girl you call a whore and she broke me. Princess, you have become my refuge. You've become a safe place and that scares me."

"You don't understand, Jeff. You've become the excitement I've never dreamed I would be thinking this way. I never dreamed I'd be experiencing these things. If you only knew what you brought into my life. I know we're just kids, but what does age have to do with it?"

"Goodbye, I'll see you tomorrow at school." He hung up and I sat back on my bed. I decided not to think about it, just live it and experience it, but I never dreamed I'd be so young. I was experiencing sex at fifteen and I didn't know what to expect next, but I was excited about it. I got my diary out and I started writing.

Dear Diary,

Today at the barn, Jeff had his hand in my panties. I'm afraid I'm not a virgin anymore, but I don't care. He wanted to have sex with me, but I stopped him. Deep down, I really didn't want to stop, but I knew I'd better. I'm sorry that Michelle and I talked about his girlfriend and called her a whore. Now I'm wondering if I'm I going to become his whore. I hope not. I want to be more to him than just that. He said tonight that I became his refuge and he has become mine. There's a whole new world in front of me. Oh my God, Diary, what am I going to do?

The next morning at school I met Michelle, and we started our day. Jeff was down at the end of the hallway talking to his football buddies. He never looked my way and I had to go through the day until we had a class together.

Civics class, Mr. Lindsay came in and I turned to Jeff. "I'm going back to the barn tomorrow after school. Do you think you can make it?"

"I'll try." Once class ended, I followed him under the stairwell and the kissing was intense. My body reacted in such away. I could feel my desire for him to put his hands on me, to do to me what he did when we were in the barn, and I knew we couldn't. Then I made a mistake. "I'm going to tell you something. I'm having feelings for you."

"Stop! Don't go there, Princess. I'm a nobody. I'm not your boyfriend, and you're not my girlfriend. We're just doing this for pleasure. I know you're experiencing new things, but don't start having feelings or think that we're going to have a relationship. The only thing we've got going is comforting one another. Your needs and my needs to have a place that I can go to. Princess, I have feelings for you, but not like you think. Don't let me mislead you, baby. I'm enjoying this more than you are." The bell rang and Jeff slipped away, leaving me standing there wondering.

Every day we met, I looked forward to, being with him. He changed. He is more gentle with me.

We went to the football game, Friday night and I couldn't wait until Saturday morning to meet him at the barn. While we watched the game Michelle and I got hot dogs and drinks and cheered for our team. But the whole time I was keeping my eye on Jeff. He was tackling the running back on the other team. I was so proud of him. He got a penalty flag for roughing the passer. Jeff seemed to really get into it, almost as if he liked hurting people. I think it's because he seemed to be hurt so bad himself. After the game, we watched the team get on the bus. We went to the bowling alley afterward and Mom and Dad took me home after we dropped Michelle off. All I could think about was seeing Jeff the next day.

I had a sleepless Friday night thinking about that. Mom got started a little bit late to take me. When we finally got there, I had no idea where Jeff would be. Maybe he wasn't there yet. Mom came in just for a moment and I started grooming my horse, and I asked her if could I stay a little bit longer since it was Saturday. I really didn't have anything else to do and she agreed.

When she went out the door, it was just a moment before I heard Jeff's voice. "Princess, come on up in the hayloft and bring your horse blanket."

"Ok," I answered. I started up the ladder with the blanket over my shoulder. When I got to the top Jeff took the blanket and spread it out between two bales of hay no one could see us.

"Lie down, Princess. I want to kiss you. I've been waiting all night long to kiss you."

"You have?" He kissed me on the lips and around my neck, but this time he went down to my blouse and unbuttoned it. I never stopped him. He lifted my bra up over my breasts. He kissed around my nipples. I was getting excited, but what he did next scared me. He jumped up and said, "Take your pants off."

"Oh, no Jeff. I'm not ready for this."
I wanted to scream!
My heart was beating out of my chest.
I didn't know what to do
I kept wondering if this was what a girl
was supposed to do.
What my mother told me
didn't mean anything now.
Was I supposed to do I resist?
I couldn't fight him.
Down inside me, I wanted him.
Suddenly, he slowed down.
I was holding onto his arms trying to stop him.
Then he took his hands
and rubbed me between my legs.
He put his lips on my nipples and licked them.
I tried to relax, but I couldn't.
Jeff reached down, grabbed my pants
and pulled them down around my ankles.
Then, he got out a rubber
and put it on his penis.
He held me down.

"Stop, Jeff, stop!"

"Listen to me, rich girl. I've been teased long enough. I want your body and I want it now!"

"Please don't! Please don't! You're raping me!"

"I'm not doing anything to you don't want me to do. Now I want some of that pussy. It's time!"

"Please don't, Jeff, don't. Don't rape me!" He lay down on top of me put his penis inside me. "Take it out, Jeff. It hurts, take it out please, take it out. It hurts!"

"It's too late, Princess. Just relax, it will stop hurting."

I lay there and he was right. It stopped hurting and then started feeling really good, but I was so scared. "Please don't get me pregnant, please don't get me pregnant."

"I won't get you pregnant. I've got a rubber on. You know what that is don't you?"

"Yes, I know what that is. Jeff, you're raping me. You didn't have to rape me."

"Would you let me do this on my own?"

"You raped me!" He kept it in me and looked me in my eyes. He had such sadness on his face. I was crying and he put his head close to mine and kissed my tears away. I hugged him around his shoulders and held him tight. He got it going back and forth, he stopped and rolled over. I looked down between my legs and I was bleeding.

"That's virgin blood. Are you angry at me?"

"I don't know. I really don't know. You raped me. Don't you understand you raped me?"

"Where did you think this was going? The way we've been kissing, the way I put my hands on you, then you jacked me off. I wanted your body and I got it."

I'm crying, I couldn't help it.

"Stop crying, poor little rich girl."

"You raped me. What am I supposed to do?"

"Are you trying to tell me you didn't like having sex with me?"

"After it stopped hurting, I liked it, but look at me now. I'm bleeding. How am I going to get home? My panties have blood in them." He took his handkerchief out and I wiped myself off. I didn't bleed much, but I was no longer a virgin. I finally got myself together. I couldn't get over, he raped me.

"Princess, pull your pants back down I want to do it again."

I didn't want to be raped again. I looked at him without saying a word, pulled my pants back down, spread my legs. We had sex again, but it was better this time. I knew I had to keep my head about myself. I knew I could never be seen in public with Jeff, but I wanted to. This time while we were having sex, he pulled my bra up and licked my nipples. I was in heaven. Finally, Jeff got off and rolled off of me. I pulled my pants back up and sat up without saying a word.

"What's wrong? Didn't you know you can't lay with a boy without him wanting to do something to you?"

"I didn't think you would rape me."

Jeff lay back down beside me, put his arm around me and cuddled. He was so soft and tender.

"Why did you call me 'rich girl' when you were raping me? Were you angry at me?"

"I'm not angry at you, Princess, but here we are now. We're having sex and you can't be seen in public with me. How do you think that makes me feel?"

"I'm not thinking about things like that. I just know I'm right here with you and I'm experiencing things I wasn't ready for. Jeff, you're a wild and crazy boy and here you are lying with me. You resent me because my family has money. Tell me the truth, Jeff, you resent me. You're doing this to me just to punish me."

"I'm not punishing you. I guess I thought maybe you just — Princess I will tell you this – No, I won't tell you anything."

"Are you still going to meet me here next Saturday?"

"Yes, I'm going to meet you here," I told him.

"Are you sure?

"Are you going to have sex with me every time I come to see you?"

"Yes, as long as you bring a rubber and keep me from getting pregnant."

"Are you ready to have sex again? You've got me so turned on. I'll tell you something, you're good. You're really good. You keep me excited."

I didn't tell Jeff I loved to hear him say that. I wouldn't dare tell him how much he excited me and how my life changed. What was I doing here with this guy? He was wild and some people hated him, but I wasn't sure why. I found myself thinking about him all the time. I lay back down, pulled my pants down and we had sex again, but this time Jeff was slow and gentle. I hugged him around his neck and kissed him on his ear while we had sex and it was wonderful. If my mom knew this, I'd be in serious trouble. If anyone knew this, I would be more than in trouble. Finally, Jeff finished. I still wanted more, but I didn't tell him.

"I'm going to tell you something. You're a pretty girl. I feel bad about raping you. You can have me put in jail. You could tell them I came in the barn and raped you."

"Listen to me. I didn't want you to rape me, and honestly, I wanted to have sex with you, but I didn't know how."

"I'm sorry. I feel bad about it now, and you're right. I guess I was getting back at you. Remember the time you made fun of me? I guess I got revenge. I better shut up. I've said too much. I went too far now. I feel bad about it," he said.

"Jeff, promise me you'll come back next Saturday. Promise me you'll meet me under the stairwell, and promise me you'll keep seeing me. You can't stop now. What would I do? There's no one else. I would never let anyone know what we're doing. No other boy would do what you're doing to me. So, promise me as long as we can keep meeting, will you come? Please meet me at the barn?"

"You really want me to?"

"Yes, I do and I want to have sex with you every time we can. I've got a feeling this is going to be a time in my life that I'll never forget. I'll never forget you."

"Maybe it's time I better go, Princess." We both stood up and Jeff took me in his arms, kissed me and whispered in my ear that he was sorry he raped me. I held onto him real tight and looked him in the eyes; he looked sad. I knew I had to wait until Monday before I could see him again. As he went out the door, he kissed me one more time. I was completely consumed by him and I tried my damnedest not to be. I was raised differently than Jeff. I wasn't used to this.

When I got home, I got my diary. I started crying as soon as I opened it. The tear stains were on the paper as I wrote.

Dear Diary,

Jeff raped me today and I bled. For sure now I'm no longer a virgin. The sad thing about this is he didn't know he didn't have to rape me because I wanted him, but I didn't know what I was doing and now I feel like I'm in a hopeless situation and I don't know what to expect next. I pray nobody finds my diary, especially my mother. This would horrify her so I'll put it in a safe place where she can never find it. I'm sure there's much more I have to say to you about what Jeff Gray has caused me to become. I feel like a different person now.

On Sunday, we went to church and Michelle kept asking me what was wrong. I didn't dare tell her that I lost my virginity, I was raped because part of me felt like I asked for it. I should've known better than to be with a wild, crazy boy like Jeff, but the excitement of him was something to experience.

October was ending and all the leaves on the trees were blowing away. Jeff and I kept meeting under the stairwell and it got more intense between us. We were having sex regularly every Saturday in the barn up in the hayloft, but Jeff began to change. After we had sex, he was so melancholy and sad. I don't know how to explain it. He was having some trouble in his family and when he would see me, I would hold him in my arms while I sat against a bale of hay.

Things were changing in my life, it's like it happened overnight. I was no longer a virgin and I was too young to know what love is, but I was sure I was in love. What else could it be? I decided to write everything down and keep track of what was going on at this time in my life. But I was sure I had to be careful because if my mother read my diary this would all be over as quick as it started. So, every time that Jeff and I were together I wrote it down anyway. I knew just enough about life to realize we could never predict what tomorrow would bring, but I was sure with Jeff Gray there was no limit to where this could go.

Chapter 3

Michelle was getting suspicious, I was making excuses to get away from her, so I could see Jeff. She cornered me. “You’ve been acting funny lately. What’s going on?”

“What you talking about? I’m not doing anything differently. What makes you say that?”

“Come on, you know you’ve been acting funny. You used to call me every Saturday. Usually, we’d go to town or go shopping and if we didn’t, you’d take me to the barn to take care of your horse, but you never ask me to go anymore. So, what’s going on?”

“Nothing, really. I’m just trying to get some time to be alone and think.”

“Think about what?”

“You know, just – things.”

“Ok then, but I’ve been feeling like I’ve been left out like you’ve got a boyfriend or something that you’re not telling me about.”

“What makes you say that?”

“Are you seeing a guy and you’re not telling me?”

“You know I’m not. Now, let’s talk about where Mom is going to take us for my birthday dinner.”

I had a hard time explaining to Michelle that I didn’t exactly have a boyfriend, but I was in another world. Jeff Gray was a different world. He was the kind of guy people had different opinions about and none of them were good. He never fit in any kind of group.

He was a loner and people couldn't figure him out. You could push Jeff, but if you pushed too far, he would explode. Unpredictable would be the best way you could describe him. They said he gave his girlfriend a bad reputation. I guess because he did to her what he's doing to me.

On Sunday morning, Michelle and I went to church together. I was trying to be myself, but I was still thinking about Jeff. He was on my mind all the time. Given what happened between us and the things I was experiencing with him, I couldn't help but think about it. I didn't dare tell anyone what I was doing.

Monday morning was slow until civics, but this time Jeff was not in a very good mood. When I sat down beside him and started a conversation, he wasn't too friendly.

"How are you today?"

He looked up at me and was slow to answer. "I'm all right."

"Are we going to meet today under the stairwell?"

"No, not today."

"What's wrong, are you mad at me?"

"Not today – just not today." Jeff sat back in his seat and he didn't speak to me. After class, he got up and I followed him like I normally do down the hallway, but he never stopped at the stairwell. He went upstairs to his next class. I was disappointed that he wasn't going to meet me there. It was the highlight of my day. The rest of the day was slow and I wondered what was wrong with him.

Michelle was acting funny around me because she was suspicious that something was going on in my life, and she was right.

That night I decided to call Jeff and find out what was wrong. His mom answered the phone. I asked to speak to Jeff. She told me in a very angry voice he couldn't come to the phone right now. I could hear yelling in the background. She asked me if he could call me back but I didn't dare tell her who I was. Something was wrong at Jeff's house and I didn't know what it was.

The next day at school, I was anxious to talk to him to see what going on. When we had class, I asked him again. "Are you going to meet me under the stairwell?"

"No."

"Why?"

"Mind your own business."

That whole week we never met. I have to admit I really missed it. Friday came around and I asked about Saturday morning at the barn. "Jeff, are you going to meet me at the barn Saturday morning? The weather is going to be chilly, but I don't care. Do you?"

"Yes, I'm going to be there. I have to get away from home. Things are not going well there."

"Is that the reason you're not meeting me under the stairwell? Are you going to tell me what's wrong?"

"No, I'm not. You wouldn't understand."

"I'm here for you. You can talk to me."

"What in the hell would you know about it? You live in a privileged home with parents who take care of you." There was anger in Jeff's voice. "What do you know about real life!"

"I'm trying to help, that's all. I just want you to know that I care about you."

"I'll see you Saturday morning at the barn if I get there."

"I hope you get there I'm looking forward to seeing you. I'm looking forward to just being with you. Do you know that?"

"Really! Is that the reason you don't tell anybody we're seeing each other?"

"Please don't do that Jeff. You know it's impossible. My parents would stop me from seeing you. Do I mean anything to you at all?"

"Ok then. When I come to the barn, I'm going to have sex with you."

"I hope so. I really hope so. Just bring a condom. I want to have sex with you, but please tell me what's wrong. You're acting like you're mad at me for something."

The bell rang and I followed Jeff out the classroom door and under the stairwell. When we got there, he was rough. He stuck his hand in my pants and groped me, but we kissed passionately. He was so angry and I didn't know why. I'd done everything he'd asked me to do with him. I gave him my body after he took it. Now it seemed he was just angry with the whole world and he was taking it out on me.

After school, I was in a daze. I could hear Michelle's voice, but I couldn't understand what she was saying. She noticed I had a faraway look on my face. I was wondering if Jeff was going to turn violent. He was rough under the stairwell and I didn't know what to expect from him.

All of a sudden, Michelle yelled at me. "Hey! Hey! Where are you? I felt like I just woke up from a bad dream.

"I'm sorry. I was thinking about something else." Michelle was almost angry, shaking her head. "What is wrong with you? I thought we were very good friends. Something is bothering you. I've never seen you act this way before!"

"Nothing is wrong between me and you, honest."

"Then why are you not telling me what's on your mind? Anyway, do you want to go to the movies tonight?"

"Yes, I do I need to get out." Then Michelle answered. "I sure hope so you know you're really hurting my feelings, Princess. Something is going on and you don't want to tell me what it is and I can't imagine what it could be."

We walked on and I explain to Michelle that nothing was going on, but she knew better and she was right. Our conversation really slowed down while we were walking. I tried to avoid answering any of her questions. We walked home and waited until it was time to go to the movie.

Mom dropped us off at the Rex Theater where Michelle confronted me again. "I want to know what's wrong with you?"

"What do you mean, what's wrong with me?"

"You can't tell me something is not bothering you. You're not the same. Even in school, you're not yourself and I want to know what's going on. What are you keeping from me?"

"I don't understand. I'm not doing anything different."

"There's something you're not telling me. I don't know how to explain it to you, but we've been friends long enough for me to know there's something going on and you're leaving me out."

"What could that be, Michelle?"

"If you're not going to tell me I'm not going to ask you anymore."

"Let's just go watch the movie. I don't know how to convince you there's nothing going on." I was sitting there thinking about meeting Jeff and about what was going to happen between us. I couldn't tell anybody about it. I had to live in my own world with Jeff. At the end of the movie, Mom picked us up. On the way home, we didn't talk much. Mom asked about the movie and I said very little. I was anxious to get home.

Saturday morning, I was up early getting ready to go to the barn. I didn't know what to expect from Jeff. He was angry about something that was happening in his home life. I had no idea what it was. It was about 9:30 AM when Mom dropped me off at the barn. There were a few people around, but not many.

The weather was starting to turn cooler for the most part. That's the best time to ride your horse, even though I wasn't riding very much. I was more anxious to see Jeff.

I was back in the stable brushing my horse when he came in. He didn't say much, but walked into the stall and shut the gate behind him. For some reason, he was very gentle. He turned me around and took me in his arms. This was exactly what I'd been waiting on. He kissed me on my cheek and on the side of my neck and I was in heaven. Then he whispered in my ear. "Let's go up in the hayloft. I want you."

I never said a word, but took the horse blanket and climbed up to the loft. He came up behind me in between two bales of hay. I laid out the blanket and we lay down together. He began to unbutton my blouse and push my bra up as he played with my breasts.

Then he did something different. This time he kissed down my stomach and around the hair down there. I certainly enjoyed that. He pulled my pants down around my ankles, put on a condom and we had sex. Afterward, I pulled up my pants and sat up against a bale of hay. Jeff crawled up in my arms.

I thought I had finally found my chance to ask him what was making him be so down. "Are you going tell me what's bothering you?"

"You have a good home life, you wouldn't understand."

"Please tell me."

Jeff was snuggling in my arms. I never felt so good in my life. This strong boy was like a child. "I got in a fight with my dad. He and my mom were fighting and I couldn't take it anymore. I opened up the front door to let him out. I wanted him to leave. He drew a knife on me and told me he'd cut my throat. Do you know what it is to have your parents fighting all the time, making your life miserable?"

"No, I don't. I can't imagine living in something like that. I'm so sorry." I hugged him and held him tight.

Then out of nowhere, Jeff went crazy. "You know what your problem is, rich girl? You don't know what it is to have problems." Jeff's voice changed. All of a sudden, he jumped up and pulled me up. He turned me around, jerked my pants down, bent me over a bale of hay he stuck his penis in my rectum.

"Stop, you're hurting me!
Please take it out, you're hurting me!
Stop, Jeff, you're hurting me!
Please stop! Stop!
Why are you doing this?
Please stop, you're hurting me!
He stopped. I had no choice but to relax.
He pulled it out.
I pulled my pants up and sat down.
I couldn't stop crying.
He hurt me and I didn't know why.
With a trembling voice, I asked,
"Why did you do that?
Why did you want to hurt me?"

Jeff sat there, looked at me and said,
"To show you what it is, rich girl.
What real-life is."
"Please don't ever hurt me again, please," I begged.

Jeff just stood there looking at me before taking me in his arms. We both sat down and I cried on his shoulder.

"You hurt me, why?"

Jeff held me tight and said. "I'm sorry. I don't know what got into me. I'm sorry I did that to you."

I was trembling and sniffing back the tears. "Please, Jeff, you're scaring me. Please don't ever hurt me again. Don't you realize how much you've changed me? I look forward to seeing you every day. I'm fifteen years old next week and you took my virginity. I want to have sex with you, look at me, please don't hurt me again."

While I was sniffing back the tears, Jeff laid me back down. I was afraid of what he was going to do, but I pulled my pants down for him. This time He was easy and gentle with me and it was so good. Jeff had such a hard home life, but I didn't want to feel sorry for him. I was caring for him. I never forgot this moment. Jeff told me the story about how his father pulled a knife on him and how bad he was hurt by it. I was looking at Jeff with a different attitude. As we sat there holding each other, I felt so alive. The pain of what he did to me was going away. I knew I never wanted that to happen again, but I felt like my life had a purpose. Jeff was hurting inside and he took it out on me. Time goes so fast when you're with somebody that you care for, but I knew I could never tell Jeff that I had feelings for him. He wouldn't have it. It was time for him to leave, but this time he kissed me softly and patiently, he held me like I meant something to him.

I knew I was too young to have those kinds of emotions, but after everything we'd done, there was no going back. I realized I was not a little girl anymore when Jeff went out the door. I didn't want to go home. I wanted to go with him. When Mom came to pick me up, it was all I could do to keep myself together after what Jeff did to me. I wasn't mad at him I blamed it all on his home life, I can't imagine living that way fighting all the time, I can understand what would drive him crazy and not knowing how to let it out, let it out on me was a different issue, I was sorry I couldn't help but more than that I didn't want to be his punching bag I wanted him to love me.

That night I called Michelle and we made plans to go to church together Sunday morning. Michelle kept asking me if I was ok. If she only knew – but I couldn't tell her that Jeff raped me, twice. I couldn't tell anybody that I was secretly seeing him. Next Tuesday I'd be fifteen years old. I never dreamed I would be raped, but I tried not to blame Jeff for it. I told myself it was just as much my fault as it was his.

It was hard putting on a front for Michelle. Then there was my mom. She looked at me suspiciously as though she knew. It was my mind playing tricks on me with the drama that I'd been exposed to.

Mom and Dad had planned to take me out for a birthday dinner. I couldn't tell anyone what I really wanted for my birthday, to be with Jeff. That would be the biggest gift of my life, to be able to be with him and nobody would care or think that I was above him. But I was glad the dinner was over. I just wanted to go to school on Monday. That one class I had with him was the highlight of my day.

When I got to school, I met Michelle, we walked in. I didn't see Jeff that morning until I got to class. I was late getting there, but Jeff was already sitting in the back. On my desk was Goldman's bag.

I sat down and looked at Jeff. He was smiling.

"What is this?" I asked.

"I don't know. It was there when I got here," he said.

I opened it up and there was a card with a sweater. When I opened up the card, it said, *Happy Birthday, Princess*. I looked at Jeff. "Did you give me this sweater for my birthday?"

"Is it your birthday? How would I know it's your birthday?" Then he said, "Happy Birthday."

"Oh Jeff, it's a beautiful pink sweater. Let me try it on." I stood up and pulled it on. It was a little bit big but I loved it. I sat back down and took all the tags off. "Thank you, Jeff. I can't believe you did this for me."

"Who said I did anything? Like I told you, the bag was there when I got here. It's probably somebody that secretly likes you."

"I love it. Thank you. It's the best gift I've ever gotten, and coming from you makes it special."

"I didn't tell you I got that for you. I don't know where it came from."

"Will you meet me under the stairwell today?"

"I wouldn't miss it. I'm really looking forward to it."

"I want to give you a special kiss for this, Jeff."

"All of your kisses are special, Princess." He had a sad look on his face as though he was sorry about what happened. It felt like Jeff was changing. I could only hope so after he said that.

I couldn't believe my ears. He changed my world so much. After class, I followed him under the stairwell and we kissed passionately. The whole time, he had his hand on my crotch and I enjoyed it. I didn't want to wait for the weekend at the barn. I wanted to have sex with him right there, but there was no way. He never said a word, but he peeped around the corner to see if anyone was looking before he faded away. I buttoned my sweater. He never did own up to buying it, but I knew it came from him.

Michelle saw me at lunch and wanted to know where I got the sweater. I was getting used to lying to her. I had no problem telling her another lie. It was more important to me to be with Jeff than being with her. I told her my parents got it for me.

Then she said, "You didn't have it on this morning."

She caught me off guard and I had to think quickly. "It was in my locker." For the time, it satisfied her.

After school, she and I walked home and I got so messed up in my lying. We were halfway home when

Michelle said something. “Princess, you are lying to me and I want to know why?”

“No, I’m not! Why do you say that?”

“Do you think I’m that dumb? Look at the sweater you’ve got on. It’s the very same one you wore this morning. You’re telling me your mom and dad bought you that sweater, the pink sweater that you had on at lunch! You are lying to me. Why?”

“Please don’t ask me, Michelle. Yes, I’ve been lying to you, but I’m not ready to tell you everything. So please leave it alone. I’ll tell you what’s going on when I can, but right now I can’t tell you. Please don’t ask me again.”

“You don’t trust me to tell me what’s going on with you. You’re changing and I’m not sure it’s in a good way. Don’t you trust me to tell me what’s happening to you?”

“Please, I can’t tell you right now, I can’t bring that sweater home until I figure out how to get it past mom because she’ll ask me where it came from and who bought it for me. That’s the reason I left it in my locker, but please Michelle, I can’t tell you. I just can’t tell you right now.”

“Is it some boy you’re not telling me about? Every time we’re around Jeff Gray you act differently.”

“How?”

“If I make a joke about him, you don’t seem to think it’s funny anymore. I know you’ve got that one class with him and I’ve been told you sit in the back right beside him every day.”

“I talk to him if that’s what you’re saying.”

"What do you talk about?"

"I ask him about his old girlfriend."

"What does he say?"

"Nothing really. Sometimes it makes him mad and I laugh at him."

Michelle kept on talking about Jeff, the whole time she was talking about him I thought about being with him, the conversation ended, I was glad. I couldn't wait till Saturday. Mom wanted me to go spend time with my horse. It kept me busy. She liked the fact that she was keeping me out of trouble.

Back at school, Jeff smiled at me when I walked into class. As I sat down beside him, he reached over and took me by my hand and looked me in the eye. Then he said something unexpected. "I'm really sorry I hurt you."

I couldn't believe my ears. He cared enough for me that he was sorry. "Please don't ever hurt me again. I want to please you."

"I'm having a bad time at home I'm not doing too good in school and I guess I took it out on you. I'm sorry. I don't really like hurting people. I'll tell you a little secret. Sexually you're good."

"But Jeff, you know you're the only boy I've ever been with. You're teaching me everything and you say I'm good. I never thought about it. I know you make me feel good."

"Princess, your body really turns me on." I heard words from him for the first time that he was having emotions about me. I hoped it was more than just being physical I couldn't tell him how I really feel. "I'm going to be at the barn in the morning, about 10. It's going to be a cold day, but I don't care. Can you come and be with me?"

"Yes, I will, but I may ask you to do things with me you may not want to."

"Ask me anything and I'll do it for you. Just ask me."

"Now you've got me excited." Jeff took me by the hand and looked around the room. Mr. Lindsay hadn't come in yet and while everybody was looking toward, Jeff put my hand on the bulge in his pants. His penis was hard. "See what you do to me. I'm thinking about you. I wish we could have sex under the stairwell."

"I do, too, I feel the same way about you."

"Would you jack me off under the stairwell?"

"Oh no, Jeff, we wouldn't have time. I'm afraid we'd get caught." Mr. Lindsay came in and started class. All kinds of things were going through my mind.

I couldn't wait for class to end. When the bell rang, I followed Jeff under the stairwell. I laid my books down and I embraced him. We were kissing and it was so good.

Jeff took my hand and put it in his pants and whispered in my ear. "Hurry, jack me off!" I grabbed him by his penis and I jacked as quickly as I could. I wanted him to get me off too. I could feel the adrenaline running through my body. The bell rang and I was still jacking him, he got off. He pulled out a handkerchief from his back pocket. I wiped my hand off, he quickly kissed me and we both were late for class. I was excited. I couldn't believe I did that in school. Jeff didn't mind taking chances. That was what was so exciting about him.

The rest of that Friday afternoon I couldn't help but think about what he had me doing, things I'd never dreamed I'd be doing. I went over in my mind about what my mama told me about sex and how easy it was to get pregnant, but that didn't seem to matter to me anymore. I was only fifteen and doing things sexually before my time. But it was how Jeff affected me to think about him and his touch on my body, how it made me feel. I was wondering how Jeff knew so much about sex. He was only a year older than I am. Who taught him the things he was doing to me or did it just come naturally for boys? It was too late for me now. I was learning from him the things he liked me to do to him and what he did to me. I dreamed about Saturday morning, to get in the hayloft with him and see where it would go from there. I really looked forward to it.

Saturday morning was cool. It was the week before Thanksgiving. Before I got to the barn, Mom came in just for a moment and then told me she had things to do, so she should be back in the afternoon. I told her to take her time. I had to clean the stall, groom the horse, and that I might go for a ride. I was going to be busy.

I was brushing my horse, hoping Jeff was in the loft, but I never heard anything. Then he came through the door. "Princess, are you here?"

"Yes, I'm back here in the stall with my horse." Jeff came walking in. When he got to the stall door, he took me in his arms and immediately started kissing me on my neck. He told me he was really looking forward to seeing me today.

My heart leaped a little bit. I whispered, "You want to go up in the hayloft?"

"Yes," he agreed. We climbed the ladder and laid the blanket out between the bales of hay. We lay down and kissed. Jeff's hands were all over me and I loved it. I spread my legs for him and he pulled my pants down and laid on me and we had sex, but this time Jeff was really slow and easy. While we were doing that, he whispered in my ear. "You're so good to me." I was breathing heavily and whispered back.

"You're taking me to heaven right now. I'm having the best time of my young life. With all my privilege and all the money my parents have, it's nothing compared to being with you."

Jeff got off, rolled over, pulled the rubber off and threw it on the other side of the barn. He sat up against a bale of hay and I lay back in his arms. I don't know what got into him, but he was so gentle like he respected me. He wasn't being mean to me, he wasn't trying to hurt me, he was holding me.

Then I made a big mistake when I asked, "How do you feel about me?"

"What do you mean? I'm here with you."

"How do you feel about me, Jeff?"

"Princess, stop now. You know this not going anywhere. All we have is the time we're together. There's no future, there's no past, it's all right now. We can't count on yesterday because it's gone, and there's no tomorrow because it's not here yet. We only have right now. Don't try to make anything else out of it. Besides, you know I can't come to your house. You know that your parents would never have anything to do with me. You know this is not going anywhere. It's only now."

Then I said, "Would you get mad if I told you I wanted more if I told you I want to be with you every day? How would you feel about that?"

"Princess, this is all we've got. Don't make any more out of it than what it is."

"If this is all we've got, hold me tight never let me go like you really want to be with me like you want me more than just to have sex. You want more from me than just right now. Can't you imagine that?"

"No, I can't!" He began to kiss on the back of my neck and around until he unbuttoned my blouse then ran his tongue across my nipples. He kissed down my belly and around the top of my hair. I never felt anything like that before. He pulled my pants down and we had sex again. We lay in each other's arms and I didn't want it to stop.

We stopped talking and had sex one more time. I couldn't get enough of him. After having sex for the third time, I lay back in his arms and we never spoke a word. I felt so warm, so safe, yet so scared. I knew he hurt me, and I had to ask myself if it was worth it just to be with him again. Without saying a word, we stood up and Jeff kissed me and he looked in my eyes. Then he turned around, went down the ladder and walked out of the barn.

Jeff matured me before my time. I was coming of age, I was in a hopeless relationship with no future. I feared the ending of it. I was in a daze and losing track of reality. My first experience with real-life was becoming painful. I finished up all the chores with the horse, but I didn't feel like riding.

Mom came and picked me up. On the way home, I guess I had a look she noticed and she wanted to talk about it.

"I passed Jeff Gray again walking," said Mom. "Do you see him here at the barn?"

I turned my head to look out the car window I tried to come up with a lie. "I don't know, Mom. I think he's got a part-time job taking care of somebody's horses. I see him occasionally, but usually, he's in somebody's horse stall cleaning up."

"You don't associate with him do you?"

"I speak to him. After all, I go to school with him."

"I hear he stays in trouble. None of the parents have anything good to say about him."

"I have one class with him. He's never done anything to me."

"That's not what I'm talking about, Princess. I'm not trying to tell you who to be friends with and who not to be friends with, but Jeff Gray is in trouble all the time. I just don't want you to get mixed up with somebody like that."

"What do you mean, somebody like that?"

"Somebody who's in trouble all the time. I hear he drinks, fighting and gave some girl a bad name."

"What you mean he gave girls a bad name?"

"Now, Princess, you know exactly what I mean. I heard he goes up to Red's Roller Rink on Friday nights and they got caught out in the car doing things you are not supposed to be doing."

When Mom said that, I got jealous. I could understand why that other girl would go out with him in a car, I wished I could. "Mom, I think he's got some problems. He has a hard time in school. I don't know anything about what girl you're talking about, but Jeff seems like he's never happy when I'm around him in class."

After hearing Mom talk about Jeff, I knew it would be impossible for me ever to see him out in public. My mom wouldn't stand for it. Jeff brought some excitement to my life. He was my first and I was so naïve. It only took a kiss for me to want more from him.

"Princess, he doesn't come around you at the barn, does he?"

"Only in passing, Mom. There are a few people in and out, so many people there boarding horses right now. I use my time in the barn, grooming my horse, clean the stall and feed. I don't have time for Jeff Gray or anybody else when I'm there."

"I'm just saying, when it comes time for you to start dating, Jeff Gray is not the guy for you."

"Why do you say that? How do you know who's for me when I don't even know?"

"Let me ask you, Princess. When I asked if Jeff Gray came around you in the barn, you hesitated to answer me and you were squirming in your seat. Are you telling me the truth?"

"Mom, nobody has ever asked me to go out on a date, especially Jeff Gray. Jeff has never said a word to me other than having a class with him. I'll tell you the truth. Jeff is a handsome guy. He's big and strong. If he did ask me out, are you telling me you wouldn't let me go?"

"Princess, I'm telling you when you start dating, you are really going to find out what boys have on their minds. That's why your father and I want to make sure the guy you date is a gentleman."

"Mother, for some reason, nobody has ever asked me to go out and you're telling me that you and Dad are going to choose who I go out with?"

"Yes, that's exactly what I'm telling you, Princess. You need to choose wisely, and Jeff Gray is not the boy we want you to go out with. He comes from a bad family, his father drinks all the time, and he has a reputation for running after women. So, I'm afraid Jeff Gray is not on your list of guys to be going out with."

"Mama!"

"Now that's enough. You understand me, Princess? We want you to have a good life."

"So, you're going to make decisions for me?"

"Yes, that's exactly what I'm going to do. Now drop it!"

Then I knew they'd never let me see Jeff no matter how old I was. It made me want to see him more, and I was going to do it.

When we got home I called Michelle and we decided to go to the Rex Theater that night. We went to the 5 o'clock showing of James Bond 007, and got hot buttered popcorn and drinks before we sat down close to the back row. The lights dimmed for the movie to start, when two girls came walking down the aisle on the left. When they got to a certain row, they walked over to the end where it was darker.

Michelle punched me in the side and said, "Do you know who that is?"

"No, who is it? Which one are you talking about?"

"The one on the left that walked in first. You don't know who that is?"

"No," I said. "Who is it?"

"That's Jeff Gray's girlfriend. You know, the one who goes to Woodlawn."

I sat there looking at her. She had long brunette hair and was very pretty. She was much prettier than me. I was jealous. I was sure now that Jeff was just using me and I wouldn't have a chance for him to really love me. I looked at her. She made me feel so bad inside. Just her looks alone put me to shame, and then Jeff came walking in and sat down beside her. He didn't see me. When the lights dimmed, you could barely tell they were sitting there, but they begin to make out.

Michelle was laughing. "I bet he's got his hand up her dress," she said.

"You think so? Here in the theater?"

R
E
X
JAMES BOND – 007
DR NO
SEAN CONNERY

"Jeff Gray doesn't care. He does what he pleases and he doesn't care who knows."

"She doesn't care either?"

"No, that's kind of girl he likes."

I was about to burst. If Michelle only knew I wished I was sitting there with him. We sat there during the whole movie, and sometimes I watched him. Jeff came walking up the aisle he looked over at me and stopped. He stood there for a moment looking at me. Then he walked on.

"Who is he looking at? Was it you?" Michelle asked.

"I don't know. I thought he was looking at you. Have you made him mad about his girlfriend?"

"No, he was looking at you."

"I don't think so. He's got no reason to be looking at me." In a few minutes, he came walking back down the aisle and sat with his girlfriend. I kept looking at him out of the corner of my eye without Michelle noticing me. I knew what that girl was doing for him because he laid his head back. I just knew she was jacking him off. I could tell, He took his coat off and laid it on her lap, what I could see from where I was sitting and she laid her head back and I knew what he was doing for her, I was jealous. I was jealous and there was no getting around it. I wished it was me.

When the movie was over, everyone was waiting in front of the theater to be picked up. Jeff stood there with his girl, holding her hand. It looked like her parents picked them up and Jeff got in the car with them. I was sure he'd be dropped off at the bowling alley. I caught him looking at me out of the corner of his eye. He knew I was going to say something to him about it at school on Monday. While we were waiting for Mom to pick us up, Michelle started asking me questions again. "Ok, Princess, what's going on? What's Jeff Gray got to do with you?"

I turned and looked at her as though I were startled that she asked me such a question. "What! What do you mean by that? He doesn't have anything to do with me."

"You've been acting strangely for the last few weeks. They're something you're not telling me."

"I don't know what you're talking about."

"All right then, if you're not going to tell me, fine. I thought I was your best friend."

"You are my best friend. The fact that I haven't said anything is because there's nothing going on. I've got a civics class with him, I think that's the reason he stopped and looked at us. He knows we're going to say something about it in school. I don't know, Michelle, maybe we shouldn't say anything to him. I don't want to push him too far. You know how crazy he can get. He's got a reputation for blowing up if we go too far with this."

"What you mean to go too far? He's not going to do anything to us. He knows better. Your daddy and my daddy would kill him, you know that."

"That's what I'm afraid of. Let's just leave him alone."

"I've never heard you talk like this before. Why should we leave him alone? He's nobody, what do we care?"

"Nevertheless, I'm going to leave him alone," I told her, just as Mom pulled up. Michelle spent the night with me and we went to church Sunday morning. Jeff never came up again and I was glad. Michelle spent Sunday afternoon getting ready to go to school. I wanted to see Jeff, but I was afraid of what he might say to me about Saturday night.

I spent Sunday night thinking about what I was going to say to him.

Monday morning started out normal. On the way to homeroom, I could see Jeff down the hallway. When Michelle and I walked by, I saw him look at me out of the corner of his eye. Of course, he never said a word. After homeroom, the morning went on, time for civics. Jeff was sitting in the back, waiting on me. I had a feeling of apprehension. I couldn't let him know I didn't like seeing him with her. Yes, I was jealous, but I sat down beside him like nothing was wrong.

"Hello." When he spoke, I thought everything would be ok.

"Hello, I saw you on Saturday night."

"Yes, I know. You were with your little snobbish friend Michelle. Did you get a good laugh at me like you normally do?"

"We didn't laugh at you."

"Really!"

"No, I wasn't laughing at you, and you know I wasn't."

"Well that would be the first time wouldn't it?"

"I'm going to tell you the truth. When I saw you with her, I was jealous."

"Why would you be jealous? I don't mean anything to you."

I didn't dare tell him how I felt, he wouldn't have it. "Can I ask you something?"

"Ok."

"Do you love her?"

He dropped his head and then he looked up at me blankly without saying anything.

"I'm sorry," I didn't know what else to say. He stopped talking to me. "Are you going to meet me under the stairwell after class?"

He turned straight in his desk and never answered. During the whole class, he never spoke another word to me. I realized I asked the wrong question. The bell rang, the class was over. He never said a word to me when he got up, walked out and down the hallway. I didn't follow him this time and I went on to my next class before lunch. I thought to myself for the first time, I hurt him but I didn't mean to. He must be really hurt and in love with that girl. I hated her. I wanted to be here for him.

The whole week Jeff never spoke to me. He sat in the same class with me while my heart was aching. Friday I got the nerve to ask him if he would come to the barn Saturday morning.

He slowly turned his head and looked at me. "Why?"

"Why haven't you talked to me all week? I want to see you."

"Why don't you take me out in public like somewhere we can be seen together, maybe the movies?" he asked. I didn't know how to answer him I really wanted to be with him.

"Please don't do this to me. You know I want to be with you. If we went out in public you know my parents would never let me see you again?"

"I don't know why you want me at the barn. If I hurt you again, would you still want me there?"

"I don't want you to hurt me. I just want to be with you. I wanted to be that girl you were sitting with at the movies. She's prettier than I am, and I bet she pleases you better than I do. I want to be here, just for you. I want you to do to me what you do to her."

"You don't know what you're saying. You don't know what I do to her. You might not like it."

"I just want to be with you. I want you to come to the barn Saturday morning and spend time with me. You don't know how much that means to me. You know a lot of girls here in school likes you. You play football, you're strong, handsome, and tough. Jeff, come to the barn and have your way with me. That's how much I want to see you. I've never had somebody as you pay me attention, and when you kissed me" – I paused – "I mean, look at me now. I'd do anything for you."

"Anything, Princess? You mean anything but be seen in public with me?"

"Just come and see me on Saturday morning."

"What time will you be there?"

"Probably about ten o'clock. I'm talking Mom into letting me stay the whole afternoon. It should get warmer as the day goes on. Jeff, I'll keep you warm in the hayloft if you come."

"I'll try to be there."

"Are we going to the stairwell today?"

"No." That's all he said. When the bell rang, he got up and went out the door. I was disappointed. He hadn't kissed me all week and I missed that.

Saturday morning after breakfast, I went back to my room and showered to get ready to go to the barn. I wanted to be fresh for Jeff. I had no idea what we would do that day. At ten o'clock, Mom and I got in the car and started driving toward the stables. On the way, we saw Jeff hitchhiking. I could feel my heartbeat pick up, I panic. I wondered how Mom was going to react if she knew Jeff was going towards the barn. I tried not to let her know I was panicking. I was almost hyperventilating when Mom asked, "Is that Jeff Gray?"

"Yes, Mom." Then I said, "Stop and give him a ride. He's probably going to the barn."

"Is he going to be there today?"

"I guess so. He's there once or twice a week, I hear."

"Ok, I'll give him a ride."

"I'm glad. I don't know what I would say to him at school if you didn't," I told her.

Mom pulled around in front of Jeff on the side of the road. I rolled down my window and motioned for him to come. "Are you going to the barn?" I asked.

"Yes," he said. Then he got in the back seat and we drove on.

While we were driving, my mom asked, "Do you have a horse, Jeff?"

"No, ma'am, the Morris's' daughter is away at college and they pay me a little money to take care of their horse."

Then Mom replied, "Princess told me she sees you down there occasionally. I didn't know if you had a horse or not."

I listened to Mom and Jeff talk back and forth. Jeff was being very polite. I knew he thought badly of me for stopping and giving him a ride, but I didn't know what else to do. We pulled in the driveway in front of the barn.

Jeff opened the car door and told Mom, "Thank you, ma'am, for giving me a ride. I appreciate it."

"You don't have a car, Jeff?"

"No, ma'am. My birthday is next week. I'll be sixteen and then I'll get my driver's license." He got out of the car and went inside the barn. I was barely keeping control of myself, trying not to let on to Mom that I knew Jeff was so moody and unpredictable, but he surprised me. It took me a moment to realize Jeff just need A chance to prove himself. I don't know what he would say to me when I got in the barn.

"He doesn't seem to be a bad guy. He was polite to me," Mom said.

“He’s not too bad. He stays to himself at school and pretty much a loner.”

“You don’t see him much at school?”

“I’ve got one class with him. He’s in a different world, Mom. I’m glad you stopped and gave him a ride.”

Then she caught me off guard by asking, “What do you mean, Jeff’s in a different world?”

“I don’t know, Sometimes I feel sorry for him.”

Then Mom said something I didn’t want to hear. “Don’t misunderstand me, Princess. You don’t need to be around people like that. We’re bringing you up for a better world, and your father and I are preparing you for college. You don’t have time for nonsense like Jeff Gray.”

I stepped out of the car and asked, “What time will you be back to pick me up?”

“How much time do you need today?”

“I don’t know. I’ve got to clean out the stall and exercise the horse some. I don’t know. If you give me about three or four hours, I have nothing else planned today. Is there anything you want me to do with you?”

“Not really, baby. I’ll be back in about three and a half hours, maybe four. There’s nothing you’ve got to do? You and Michelle going shopping or to the movies?”

“No, Mom, there’s nothing else.” After she drove away, I walked into the barn, I didn’t see Jeff anywhere. I looked up in the hayloft where I found him sitting on a bale of hay. I climbed up the ladder and sat down.

"Thanks for picking me up," he said

"I didn't know if you'd take a ride from us or not."

"I wanted a ride, but I was surprised to see you offer."

"Thanks for being polite to Mom. She said you were nice."

"Would she have said that if she knew I was fucking you?"

"You don't need to talk that way. I told her to pick you up and she did. Now you're being mean about it." I felt bad that Jeff resented me and my family.

"I'm sorry. Thank you for picking me up." Jeff stood up to take me by the hand, then sat me down with my back against a bale. Next, he did something strange. I thought we were going to have sex, but we didn't. He sat down in front of me and leaned back in my arms and I held him. With the back of his head on my left shoulder, I stroked his forehead and back through his hair. He had such thick hair and he smelled good.

Then he asked, "Why did you ask me how I felt about her?"

"I didn't mean anything by it. I just wondered," I paused. "I wondered why you're here with me if you love her."

"I don't know, Princess. Do I love her? Yes, maybe I do – to the point, it hurts. But here I am in your arms and you feel good. I feel like I can come here with you and hide. Princess, the whole world is against me and you know that. I'm never going to be anything or anybody. That's why when you asked me things about feelings..." he stopped before he could finish his thought. "We've got right now, the two of us. There's not even the next minute, the next second, there's no yesterday, it's just right now. I'm lying back in your arms and you're stroking my hair and right now I feel at peace with you. You can't get attached to me, you know that?"

"It's too late, Jeff."

"Don't you ever get attached to me. You have a future and it's not with me. I took your virginity, but we are not going to be together forever. Are you sorry that I did that to you?"

I thought for a minute before I answered him. "No, I'm not. I'm not sorry. The only thing I'm sorry about is that I know deep down we can't be together and I want to be. I wish you thought differently about me. Is sex all you want from me, Jeff? I guess I'm fooling myself and I'm giving you my body just to keep you."

He never answered, but for some reason, I slid my right hand in the front of his pants, grabbed him by his penis and played with him until he got hard. I just lay there doing it to him. He never said a word. I don't know why I did that. I guess it was because I wanted to have sex. After that, he stood up and I did, too. I pulled my pants down around my ankles and spread my legs for him to have sex. I couldn't tell him how much I was enjoying it. We lay there and he played with me until we had sex again. I couldn't tell him how much I needed him because I was afraid he would feel trapped. I was in heaven, and I was experiencing orgasms for the first time. I wouldn't let him up now that he had a finger in me. I was responding to every touch, we had sex for the third time. It was unbelievable.

We put our clothes back on and Jeff lay in my arms like a child. I was happy to hold him. "I'm going to be sixteen next week, Princess."

"I'm giving myself to you for your birthday. I wish I had more to give you and honestly, Jeff, you've given me more than I gave you."

"What do you mean? I didn't give you anything. I took from you."

"You gave me things that a girl like me never thought she would experience with someone like you. I don't think you realize you're popular in school. People won't say things to your face because you're strong and they're afraid of you. I've heard girls talk about you and some of the guys talk about you on the football team. You don't give yourself credit. But you're here with me and you put me in heaven with your touch."

"Nobody gives a damn about me, Princess!"

"You gave me the best I've ever got in my life for my birthday." We lay there for a little bit longer. "I better go. Thank you for the birthday present. You've made my birthday," he said.

"I forgot to ask you something. You don't have to tell me if you don't want to. Am I as good as she is to you?"

"I'm sorry, Princess, it's not that you are better than each other. She broke my heart and I take it out on you. Don't ask me that question again. My problem is that I know I will never end up with either one of you. You don't understand I have no future, but you give me peace, baby."

"Will you call me that again?"

"Call you what?"

"Call me baby. I know I'm being childish, but I like you calling me that. You know you're turning me into a woman before my time, what am I to do?"

Jeff climbed down the ladder and walked out the door. I had no idea what was ahead of me or what next week would bring, but knowing Jeff, I was sure it was going to be exciting.

Chapter 4

On Monday, the only thing I had to look forward to, seeing Jeff in civics class. When that class started, I sat beside him and everything seemed to be fine, I followed him under the stairwell. It really made my day. The day ended with no problems and I felt that everything was going smoothly except I didn't know where this was going to end. I knew it was coming. I just didn't know-how.

Something happened Thursday that no one could understand. When the last bell rang, I came out of class and saw Michelle. We got together and looked down the hallway. There were a bunch of people and a big commotion going on.

We walked that way and Michelle asked Tony, one of the football players, what was happening.

Tony looked around and said, "Jeff got in a fight."

I leaned around the door and looked in. Billy Evans was sitting on the floor.

"It was Jeff Gray?" I asked. I tried to maintain my composure in front of Michelle. I couldn't let anybody know that I was worried about Jeff.

We walked out the front door and looked down the street, Coach Surber was talking to Jeff. When the coach let him go, Jeff glanced up and saw me. I felt so helpless because I couldn't go to him and find out what happened.

Tony told us he heard that Billy was picking on Jeff's cousin Milo. Everyone knew that Billy was a bully, but he picked on the wrong guy when he picked on Jeff's cousin. Jeff told him to leave Milo alone, from what Tony heard. The word spread quickly that Jeff had knocked Billy out. The next day, the rest of the class said Billy shook his fist at Jeff and told him he would give him some of it when the bell rang. Billy started towards Jeff, who knocked him out with an overhand right. They say Billy was lying on the floor. Jeff walked out the door and down the street before the coach went after him and called him back to tell him he had hurt Billy.

This was the day before Jeff turned sixteen.

When I saw Jeff the next day, he wasn't talking about it. We did meet under the stairwell, but Jeff wasn't talking to anyone. I felt so sorry for him. And when the last bell rang for the first day of December, Jeff's 16th birthday, he was expelled from school, that's what people were saying.

I found out later they only suspended Jeff, not expelled him, and he had to come back with his parents before the school board to get him back in school. Jeff had a history of talking back to the teachers. I didn't know, but before I started seeing Jeff, he got caught drinking while on the football team, and after this, everything added up and the school board decided it was best to suspend him.

I was brokenhearted. I didn't know what was going to happen. After Friday, Jeff would not be at school and nobody knew when he was coming back or if he was coming back at all. The whole town was buzzing about it and a lot of people were glad Jeff did what he did. Billy was big and bullied a lot of people and got away with it until he met Jeff Gray.

I wanted to call Jeff, but I was afraid to. I didn't know what to say to him. A week went by before anyone saw Jeff again. I was surprised his mom brought him by the school to get homework assignments so he wouldn't get behind. That was a good sign he was coming back, but it would still be a while before I would get to talk to him.

I had to wait until I was sure that Mom and Dad were busy doing something else before I went to my room and I dialed Jeff's number. Luckily, he was the one who answered the phone.

"Jeff, I'm glad you answered the phone. How are you?"

"I'm all right. I'm surprised you called me."

"I've been worried about you."

"Why would you worry about me?"

"Jeff, please don't do that. You know I care."

"Princess! You stop right now. I've told you."

I interrupted before he got through talking. "Jeff, you can't stop me from having feelings for you! And being worried about you!"

"Damn, I told you! Look what I've done to you. I'm no good. This is just a moment in your life, so what are you thinking?"

"You can't stop me for caring about you."

"Princess, you gotta stop."

"It's cold now, but I'm going to be at the barn this coming Saturday probably about eleven o'clock. I was hoping the day will get a little bit warmer and I want to see you. I'm going to have the whole afternoon to myself. I'm leaving it up to you, but please come and see me."

There was silence on the phone for a moment. "I've got to go, Princess. Goodbye." He hung up without telling me if he was going to come to see me or not.

That night, my parents got into a discussion about everyone around town talking about Jeff. I knew Dad was going to ask me about him.

"Princess, do you have classes with Jeff Gray?" he asked.

My mom looked over at me. I held up my head up, looked at Dad and replied, "I had one class with him until he got expelled. civics class with Mr. Lindsay."

"Is he coming back to school?"

"I don't know, Dad. Everybody in school was talking about him. I hear there's a lot of guys in the eighth grade that was glad Jeff did what he did. Everyone knows Billy is a bully."

"If he comes back to school, I want you to stay away from him," Dad told me. "I don't want you to be around somebody like that."

Then Mom spoke up, "I met Jeff one time when I was taking Princess to the barn. He seemed like a pretty nice young man. He was polite to me."

"You mean to tell me Jeff Gray was at the barn with our daughter?"

"Dad he never comes around me. He stays to himself and he takes care of the Morris's' horse while their daughters in college. He never comes around me, and besides, he doesn't like me."

"What do you mean he doesn't like you?" Dad asked.

"He's only said two words to me at a time the whole year. Well – he's said more than that."

Mom swallowed her last bite of food and asked, "What did he say to you, baby?"

"This was a while back, Mom. He called me a little rich girl, that's all."

"Is that what Michelle was talking about the other day. Something about Jeff went by you or something like that?"

"I don't know what Michelle was talking about. She asked me about Jeff one time and I told her it was nothing. Sometimes we – sometimes we make fun of Jeff and it makes him mad. I told Michelle I wouldn't do it anymore because I was afraid of him."

My dad stopped eating and looked at me. "You stay away from that boy. If we're lucky he won't get back in school. We don't need that kind around to start with."

When my dad said that, it made me sad. If my parents knew how I felt about him they certainly would have a fit, but it's too late. I didn't know what to think, but I knew for some reason when I'm with Jeff, I felt different. I knew I wasn't supposed to, but I liked what he did to me and I liked pleasing him. It was too late, I thought to myself. It's too late and there's no hope for me.

When I got to school, all Michelle could talk about was how mean and crazy Jeff was. Everybody said he was unpredictable. When Michelle noticed I wasn't responding, she stopped and said, "You don't seem to be interested in talking. You know I've been suspicious. Every time we go by him or around him you act funny."

"What!"

"There you go again, acting funny."

"I'm not acting any different."

"I don't know, we used to run around on the weekends together. Now it seems like you're always busy and you don't have time. All of a sudden we don't talk on the phone like we used to. Something is going on and you're not telling me what it is."

"I don't know what's going on, Michelle. I feel different and don't ask me why because I don't know."

"Ok then. I'll see you later."

The bell rang and we went to our homerooms, school was different now that Jeff wasn't here. It was as if I had nothing to look forward to. There was not a lot of excitement going through the day and when I got to civics class I sat in the back beside Jeff's empty desk. when class was over, I asked our teacher, "Mr. Lindsay have you heard anything about Jeff Gray? Is he coming back to school?"

"Princess, I couldn't help but notice you always sit in the back with Jeff. Why are you asking about him?"

"Well, I just wondered. He was always pretty nice to me and he was fun to talk to. I mean, you know Jeff's different, and I'll just wonder if he was coming back to school?"

"Yes, you could say Jeff's different, that's for sure, but I think he has to come back with his parents and talk to the school board. That's the last I heard. I don't know when it's going to take place, though."

"I was wondering. I think a lot of people don't give Jeff a chance."

"I think you're right. A lot of people don't give him a chance. He seems to have something on his mind all the time. I don't think he has a very good home life and there were some rumors about some girl. As young as he is, you wouldn't think anything like that would be a problem. Has he ever talked to you about such things, Princess?"

"Not really. I think he resents me. He called me a spoiled little rich girl."

"If I hear anything, I'll let you know."

I turned and walked out of the classroom. I had to walk up the steps where Jeff and I usually met under the stairwell. I missed him more than I realized. I missed him so much that I could imagine being with him. I was glad it was Friday because I was hoping he would be at the barn on Saturday. Although the days were cold, I hoped he would show up. The rest of the day went really smoothly. Michelle and I made plans to go to the movies on Saturday night.

I lay in bed Friday night thinking about Jeff. I wanted to see him and wondered what was going through his mind about school and his future. Did he even care about his future? He told me he had no future.

Saturday morning, I got ready to go to the barn. On the way, Mom asked me if I thought Jeff was going to be there. "Has anyone heard about Jeff Gray? What's going to happen to him?"

"No, no one knows. I asked Mr. Lindsay about him and he thought that his parents had to come and talk to the school board to get Jeff back into school. You know, Mom, he turned 16 last Friday, so he's old enough to be expelled. I guess that's the way the law works about being of age."

"If he's at the barn today, Princess stay away from him. You know what your dad said."

"He has nothing to do with me, Mom. Because we've got money, he resents me. He's as much told me to my face in school so I don't expect to see him and if I do, he won't come around me."

"You be careful."

"Mom he's not going to do anything to me. He's not that kind of guy." I was afraid on the way to the barn we may pass him, didn't see him anywhere. I was relieved, on one hand, and was worried he wasn't going to be there. It was ten-thirty when Mom dropped me off. I went inside, Jeff wasn't there. I started grooming my horse and cleaned out the stall.

Then I heard Jeff's voice. "Hey, Princess."

I looked up and Jeff was in the hayloft looking down at me. "How long have you been here?"

"About an hour."

"Why didn't you say something?"

"I was waiting until you finished with your horse."

"I still need to throw some hay to her."

"Come on up."

"Ok, I'll be up in a minute."

I finished what I had to do, grabbed a blanket and went up to the hayloft with him. Jeff was in a mood I'd never seen him in before. I could feel he was so sad. He had a very solemn look on his face when I said, "I've missed you."

"Why would you miss me?"

"Because I don't understand you. You don't care anything about me, do you?"

"What am I supposed to care about with everything else going on around me," Jeff asked.

"Are you going to come back to school?"

"I don't know. The principal called my parents. I'm supposed to go back with them and sit in front of the school board."

"What are you're going to do?"

"I don't care anymore."

"You've got to care; you've just got to."

"You don't understand. You come from a privileged home with money anything you want, but you know what you've got that I would love to have?"

"I don't know. What do I have?"

"Peace, peace in your home not having parents that fight all the time. I'm talking about the real fight. My mom and dad fight all the time and that's the reason my dad drew a knife on me. They were fighting and I got in the middle of it. You've got in your house what I'd like to have in mind, peace, just peace of mind. I try not to blame my parents. They're doing the best they can, but they just," he paused. "I don't know how to explain it to you, Princess. How would you like to go home from school on your 16th birthday and walk in the door and there's a big dinner on the table with a birthday cake, but nobody is there? It's just my mom and she already got the word that I've been expelled. I sat at the table with all that food while my mom was washing dishes crying. There were no candles on the cake, and I ate by myself. There was no celebration. I never had a piece of the cake. I just ate my dinner and I wanted to die.

I took Jeff in my arms and we lay back against a hay bale. I held him and he was almost in tears. I didn't know what to do for him, but it hurt me to hear how he spent his sixteenth birthday. He was right. I couldn't imagine that. I held him for a while, and I have to admit, I felt good holding him. He had his head on my shoulder and my arms around him. I could feel his heartbeat against my body. He was in such a sad mood. We lay there the whole time. He never asked me for sex or made any mention of it. We just lay there together. I was hoping he was starting to have feelings for me more than just sex and that he really was falling in love with me, but I guess I was asking too much. I don't know how long we lay there. I didn't want to let him go. Jeff was like a little child, but I thought about the people that hated him or feared him, and I remembered the times I'd made fun of him and now I hurt him. I could feel his pain at the same time, but I couldn't imagine having that in my house, and I realized I had such good parents.

For no reason, he got up and looked at me with some compassion in his eyes. I was hoping he would come out of this and that he would really have feelings for me. He started to go and I asked, "When will I see you again?"

He took a deep breath. "Do you really want to see me again knowing I'm nobody and never will be?"

"I know what you are. Like you told me, there's no yesterday, there's no tomorrow it's just right now it's just that moment under the stairwell just the hour we have here in the barn. I'll settle for that, Jeff if you will."

He turned and went down the ladder and walked out the barn door without telling me when I would see him again. When he left, I began to cry. I was crying for something that I knew was never, ever going to be. We wouldn't have a future, just like he said. We've only got these few moments, that's all we will ever have. Now I realized being this young I knew nothing about real life and the things people like Jeff go through. It made me think for the first time in my life how privileged I was and I better not take it for granted. It's true I was privileged. I had a good home life but right now I was so unhappy.

A week went by and I never heard a word from him. I didn't dare call him. I really wanted to, but I was afraid. When he told me how he spent his sixteenth birthday I wanted to cry and I did. I was only a year away from my sixtieth birthday and I expected to have a big celebration, but Jeff had none of that; he had nothing but heartbreak.

Every day at school I would look back in the corner where we sat. Without Jeff, the whole room seemed empty. Each day was the same, but Michelle started aggravating me. She kept asking why I was so moody. I told her I had things on my mind. Then one day she really pissed me off.

"Listen to me, girl!" Michelle said. "Ever since Jeff Gray was kicked out of school, you've been acting like it's the end of the world. I want to know what he has to do with you?"

I hung my head so she couldn't see my face turning red. I didn't want to talk about Jeff. I couldn't stand it, I missed him so bad. "Why do you keep bringing Jeff up?"

"Listen, this started not long after school started this year. You started changing and I could tell you aren't telling me what's going on. Now please tell me what is wrong with you?"

"There's nothing wrong let's just go to class." The bell rang and we went our separate ways.

She was right I couldn't get him off my mind I missed the excitement of kissing under the stairwell. I tried my best to show I was the same, but I couldn't control it. I missed him that bad to the point of being miserable. I was sure it was over and that I would probably never see him again and I had to get over it. I knew I was having more than just feelings for him. I wanted to use the L-word, but I didn't because he told me never to say it. He wouldn't let me say it. I wouldn't even admit to myself how I felt about him. I was so miserable I didn't want to go home. I couldn't control myself. I was down and hurting inside. I hated feeling like that I just knew Mom would realize something was bothering me and I had a feeling she knew what it was.

When I got home, she started in on me, wanting to know what was wrong with me. At the dinner table that night, Mom started to ask me questions. "Has Jeff Gray started back to school?"

I looked up from my plate at Mom. Dad said, "I heard he was down at the pool room the day before yesterday under the Rex Theater. They say he hit some guys upside of his head out of nowhere. I'm not sure what it was about, but they told Jeff not come back. That boy is no damn good."

When my dad said that, my heart cracked. He must really be hurting. Then Mom asked, "Princess, do you feel all right? I mean you seem to be somewhere else. Is something bothering you?" She put me on the spot.

Dad looked at me at the same time and said, "Yes, I've noticed you don't seem to be your happy self."

"Are you and Michelle getting along?" she asked.

I had no choice but to answer them. "Everything's fine. Everything is ok at school, but Michelle is asking me the same thing. What am I doing to make you guys think there's something wrong?"

"I'm just saying, baby, you seem to have something on your mind that you just can't let go of. Something is really bothering you."

"There's nothing going on. What am I doing to make you think something is bothering me?"

Then my dad asked, "Princess, what do you know about Jeff Gray?"

I almost froze in place I didn't know what to say. "Dad, I don't understand why you are asking me about him."

"I was down at Higgins' filling station a couple of days ago when they were talking about Jeff. This guy from Woodlawn said Jeff was messing around with his daughter. He's ready to kill him."

I told Dad, "I had one class with him and now he's gone and nobody knows if he is coming back to school or not."

"Well, Christmas is coming and that should cheer you up." Dad continued to eat, but he and Mom looked at me and things got quiet. We finished our meal and Mom asked me to help her wash the dishes, which meant that she wanted to talk to me away from Dad. He went to the living room to watch the local news. Mom and I got up all the dishes and carried them to the sink. That's how we did it, she washed and I dried. I knew what she was going to ask me. I had no idea how I was going to handle this.

"Ok, baby, tell me what's on your mind. Do you think I don't know that something is bothering you? I am your mother; I know when something is bothering you. Are you going to tell me?"

I took a dish out of her hand, rinsed it off, then dried it with my towel. I laid the plate down and turned around and looked at her. "Mom, let me ask you something personal. I'm almost sixteen, and I think I can ask you this question from a daughter to her mom."

"Ok, you're saying it's personal. If that's the case I don't know if I can answer it."

"Was Dad your first?"

"Princess! Where did that come from?"

"Mom, I need to know. Was Dad your first love?"

Mom looked around the corner to make sure Dad was watching TV. She knew he couldn't hear us and she looked back at me. "I don't know why you're asking me this, but no, he was not my first love. We very seldom end up with our first. Some do, but most of the time we never end up with them. There's an old saying, Princess, the first cut is the deepest. It's because it's all new to us. A boy is paying attention to us for the first time and his touch to our bodies, the way he talks to us, is exciting. The way we feel when we're not with them. Our imagination runs away with us. We find ourselves doing things we never thought we would do. We get so overcome with the attention that we mistake it for love. Then when that boy is gone, we can never forget him. But it serves one purpose, Princess. When we do meet the right one, we guard ourselves against being fooled again. We judge the boy by how he treats us how he feels for us, and there's a trust that grows between two people. We used to call that chemistry. You've got to trust a man that he will be there for you when age diminishes your beauty, that he'll put you above everything else in his life and you can trust that he truly loves you for who you are. When I say chemistry, I mean you're both going in the same direction. There's no longer just you or him. You become one, and that's when lovemaking is a reward of becoming one with each other. You never have sex, you could only make love. There's a difference, and when you get old enough you'll have to find out the difference. Baby, you asked me for a reason. What is it?"

"Mom, I can't tell you. I just can't tell you."

"By any chance, does Jeff Gray have anything do with this?"

I took another plate out of her hand, rinsed it off and began to dry it. I was slow to answer her. "No."

She looks at me. "Are you sure he has nothing do with the way you're acting? Are you telling me the truth?"

"Mom, I never said anything about Jeff Gray. Why did you bring him up?"

"Because every time I've been with you and he was around I could see a twinkle in your eye. You can't fool your mother. Then you're asking me about my first, and two and two go together, baby."

Then she grabbed me by my shoulders and looked me in my face. “Princess, I’m not going to ask you this again. Whatever you’re into, baby, you be extremely careful. I don’t know if Jeff Gray has anything to do with you or not. I don’t want to know now and I don’t want to break your trust in me so I’m not going to ask you again about him. You never said it was him, but I’ve got a feeling it is. I remember my youth. To answer your question, your dad was not the first. There was one who was wild and crazy. My parents hated him, but when I was with him my world was so exciting. I’ll carry it to my grave and your dad knows about him. But remember, Princess, I love your father. I’m sure he had an idea that he wasn’t my first love, but he wanted to marry me anyway. He loves me and I love him. All I had with that first guy was a good time and I was too young to realize you can’t live off of good times. That guy was never there for me. He just disappeared and left me not knowing what happened to him. Princess, I would never have any peace in my life if I married that guy. We have a good home, a good life, and you’re going to get a good education. I wasn’t thinking about those things back then. You are growing up, baby, and I’m concerned for you because I’m your mother. You’ve got to be careful. You have a future and you can’t mess it up so easily by making wrong choices. Always remember that.”

We finished washing the dishes and when we were through, Mom hugged me real tight and whispered in my ear, “Be careful, Princess, be real careful. Remember, baby, you can really mess up if you're not careful."

I went to my room and looked at myself in the mirror. I realized my life was becoming complicated and I didn't like it. That was the first time Mom talked really honest with me. She knew something was happening in my life, and she knew it was Jeff. No one liked Jeff, I guess it was only me and the first love that liked him. I wondered what the girl that broke his heart did. She loved him and I was so afraid I did too because it hurt.

Chapter 5

After the holidays, I didn't hear anything about Jeff. Nobody said anything, and there were no rumors floating around. We assumed he wasn't coming back. I changed my attitude about people. He changed my world. It was different now and I guess I owed that to Jeff. Before he came into my life, I viewed people less. I didn't give much thought to what other people went through that didn't have the things that I have.

My Christmas was wonderful, as long as I didn't think about Jeff. I had very expensive gifts. I was pampered and I didn't think about people who had nothing and were struggling to go through life. I didn't realize I had the one thing that Jeff wanted more than anything else and that was peace in his own house. I never heard my parents argue or get mad at each other, at least not in front of me. Jeff told me about his mom and dad how they would fight, that he couldn't take it anymore. I just knew I'd never see him again. It was painful for me. I knew I had everything, everything but Jeff.

When school started after Christmas, in homeroom I talked to Michelle and went to my classes. Then it was time for civics. I really didn't want to go in that room. I knew it was going to be empty. I shuffled my feet and was slow getting to class. Mr. Lindsay had a bad habit of being late, so I knew it was no real hurry. I walked through the door and I looked up to see Jeff sitting in the back corner. I stopped dead in my tracks, looking at him. My chest was pounding and he smiled at me as I walked. I didn't take my eyes off of him as I sat down.

"Hello," he said.

I smiled. "Hello."

We both sat there looking at each other. I knew I was smiling and to my delight, he was too.

"Are you back in school for good?"

"Yes. My folks went to the school board and got me back in on probation."

"What does that mean?"

"I can't get in trouble anymore or I'll be gone for good. Let's not talk about it. You want to know something?" Jeff asked with a big smile on his face.

"Yes, I do."

"Do you know how much I missed you? I thought about you all through Christmas. I knew you had a good Christmas with your family. I couldn't get you off my mind. I missed you."

I looked in Jeff's eyes. I never heard such sweet words coming from him. I couldn't believe he missed me. I didn't want to tell him about my Christmas. He knew I was a spoiled little rich girl and he resented me for it. The way he was talking to me now made me feel good. I didn't know how to tell him that I had changed, that he opened up my eyes to other people's needs and wants and the things they didn't have, especially having peace, like in my house. So I decided to ask him about his Christmas. I hoped that wasn't a mistake.

"My Christmas was ok, but not hearing from you, it wasn't the best Christmas I've had. What about you?"

"Believe it or not, for once, it went smoothly. I didn't expect that we had to go to the school board. I worried that my parents wouldn't get along, but it was like it used to be when I was growing up. They didn't get into a fight this time. The worst part about my Christmas this year was thinking of you, and that I know I'm never going to be good enough for you. I fear that, but I felt the same way about the other girl. I won't mention her name to you. You know who I'm talking about. You say you worried about me during your Christmas. What did you miss about me?"

"I missed you kissing me. I missed you holding me. I missed hearing your voice. Jeff, I missed everything about you. I worried so much and I want to tell you something that you don't want to hear."

"No!"

"Please Jeff, let me tell you how I feel about you."

"No, please don't say it. Let it go. Can I tell you something now?" Jeff asked.

"You know you can."

"Do you know how much I want to have sex with you?"

I wanted to hear him say that, but at the same time, I was disappointed. I was hoping he wanted me because he loved me.

"I missed having sex with you. Are we going to meet under the stairwell today?"

"Better not. I have to put my hand in your pants."

"I'm glad to hear that."

Then Mr. Lindsay came in and class started. He made an announcement. "Welcome back, Jeff, we missed you. I hope you kept up with the homework assignments that I gave you."

"Yes sir, I did the best I could."

Then Mr. Lindsay said, "Perhaps Princess could help you catch up in the library."

"Yes sir," I said. "If Jeff wants me to, I'd be glad to do it."

"How about it, Jeff?"

"Yes sir, when can we start?"

"I'll try to coordinate your study halls. Perhaps you could do it in the library here in school. Would then be ok, Princess?"

"Yes sir, that would be fine with me."

"Then it's settled."

I was glad to do this. It gave me a chance to be with Jeff a little bit longer in the day and I was looking forward to it. Jeff and I could sit in the library where we could really talk and I could ask him so many questions. The class was almost over when I told Jeff, "You better meet me under the stairwell. I've just got to kiss you."

"Just follow me." The class was over and I followed him under the stairwell and around the corner we went. I laid my books down and wrapped my arms around his neck. We kissed deeply. I had missed this so much. Jeff put his hand in my panties, I spread my legs a little bit and he put a finger in me. I closed my eyes, he worked just enough that I got off. He pulled his finger out and stuck it in his mouth. He grinned at me and told me how sweet it tasted. I couldn't believe how wild and crazy he was. I was back in heaven. He looked around the corner and slipped away with me right behind him.

Yes, I was in a better mood now and I guess it showed on my face. Michelle said something about it and my mom even told me she was glad to see me cheer up. I didn't tell her that Jeff was back in school and she didn't ask. I was glad she didn't. The next day at school, Mr. Lindsay told me and Jeff that he'd arranged a few things so that at the end of the day Jeff and I could meet in the library and if need be, we could stay after school. I was excited I could spend more time with him right out in public where everybody could see us and nobody would question what we were doing.

When Michelle found out about it, she started laughing. "You're going to have to sit with Jeff Gray!"

"What am I supposed to do? Mr. Lindsay wants me to help him to make sure he stays up with the rest of us after being out of school so long. I want to help him."

Michelle noticed I wasn't laughing about it. I had to go home and tell Mom that I'd be staying over after school.

Sitting at the table eating, I decided to come right out and tell Mom in front of Dad. "Mom, I volunteered to stay after school in the library to help someone with their studies."

"That's nice."

"Mr. Lindsay wants me to help this guy with his lessons to make sure he keeps up, so I volunteered I will be late getting home."

"Oh, that's nice of you. Who is it?"

"Jeff Gray."

My dad stopped eating, looked at me laid his fork on his plate, and said, "No you're not!"

Mom responded, "Now, Doug, all she's doing is helping him keep up. I don't see anything wrong with that."

"She is not staying after school with Jeff Gray and that's final. It's not going to happen!"

"Please, Daddy, I'm just going to help him. We're going to be in the library. Why can't I do that?"

"I don't want you around him! That's all there is to it, that's enough!" He was raising his voice to me. He never did that.

Then my mom told him, "Doug, I think we should let her help him. I see nothing wrong with that. They're going to be in school and I don't see any problem with it."

"Why can't he get someone else to help him!"

"I'm in the same class with him, and Mr. Lindsay asked me to help him."

"Coach Lindsay, he's your teacher?"

"Yes, civics."

“Doug, I see no harm in it. She’s going to be able to help him. Don’t we want our daughter to be helpful to people?”

“How are you going to get home if you stay after school?”

“I’ll pick her up,” Mom said. “We should let her do it.”

“Please, Daddy, I want to help him. I’m going to college to be a teacher. This would give me a chance to see what it’s like to teach someone.”

“Ok then. If you want to help him, I want you to be ready on time when your mother comes to pick you up.”

“I can call her from school and be ready when she gets there.”

We finished eating, Dad went to watch TV watching the news. Time to wash the dishes. I turned to her and said, “Thanks, Mom.”

She knew what I meant. “When did Jeff start back to school? You didn’t tell me.”

“He was in civics class on Monday, he came back after the holidays.”

“Princess, I know something is going on between you and him and I’m afraid for you.”

“Mom, there’s nothing going on between me and Jeff. I’m just going to help him with civics.”

“Princess,” Mom stopped talking and looked around the corner to make sure Dad was watching TV. Then she came back and continued, “Remember me telling you about the wild and crazy boy that my parents hated that I had the time of my life with?”

"Yes."

"There was nothing going on between me and him, either."

I looked at Mom. She had that a grimace, a look of regret on her face that I didn't see very often.

"Mom, you look a little sad," I said. I wasn't sure why, she returned my look, with a smile and I smiled back at her.

"Baby, just..." She never finished the sentence, but I had a feeling she knew.

We finished washing the dishes and I dried my hands off. I hugged her and told her that I loved her. She stood there holding me and whispered, "My little girl." There were tears in her eyes. Maybe she knew what was going to happen to me in the end.

The next day at school I was all set, to stay over and spend more time with Jeff. I didn't care if it was in the library. We would be in private and we could talk. I thought I might force him to say something to me. Maybe at least that he liked me for more than just sex.

In civics class, I informed Mr. Lindsay that I was going to help Jeff, after school and that Jeff agreed. We met under the stairwell, we kissed as young lovers would. I told Jeff I'd see him in the library after our last class.

During lunch, I spotted him at another table. Michelle was sitting with me and she had to make a remark about him. "Look at that dumb ass, he looks like he needs help." I acted like it didn't bother me. I didn't know what else to do, but I couldn't laugh at him. I just wanted to be with him. I wanted him to touch me, and do wherever he wanted to do with me.

After school, we met in the library, found a table to ourselves close to the windows and sat down across from one another. I was in heaven being with him even with the table between us. Just being with him meant everything to me. We read a little bit out of the civics book, but Jeff kept looking at me. We started talking, I found my opening.

"Did you really miss me while I was out?" he asked.

"Yes," I said. "If you only knew how much I missed you."

"I had a lot to think about, Princess, school, family, my future."

"Did you think about me?"

"I thought about you a lot, how sorry I am that I raped you. I regret that."

"You didn't have to take advantage of me. I would have given myself to you, that's how I feel about you."

"I lost my mind that day. I was hurting inside, I like you so much it scares me," Jeff said.

"Then tell me. Tell me you love me."

"I can't"

"Why not?"

"If I thought there was some hope I would. You've got a future, I don't."

"Why won't you? Why can't you say those words? I guess I was hoping for too much from you," I said

"I can't, just can't," he answered.

"You told me there was no yesterday, there's no tomorrow, there's just right now. Tell me you love me for just right now, just this moment. I'll settle for just right now. Maybe tomorrow there'll be another right now. We've got this moment. Tell me you love me. Tell me you want to be with me, just for right now. Just this moment. Each day we see each other there will only be right now."

He answered me, "Princess if I tell you I love you, it will only be for that moment. No yesterday, no tomorrow, only right now. Can you settle for that?"

"Yes, I can. And every time I see you it will be a right now moment. That's better than nothing."

Jeff sat back in his chair and looked at me. A tear ran down his cheek I don't know why. He'd been told all of his life that he was no good and that he would never be anybody. It seemed like the whole town told Jeff that. What happened to make them feel that a way about him? I didn't know, I just knew to me he was becoming everything in my life. How do you explain the sadness on someone's face? Jeff wanted somebody to love him. He didn't know how to accept it. He kept telling himself he was a nobody. His family's environment was killing him, and I wanted to help him because I was so in love with him. I wouldn't dare tell him I noticed the tears because tears were starting to run down my cheeks. I felt so close to him, and I could feel his pain, I was hurting with him.

I read some more out loud from the civics book. Jeff had a hard time concentrating. I did everything I could to help him. Time run out so I had to go call Mom. Jeff and I went outside to wait for her. He wanted to leave before she got there, but I wouldn't let him. I don't know why he wanted to leave. He kept saying he wasn't good enough for me. It hurt me to see him like that. He walked down the street in front of the school and Mom passed him on way to pick me up.

"Was that Jeff I passed?"

"Yes, Mom."

"I would have given him a ride if he stayed around."

"Would you really?"

"Well, yes. Why wouldn't I?"

"If Dad found out, he would be mad."

"What your father doesn't know won't hurt him, will it?"

I looked over at her. She had a big smile and we both laughed out loud.

"How did your session go?"

"Mama, I don't know. I feel sorry for Jeff. He has a really bad home life, and he puts himself down all the time."

"He puts himself down in front of you?" Mom looked over at me for a second before she focused back on the road.

"You know how I feel about it, don't you?"

"I'm afraid I do, it worries me."

"What are you worried about, Mom?"

"Baby, your mother was young once. I made a mistake telling you about my past, and I wish – well I shouldn't have told you about it."

"Mom, I'm fifteen now. I know I don't know anything about the real world because you and Dad protected me from it, but Jeff brings so much excitement in my life. I can't help it, Mama."

"That's what I'm worried about. Excitement can make you do things you shouldn't do and you make bad decisions that you could regret and hurt your future. I'm going to stop at the Dairy Bar and pick up sandwiches for supper. I know your daddy would want a hamburger. What do you want?"

"I'll take a hamburger and fries." We stopped and got sandwiches and went home. Dad didn't say a word or ask me anything about Jeff. I think he was preoccupied with his business.

The next day at school I got a surprise. Jeff had gotten his driver's license and a car to go with it. In civics class, Jeff turned to me and said, "You told me that you want me to tell you that I loved you. Now if I tell you I love you, when are you going out on a date with me?"

Now I knew I was in trouble. He put me on the spot. How was I going to answer him after begging him to tell me he loved me? "You know I can't."

Jeff turned around in his seat, folded his arms, and sat there with a really solemn look. I felt so uncomfortable. He never spoke another word during the whole class. I didn't dare ask him to meet me under the stairwell. He did have a point. I asked him to tell me that he loved me, but I couldn't go with him in public.

When the bell rang, Jeff got up and left. I sat there a moment not knowing what to do or say to him. There was no way my mom would let me go out with him. God forbid if Dad found out. I never saw Jeff for the rest of the day. He went out for lunch now that he has his own car.

I was down again and Michelle noticed. I didn't want to talk to her about it. It was the middle of January and too cold to go to the barn and stay any length of time. I went long enough to feed my horse and make sure everything was secure. Mom stayed with me until I got it done. That meant that I was only seeing Jeff at school. He had his car and I couldn't go out with him. I desperately wanted to. I dreamed about it and even fantasized about it. We stopped meeting under the stairwell. I don't know why because Jeff was still nice to me. It was as if he changed his attitude towards me. I could feel it.

When we were talking in Mr. Lindsay's class, Jeff never mentioned that he was getting a car. I think he was using it to put me on the spot to see if I would go out with him, and he knew I couldn't. I felt like he did it just to hurt me. Something was wrong and I wanted to know why. So I came right out and asked him. "You're acting differently towards me. We're not meeting under the stairwell and you're not talking to me like you used to. I want to know why. Are you seeing the girl from Woodlawn? If you are, I understand. She's much prettier than I am, and she probably pleases you better than I do. I guess she can go out in the car with you and I can't. Is this what you're doing?"

He turned and looked at me he was slow to answer. "Let's say I am seeing her. Why should you care?"

I lowered my head and slowly looked up at him. Then I came right out and said, "Because I'm in love with you and I'm jealous of her. I wish I was her if that's what pleases you. I can't go out in public with you because I don't want anything to happen that would keep us from seeing each other. I knew you were turning sixteen and you were getting your driver's license, but you never told me you were going to get a car. Where did the car come from?"

"My uncle gave it to me because I couldn't afford to buy one. So he gave it to me to drive to work and school. I'm going to answer you, Princess, about the other girl. She hurt me very much and I'm afraid to fall in love with you because I've been hurt so much already and I'm only sixteen. Everything in my life is wrong and it started with her and now you're telling me you're falling in love with me. I didn't mean for that to happen. I was just using you. I need to get away from you before something serious happens before I do something to you that we will regret. She's not better than you, not in any way at all. You tell me you're falling in love with me, but are you going to hurt me in the end? I've told you before, we can only have a moment. You're nothing like her, Princess. I know you're probably a better person than she will ever be. What can I tell you about her other than it's a lot of pain for me? Her parents hate me as much as your parents hate me, and I don't blame them. I was never taught anything about how to act around people. Every time I think things are good for me, my parents go crazy and it drives me nuts. That's the reason I feel like I'm not worthy of you. All of this wasn't supposed to happen between us, Princess."

Looking at Jeff's face the whole time. He was talking to me, he was hurting. "Listen to me, Jeff. I want to go out with you so bad. I want to sit in the car with you and go on a date as other girls do. I want to be happy, but when I'm with you, if you're not happy, I'm not happy because I love you and I want you to be happy. What happened between you and her? Is it over for you with her?"

"Yes, it's over. Whether I like it or not, it's over."

"I want to be here for you. I want you to want me like you say you want her. I want you to love me. I want you to want to be with me all the time, but I know I can't be her."

"Stop! I don't want you to be her. I don't want to go back to that. I've messed everything up, Princess. I wish I never kissed you. I didn't see this coming."

"I'm so glad you kissed me, Jeff."

"Princess, there'll be other boys to kiss you who want to do what I've been doing to you."

"It's too late, Jeff. I don't want anybody else."

"What are we going to do?"

"You'll see me as much as you can, as much as we can, we'll sneak around if we have to. I'll do what I have to do to see you, to get in your car with you and sit beside you and experience everything there is about you as long as I can."

He grabbed me by the hand, looked at me and shook his head. "Ok."

We decided to meet in the library that day after school. I was thrilled. I called Mom at the end of the day and told her I was staying over and she didn't ask me why, but I'm sure she knew.

After the last class, I walked through the door in the library. Jeff was sitting at the table by the windows. He liked a lot of light and I did, too. I sat down across the table from him. To my relief, he was smiling.

"You seem to be in a good mood since we talked."

"Yes, I am."

"I've got to make a confession. I miss meeting you under the stairwell."

"I have a confession, too."

"Do you miss meeting me too?"

"Now that I've got this car, at least I can get away from home when all the fighting is going on, but then I get aggravated because I can't come and pick you up."

"You want to come and pick me up? Oh, Jeff, I do want to go out with you I don't know what I'm going to do. I miss you so much," I told him.

"When my parents get to fighting, when I can't stand it anymore, I get in my car and take a ride. I went out to Iron Ridge and pulled up in the woods just to be by myself. I had some beer and I sat there listening to the radio, I was thinking about you. I looked in the big back seat in my car and I could imagine you rolled up in a blanket naked. I really got a hard-on just thinking about you."

My face turned red as Jeff talked that way. I couldn't let him know it aroused me, that I wanted him. Without saying another word, he stood up and reached out for my hand.

"Come on," he said.
"Where are we going?"
"Come on, I'll show you."
We walked down the hallway.
There were a few people in the hall.
Then Jeff let go of my hand.
"Follow me."
"Where are we going?"
"Just follow me, I'll show you."
We walked halfway down the hallway,
around the corner
and came to a door.
Jeff left me standing there
as he peered around the corner
to see if anybody was looking.
Then he opened the door
and we both walked in.
It was the janitor's broom closet.
He shut the door behind us.
"Take your panties off."
"What are we going to do?"
"Just take your panties off."
I slid my panties to the floor

and left them on one leg
Jeff turned around and grabbed me by my waist
and sat me up on the table.
“Spread your legs open.”
Jeff dropped his pants and stuck it in me.
He grabbed me by my butt,
and pulled me close to him.
I put my arms around him,
and we began to have sex.
I moaned with pleasure.
“Oh Jeff, you’re so crazy and so good.”
With every stroke of his body, I was moaning
“Do you like this?”
“I can’t believe we're doing this here in school.
God, this is thrilling.”
He kept stroking me
and with every stroke, it got better.
This was the best he’d ever been to me,
and it was a thrill.
We could hear people outside walking by,
but Jeff never stopped.
I wouldn’t let him.
Then he said the one thing
that I’ve been waiting to hear.
“I love you, Princess.
God help me.”
I held him tight.
I wouldn’t let him stop.
He kept on and it was good.
I was getting off.
I could feel it not once but twice.

"Jeff, you're so good."
He threw his head back
and took a deep breath.
he pulled out just as he got off.
"God, I've never experienced anything like that.
Oh, Jeff, I love you.
I'd do anything to go out with you.
I don't know-how,
but I've got to get in the back seat of your car
I want to hold you,
I want to do this again."
"How do you think it makes me feel
that we can't be seen in public together?"

I jumped off the table and put my panties back on. We stood there holding each other. Jeff was shaking, and so was I. We held each other and finally, he opened the door. After he peeked out around the corner to look down the hallway, he motioned for me to come and we walked back to the library as though nothing had happened. I stopped in the bathroom on the way and so did Jeff. When I got back to the library, he smiled at me.

"I don't want to go home now. I want to go with you," I told him.

"I want you to come with me, but you know this is not going to be forever, it's only right now, you know that. It's just this moment. Remember that. It's this moment."

"It may be this moment, but I love you every moment. Do you hear me, Jeff? I don't care. I love you more than this moment."

"Listen to me, Princess; this will have to end one day. I'm not the one you will be marrying, you know that."

"I don't care. Let's live it as much as we can. I know this is not going to be in the end, live it, as long as we can, Jeff, please?"

We tried to read a bit more out of the civics book, but neither of us could concentrate after what just happened.

"Did you mean it?" I asked.

"Did I mean what?"

"You know, you told me you loved me. Did you mean it?"

He paused. "Yes, I love you enough that I know you can break my heart. I don't know if I can take it anymore. God help me, I've treated you wrong. I'm sorry for it. I've got you doing things you shouldn't be doing."

"Stop, Jeff. I know what I'm doing."

"No, you don't. You don't know what you're doing, how could you? I'm the first and only guy you've ever been with. This is all my fault. I will have to live with it the rest of my life because I hurt – I hurt you – I raped you. Now, look at us. I'm responsible for what you're doing now. I regret that so much, Princess. You know why I regret it?"

"I don't care Jeff. What's done is done. I know that I love you. I know it hurts when I'm not with you. I know I hurt when you tell me about your family life. You put yourself down, but it hurts me when I hear you talk that way. I know enough to know you may be right. This is just for right now. All I can say let's just live and enjoy every precious moment. Please stop putting yourself down. You've become everything to me, and I know I'm young and naïve, but when I'm with you, I feel so excited, so anxious. I know when you're fucking me –."

"Stop talking that way," he interrupted. Look what I've done to you. You never talked that way before, using that word. You didn't know what fucking was until I raped you."

"Stop, that's behind us. I know this. I'm going to find a way to go out with you in your car. I don't know-how, and I don't know when we're going to spend time together. We're not far from spring. School will be over for the year soon, and I'm going to enjoy this summer with you one way or another, you understand me, Jeff Gray? I love you and you can't stop me from loving you."

He sat back in his seat and looked at me. For a moment, we stared into each other's eyes and finally, Jeff said, "I've created a monster. In spite of everything, you're determined to stick with me. I hope you don't regret this, I long to see you every day and when I can't see you, I know what it is to have a broken heart. I'm so afraid you're going to find out the hard way."

It was time for me to leave and I went to the telephone to call mom. Jeff waited on me in the library and we sat together until she came. I looked out the window I saw Mom waiting.

When I got in the car, I was quiet. I believe Mom could sense something happened to me. Maybe it's because I felt guilty. I just got through having sex in school. I still couldn't believe we did that. God, Jeff was right, I'd become a monster.

" Is something wrong?" Mom asked.

"Mama, everything's wrong and everything is right."

"Oh my God, Princess, I'm not going to ask you how your session went. I believe I know this crazy boy is taking you places you've never been before."

I looked over at her. I could feel the solemn look on my face. I didn't lie to her.

"Yes," I said, simply.

She looked straight ahead and drove on home. We didn't talk about it again all through dinner, I tried to keep smiling so Dad wouldn't question me. *God help me*, I thought to myself. Jeff told me he loved me. *What am I going to do now*?

We met in the library for two more days that week, I didn't go with him to the janitor's closet again. I kept thinking about how fast my heart would beat, how it made me feel for him. I've got to admit my panties got wet just thinking about, Jeff would take a chance. Just that chance of getting caught got my adrenaline running. It was almost like I was a thrill-seeker, and I burned thinking about it. I was afraid it was taking too much of a chance, but I admit I enjoyed it. Jeff was nice to me and had a better attitude. I felt like he really did care for me now, and that made a difference in my life. Someone cared for me not just for fun, but for keeps. I hoped I wasn't fooling myself, not knowing the real world. I didn't care anymore. I looked around to see if anybody was watching us, and then I walked back to the table and kissed him goodbye for that day.

Chapter 6

The following week, Michelle and I were sitting in the cafeteria eating lunch when Tony, one of the football players, came by and sat down with us. To my surprise, he sat beside Michelle.

"Are you going to be able to go out with me this weekend?" he asked.

Michelle looked at me and then back at Tony. "Yes, my mom said I could go."

Tony smiled, "Great, I'll pick you up about six-thirty and we'll go skating."

"Great," Michelle said. "I have to be home by eleven."

"Shouldn't be a problem. I'll see you then." Tony finished his lunch and got up and left. I was sitting there surprised.

"Tony asked you to go out with him? When did this happen?"

"You've been so busy. I thought maybe you were mad at me. I was standing in the hallway waiting on you, and you never showed up. Tony saw me and we started talking. Then he asked me to go out with him. Mom said I could go, so we're going out this Friday."

"Isn't he good friends with Jeff Gray?" I asked.

"I don't know, I know they played football together last season. Tony is so cute. I think I could really get to like him."

"Yes, Tony is cute. And your parents said you could go?"

"Yes. This is going to be my first date."

Wheels began turning in my mind about how I was going to tell Michelle that I'm seeing Jeff. I wondered what she would think. The good thing was, Jeff and I planned to meet in the library after school. I couldn't wait to tell him what Michelle and Tony were doing. Maybe if I could talk them into taking me with them, it could be a way that I could see Jeff.

At the end of the day, I met Jeff, I told him I had a surprise. "Are you and Tony good friends?" I asked.

"Yes, why?"

"Tony is taking Michelle skating Friday night."

Jeff turned and looked at me. "Really! Taking Michelle out?"

"Yes, I was as surprised as you are. Michelle told me today at lunch."

"That's interesting."

"Think about it, Jeff. If I tell Michelle you and I are seeing each other and you know Tony, I think maybe we can work something out. I could go with them and meet you somewhere."

"You know how Michelle feels about me. If you tell her about us, she could ruin everything. How do you know you can trust her? You know damn well when you talk to her and she asks what you were doing, you can't trust her enough to tell her about us. Do you want to take that chance? Dammit, Princess!"

"That's not fair Jeff," I said, looking sad.

"I didn't mean it. I'm just frustrated because I can't take you out. I really want to."

"Are you and Tony close enough that you can tell him about us?" I asked.

"I guess so. I haven't told anybody about us, because I never thought there would be a reason to, but here we are trying to come up with a way to see each other. It sure would be nice to be away from school and get you in my back seat."

"I'm ready for your back seat," I said, smiling.

"How do I tell Tony? Do you think you can trust Michelle? You know she hates me."

"She doesn't really hate you. We just thought we were better than everybody else. I don't hate you; you know I love you."

"Let me talk to Tony first, but let's wait till they have their first date. It's too soon."

"I think you're right. We'd better wait and see what happens."

"You want to go to the janitor's broom closet?"

"Yes, I do but I'm afraid to. I'm not going, as much as I want to."

"I didn't think so. Are you going to be at the barn this Saturday?" Jeff asked

"Let's see how the weather is." The rest of the time in the library we read a little bit then Jeff put his hand under the table on my leg. I wanted him so badly, but we waited.

When we had a class together that Friday, I ask Jeff to be at the barn Saturday morning. The weather forecast looked like it was going to be in the fifties, and that would be ok in the hayloft. I was anxious to hear from Michelle about how her date went. I hoped it went well so that I could tell her about me and Jeff.

When Mom dropped me off at the barn Saturday about 11 o'clock, there was a car in front of the barn I'd never seen before. It was an older car, light green, with four doors, and a sun visor above the windshield. I had no idea who it belonged to. I thought maybe it could be Jeff's. I made plans with Mom before I went in to have at least a couple of hours. I wanted to spend more time with him.

He was already there working on the stall and the horse he was taking care of. When I walked in, he came over to me. To my delight, we embraced and kissed. He helped me clean out my stall, and I couldn't wait to finish. I wanted to go to the hayloft.

"Is that your car out there?" I asked.

"Yes."

"It's beautiful. What kind is it?"

"1956 four-door Pontiac. In its day, it was a luxury car. Did you see the Indian head on the hood?"

"Yes, I noticed it looks like it reflects. I can't wait, Jeff. Let's go to the hayloft." We spread the blanket and lay down together. He was in no rush. I lay in his arms. It was warm and cozy. It seemed like Jeff was different now; he was kind and gentle and thoughtful. He was slow to touch my body. I could feel the bulge in his pants pushing against me. I reached down and grabbed him by his penis, then he unbuttoned his pants and I unbuttoned mine. Every time I had sex with him it was wonderful. I'm judging that on the basis Jeff was the only guy I'd ever had sex with, but my problem was I couldn't imagine having sex with anybody else. Every time I was with him, I felt so safe and secure. I was so sensitive to his touch. We played around with each other, and it was so warm lying with him. I couldn't help myself; I was ready to go again and so we did. We both got off, then snuggled in the blanket.

He asked me about Michelle. "We're going to have to wait and see what happens," I told him.

"I hope those two hit it off. If they do, I've got an idea," Jeff said.

"What are you thinking?"

"Tony took Michelle to Red's Roller Rink, right?"

"Yes, that's what they said at lunch."

"I can park behind the skating rink and nobody would ever know I was there. If you could talk Michelle and Tony into it, maybe they can take you with them. Your mother would never know the difference. Instead of going into the building, you can just walk around back. I'll be waiting for you and we can sit in the car until you have to leave."

"That would be wonderful. Nobody would know I was there; I can't wait!"

"We have to wait to see how Tony and Michelle get along before we say a word to either of them, but I hope this works out. Maybe someday we can be seen in public together," Jeff said solemnly.

"I don't care what we have to do as long as you're willing to see me, that's all that matters to me. Please don't think bad about yourself, this is more my fault then it is yours. I think my parents did the wrong thing telling me I was better than everybody else. I'm not, Jeff. I'm so proud to be with you. You're taking me places in my mind, in my heart. If only you really knew what you're doing to me. Forget about the sex, as much as I like it. Please, let's do what we have to do to be together. Even if it's just for a moment, let's enjoy every moment of it." We had sex again, and it was so precious to me. Jeff had to go and it wasn't long before Mom would be picking me up.

Late that afternoon, Michelle called me. While we were talking, I waited for an opening to ask how her date went. She came right out and told me. "I had a good time skating I really enjoyed it. Tony's a nice guy. I'm hoping he'll ask me out again."

"I'm glad to hear that. I'm surprised he hasn't already asked you for this coming weekend."

"I hope he does. He's got a nice car. Of course, it's his dad's. He's thinking about taking me to the drive-in. I'd really like that. I'm sure my mom would let me go, I hope so anyway."

"You talk like you're ready to start dating. I don't know what I'll do."

"What do you mean you don't know what you'll do?"

"You've got somebody taking you out. Nobody's asked me."

"Are you sure? I think you've been seeing somebody for a while. That's what you've been keeping from me. Come on, Princess, tell me the truth."

"What makes you say that?"

"The way you've been acting for the last few months. We don't do anything together anymore, you've always got something else to do. You come up with some excuse that you have something else to do that I'm not part of."

"There's nothing going on, I'm glad you're enjoying yourself with Tony. I wish I had somebody."

"Are we going to church together in the morning?"

"I guess so. I'll see you there. I have to go now, talk to you later."

When Michelle hung up, I still wasn't sure how to tell her about Jeff. I just felt like she wasn't ready and had no idea how she would react. If she knew what I'd been doing with him the last few months, I don't believe I could tell her. I decided I better keep it to myself.

I met Michelle at church Sunday. She was excited about dating Tony. They had a good time roller skating. I was afraid to tell her what I had in mind, but I was sure listening to her, she was not ready to hear what I wanted to tell her about me and Jeff. So, I just listened. She was excited and happy about her first date. I was happy for her, but deep down it hurt me that Jeff and I couldn't go out together. I kept thinking about how I was going to tell her I was jealous over her freedom to date whom she pleased. Just because of Jeff's reputation, everybody hated him, we couldn't be seen in public together because my parents wouldn't have it. I had no idea if the relationship was going to grow or not, but deep down I was hoping it would. If I could get the nerve up to tell Michelle what I'd been doing, maybe she would agree to help us see each other. Tony and Jeff were friends, and there were all kinds of possibilities. I could visualize a great summer in front of us. The four of us just having a good time, what a good summer it would be if we could slip away. There were all kinds of places we can go. Claytor Lake, New River, Mount Rogers, Buffalo Mountain, or Floyd County. We could hike and take a picnic lunch. We could get together now that Tony and Jeff each had a car.

I had to wait until Monday to tell him what I'd heard from Michelle. Michelle couldn't shut up. I sat patiently and listened to her go on and on about Tony. Then she told me something that made me more jealous because when Tony took her home, Michelle said he kissed her. She really enjoyed it, and I've got to admit I was a little bit jealous over that because I wanted Jeff to come and pick me up and take me out and bring me home. I shook it off and I was glad for Michelle, and a little bit sad for myself. Then I laughed at myself because Jeff would say, "Poor little rich girl."

At school the next day, I didn't get to talk to him until we had a class together. "Did you have a good weekend?" I asked.

"Yes."

"Did you see Tony over the weekend?"

"As a matter of fact, I did, down at the pool room."

"Did you ask him about Michelle?"

"No, I think it's too early."

I sat back in my seat anxious to talk to Michelle, hoping Jeff could talk to Tony and maybe get something together before summer. Spring was getting close, and I was hoping this could be the best summer of my life if things worked out.

"Are we going to meet under the stairwell today?"

"I'd like to. It's been a whole day and night since I've seen you."

"Me too." As we sat through class, Jeff would reach over and touch me, goose me, tickle me. He had changed so much, he really loves me. I was so afraid things were going to mess up because it was going too smoothly. When the bell rang, I followed Jeff to the stairwell and I laid my books down and we kissed. This time Jeff pulled my dress up in the back and grabbed my butt and squeezed it. I loved everything he did to me, I couldn't get enough of him.

"Are we meeting in the library today?"

"I can't today. I'm trying to get a part-time job. I have to leave right after school."

"Where are you trying to get a job?"

"Higgins' gas station, pumping gas. I've got to make some money to keep gas in my car."

"My dad hangs out there. He stops and talks to everybody."

"I know, I know. He frowns when he looks at me like he was saying, *If I caught somebody like you around my daughter, I'd shoot you*. But if you were my daughter, I'd hate me too."

"You would?"

"Princess, if you were my daughter, I'd never let any boys get close to you, especially someone like me."

The bell rang and we had to go to class. I wished Jeff wouldn't talk that way. Now that I knew him, I looked forward to going to school every day just to see him.

Another week went by, and Tony and Michelle went out again. Honestly, that's all I could hear her and Tony. All the time I was keeping Jeff a secret from Michelle, I wished she would shut up about Tony. I'll have to admit jealousy was overtaking me.

Then one night at home, I was helping Mom wash dishes after dinner and she casually said, "I hear Michelle is dating someone now. I spoke with her mother."

"Yes, that's what she told me at lunch. Michelle likes him, I think."

"There's nobody asking you to go out?"

"Not really. There was this one guy, but I don't like him."

"Oh, you don't like him? Who was it? Was it Jeff Gray?"

"Mama, you and Dad wouldn't let me go out with Jeff Gray and I know that."

"Has he asked you out, Princess?"

"Mama, please, leave it alone. I know you won't let me go out with him."

"Do you want to go out with him?"

"I'm not going to lie to you. I'd go out with him in a minute if you would let me go."

Mom didn't respond. I knew deep down she knew I was seeing him. "Mom, you told me about that guy in your life. What did you do?"

Mom looked around the corner to make sure Dad was watching TV. She came back to the sink and looked at me. "Princess, I'm not going to answer that and I'm not going to tell you to go out with Jeff Gray. I'm not going to say anything at all. If you decide to go out with him, just remember your age and what a small town you're living in, baby. You can get in serious trouble before you know it. The rumors would spread like wildfire."

Mom had tears in her eyes. She wiped her hands off, hugged me and she whispered in my ear. "Princess, whatever you do – I shouldn't tell you this as your mother, but whatever you do, baby, be very careful. You're headed for trouble. If you're not careful, you're headed for a broken heart. You've got to remember when you doing things you know you're not supposed to be doing, you're not in the real world, but the problems are real and they will catch up with you. When you're out, I want to know what you doing and I will worry because you're my daughter and I love you. I know this is a time in your life that will never come again. One day you'll only have memories and you can never let them go. I'm speaking from experience, baby. I made a mistake, and I've been paying for it ever since."

I wasn't sure why, but I could feel the warning she was telling me. She still didn't answer if she would never let me go out with Jeff and I would never, ever ask her again about it.

A couple of weeks went by and Jeff and I slipped away every chance we got. We were trying to be patient talking to Michelle and Tony to see if they would help us meet each other away from school. Three weeks in a row Tony and Michelle were dating every weekend. I finally got brave enough without Jeff knowing it to tell Michelle what I'd been doing. I was waiting for the right moment. Michelle was acting like I was when I first started seeing Jeff. She was on top of the world. She was smiling every day and all she could talk about was Tony. I was wondering if he was doing what Jeff was doing to me. If he was, I would be more comfortable telling her. So at lunch one day, I started that conversation, hoping to find an opportunity to tell Michelle everything.

Lunchtime in the cafeteria, Tony sat with us. He and Michelle constantly stared at each other while they ate, smiling. Jeff never ate in the cafeteria anymore. He had his car, and he drove down to the Dairy Bar to eat lunch. So, every day at lunchtime it was me, Michelle, and Tony. I started feeling uncomfortable as though I were intruding on their time. When Tony excused himself from the table, I took a chance and started talking to Michelle, hoping the conversation would lead where I wanted it to go.

"Looks like you and Tony are really getting along," I said.

She smiled at me and said, "Yes, I really like him. He came by the house to talk with Mom and Dad, and they seem to like him."

"When you go to the movies, do you make out?"

"Oh yes, and he's good, too. I've only I've got one problem."

"What could that be?"

"Tony's hands start roaming. I almost let him in my panties last time."

"Really! Are you going to let him do that?"

"I don't know. I like it, but I keep thinking, what Mama told me."

"Do you want to give up your virginity now?"

"I never thought about that. I guess. I don't know. I really didn't think about it. I just knew it felt good. I'm afraid to let him do it."

"It must be exciting for you?"

"I shouldn't have told you anything about it, but you're my best friend and I really need somebody to talk to."

" Can I tell you something without you going silly on me?"

"Of course, I know you've been keeping a secret from me. Are you going to tell me about it now?"

"I don't know if I should or not. I'm afraid to tell you, but I'm about to burst."

"Are you finally going tell me about Jeff Gray?"

"You knew! You knew about Jeff?"

"No, but I had my suspicions. I know you have changed. I knew something was going on, but I wasn't sure if it was Jeff or not."

"Michelle, I've been seeing Jeff for a few months now. I'm having the time of my life, but I was afraid to tell you. I knew you'd laugh at me. We've always made fun of him, but he's wonderful." I could feel my face turn red; my heart felt like it picked up a beat. I was tingling all over telling Michelle about Jeff. I didn't know whether to be embarrassed or ashamed or happy that I was getting ready to tell her how I felt about him.

"He's wonderful? What do you mean by that? What have you been doing to make you say he's wonderful?"

"Listen to me when I tell you he's wonderful in every way."

"Ok, Princess, I get that he's wonderful – in what way specifically?"

"He's – he's, I don't know, I better not tell you."

"You've opened the door. I've got to now. He's wonderful in what way?"

"I lost my virginity; we've been having sex." We looked at each other across the table. I don't think she knew what to say next.

"You what!"

"Jeff and I have been having sex for a few months now and I'm having the time of my life. That's the reason you haven't been going to the barn with me. It's because Jeff has been meeting me there. We go up in the hayloft. I couldn't tell you. I didn't know how you were going to react. Can you keep it to yourself? Can you keep a secret?"

"I knew there was something going on with you. You've changed, but I would never dream you were seeing Jeff Gray, not in a million years. How did this happen?"

"You will laugh when I tell you how. I was sitting beside him in class before Mr. Lindsay got there or came into the room. Jeff and I were talking, and I don't know why, but he kissed me right on my lips. It just took me by surprise and the first thing I knew was I wanted him to kiss me again. We started meeting under the stairwell before the next class. It really got intense, and then I started asking him to come to the barn on Saturday. Before I knew it, we were in the hayloft. At first, he started rubbing me between my legs, then finally I let him in my panties. He put his finger in me and I've been loving it ever since."

"Really, he put his finger in you and you liked it that much?"

"I liked it enough that we're having sex every time we meet, and I look forward to seeing him. Michelle, I'm not going to tell you what to do with Tony, but I need to ask you a favor."

"A favor, what could Tony and I do for you?"

"Jeff doesn't know I'm telling you this. He's worried that something's going to mess it up. If my mom and dad found out I was seeing him... you know everybody in this town talks about Jeff because he does what he wants and he doesn't care what people think. He's got such a bad reputation. Since I've been seeing him, I know why he thinks the way he does. All the fights he's been in, he's just different than everybody else. I'm finding out more about him every time we're together. It's no secret that he drinks, as young as he is. My parents would think he would be a bad influence on me, and they're right, he is, but I love him because of that. If they found out, they'd never let me see him again. So we're trying to find a way that we can meet each other away from school and not worry about getting caught."

"So, I'm guessing you want me and Tony to help you two guys meet up?"

"That's exactly what I'm asking. We thought maybe you and Tony would help us. I mean I don't know what Jeff has in mind. Please Michelle, please don't ever tell anybody about this. I don't want to do anything to mess it up." I took a deep breath. After telling her what Jeff and I were doing together, I was anxious to see her reaction.

"You and Jeff? You and Jeff Gray are having sex?"

Yes, I love him, I love everything about him. He's had such a hard life."

"Wait a minute. What about his girlfriend that goes to Woodlawn? What happened to her?"

"I'm not sure what happened to her. All he told me was that she broke his heart. We've both seen her, she's much prettier than I am. I don't know what happened between them, but he's not telling me much about her. I don't know, Michelle. Even though I don't know anything about her, I'm so jealous of her. I was his refuge. He told me he loves me, Michelle. It took a while, but now I'm so in love with him. I know you're thinking how do I know anything about love. I can't explain it, but I've never been happier than I am right now. So now I've told you everything. Please, Michelle, you can't tell anybody."

"There's nobody I could tell. I don't want to mess this up for you. Can I say something to Tony?"

"No, please wait until Jeff talks to Tony. But if Tony agrees, do you mind helping me out so I can see Jeff?"

"Sure, but how can we help you?"

"We'll just have to let Jeff and Tony figure something out." The bell rang and lunch was over. Michelle and I went to our classes. She left me in the hallway wondering. I was scared she couldn't keep it to herself. I knew I had to tell Jeff what I'd done. I hoped he wouldn't get mad at me.

I worried the rest of the day and all night. I didn't sleep because I was trying to convince myself I did the right thing telling Michelle, but I still had to face Jeff.

The next morning, Mom kept looking at me at breakfast. After Dad had left, she asked, "Princess, are you all right?"

"No, Mama. I'm not all right."

"What's bothering you?"

"Everything, everything is bothering me, Mom."

"Baby, at your age what could bother you? You're still in school and getting ready for real life."

"You're right, I am getting ready for life, and it's so complicated."

"Princess, I've got some bad news for you. The older you get the more complicated life gets, but you've got to mature and adjust to it."

"I know."

"Let me guess, Jeff Gray's got that kind of influence on you now?"

"Mama, why do you bring him up?"

"What else could it be? this is just a phase. Now, you know there's no future with somebody like Jeff. The only reason he's in Galax High School is that he can play football. He's good for nothing else."

I tried not to answer her, but she kept on until I lost my temper with her. "Mama, I cannot live my own life. Why can't I see who I want to see?"

"Don't you raise your voice to me like that, young lady! I'm your mother, that's why. I say who you can see. You're only fifteen years old and as long as you are underage, you're ..."

"Why did you stop, mama? What were you going to say to me? As long as I'm what? Why don't you finish telling me what you're going say?"

"Because I remember my mother telling me the same thing. Just slow down, Princess, don't be so quick to grow up. The world is changing around you, and you are changing. Just slow down. Please, baby."

I hung my head and stared at my plate. "Mom, I want to see Jeff Gray."

She walked around the table not once but twice. Stopping on the other side of me, she sat down, put her elbows on the table and her head in her hands and began crying. Sniffing back the tears, she looked up at me.

"I don't know what to say to you, Princess, but you're headed for a lot of trouble. I'm talking about trouble that will follow you to your grave, baby. You don't know what you're doing, you're blinded and you don't know it. How long have you been seeing him?"

She put me on the spot, but I decided to tell her the truth. "Right after school started."

"I thought so, I watched you change. I knew something was going on and I knew I couldn't stop it. I couldn't help you get through it. Princess, I'm not going to ask you what you want with this boy. I don't want to know."

"I'm sorry, I didn't mean to raise my voice to you, but with you and Dad, I just feel like I can't make my own decisions."

"You're not supposed to make your own decisions, you're still a child. It's too soon to think about anyone boy! You've got a full life in front of you."

"Mama, what did your parents say to you when you had a wild and crazy boy in your life?"

"Baby, they said everything to me that I'm saying to you, and I didn't listen. That's the reason I'm so worried about you. I don't know what to do to convince you. I made a big mistake by not listening to my mother, and I'm still paying for it. Princess, you've got to listen to me!"

"What did you do then, Mom?"

"I'm telling you, Princess, stay away from Jeff Gray. Do you understand me? You stay away from him!"

I finished getting ready for school. This was one of the saddest days ever since I met Jeff. I was forbidden to see him and I knew I couldn't stop. I also knew my mother was keeping a secret from me, but I didn't know what it was. She trusted me enough to tell me about her past, but now it felt like she didn't trust me to make my own decisions.

When Mom dropped me off at school, she kept looking at me. Before I got out of the car, she told me, "Baby, I love you. I just don't want to see you hurt."

I looked back at her and replied, "Mama, I'm already hurt because you don't trust me and you think I can't make the right decisions." I turned around and walked into the school to meet up with Michelle.

"What's wrong, Princess? You look like you're stressed out."

"I got into it with my mom this morning. I raised my voice to her and she's not happy with me."

"I hate to stick my nose in your business, but what was it about?"

"You can guess."

"Did you tell her you were seeing him?"

"No, I told her I wanted to see him."

"She didn't like that?"

"Not at all, and she told me that I couldn't. That's why I need your help. Spring is here and I'm going to see him one way or another."

"I didn't talk to Tony last night. You didn't call, so I guess Jeff will talk to him today."

"Probably not until I tell Jeff I told you. I dread telling him. I know he'll get mad at me."

"Why would he get mad at you for telling me?"

"Because you know how we made fun of him. He thinks you hate him."

"He thinks I hate him?"

"Michelle, you and I both stood back and laughed at people and made fun of them and never thought anything about it."

She answered, "We were just too young to know any better. Now that I've met Tony, I regret making fun of anybody."

I looked Michelle straight in the eyes and said, "Now that I'm in love with the very boy that I was making fun of has taught me a valuable lesson. When you put yourself above people, you really lower yourself beneath them.

"I guess when you put it that way we were wrong."

"I'm going to homeroom. I'll see you later." I started walking down the hall. I saw Jeff glance at me and take a second look as he passed by. I'm not sure why. I guess because he could see I was down. It showed on my face, but it made me feel good to think he was worried about me.

My first class was slow as molasses, but then it was time to have a class with Jeff. I didn't know how to approach this, but I hoped he wouldn't be mad.

When I walked in, Jeff met me. He was waiting for me.

The first thing he said, "What's wrong with you? Did somebody say something to you? Did they hurt you in any way? If they did, I'll take care of it."

That made me feel good, he was ready to defend me. *Maybe he does love me,* I told myself. "I got into an argument with my mom this morning and it made me feel bad. I've got something else I have to tell you. Please don't get mad at me, but I told Michelle about us."

"You did what!"

"I told Michelle about us. I'm hoping you'll say something to Tony. Summer's coming and school will be out soon. We've got this whole summer in front of us, Jeff. I'm going to see you one way or another."

"Damn, Princess, I don't know. Do you think Michelle can keep her mouth shut?"

"I hope so. I told her I put a lot of trust in her. She likes Tony and we're waiting for you to talk to him about it. Here's what I'm thinking: Tony takes her to the skating rink up at Reds. They can pick me up and I could tell Mom I'm going roller skating with them. She'll let me go with Tony and Michelle and you can be there to meet me."

"Now I've found out something about you I didn't know."

"What's that?"

"You are a schemer. You figured out how we can meet. There's one good thing about Red's Roller Rink. I can park behind the building and nobody will ever know that I'm there. While Tony and Michelle are skating, you can sit in the car with me."

"I knew you'd like that idea. It's starting to warm up so it wouldn't be too cold to sit out there with you."

"I can guarantee you if you sit out there with me, you won't have two worry about getting cold." We both laughed and looked in each other's eyes. I wanted to kiss him right there in the classroom, but Mr. Lindsay walked in and class started.

"When are you going to talk with Tony?" I whispered.

"I have a class with him right before lunch. I'll see if I get a chance to say something then."

"Are we going to meet in the library today?"

"Yes, I'll see you there."

"Are we going to the stairwell today?"

"Not today. I know I'll see you in the library after school."

During lunchtime, Michelle and I waited on Tony. We already got our trays when he showed up, Jeff was with him. I didn't know if Jeff was going to sit with us. I was ashamed of myself. I loved Jeff, but I was afraid for him to sit beside me in public. They went through the cafeteria line and got trays. Jeff was behind Tony and when they got to the table he sat beside Michelle. Jeff sat one seat over from me with a chair between us.

That's when Tony said, "Damn, Jeff, why didn't you sit beside Princess?"

Jeff looked at me. I was almost crying. I was embarrassed and hurt and afraid, it unnerved me, I was ashamed of myself to love him and was afraid for him to sit with me in public it was for fear that somebody would talk and it would get back to Mom. I stumbled talking I tried to fix it, I was so obvious.

"You could sit beside me, I wouldn't mind," I told him.

"That's ok, I can sit right here, I'm going to talk to you guys. Tony, I need to ask you something, then you'll know why I didn't sit beside Princess."

"That sounds really serious. What's on your mind and how can I help?"

Jeff looked at me, then back at Tony. "Tony, Princess and I've been seeing each other since school started."

"What! Do you mean *seeing* each other? You see each other every day here in school, big deal."

Michelle and I both let the guys talk. "No, Tony. I guess you could say we've been spending time with each other since school started. Princess's parents won't let me date her, and that's the reason we want to talk to you and Michelle."

"What do Michelle and I have to do with this? Do you want to double date or something?"

"Something like that, but we can't be seen together in public. If it gets back to her daddy, he'll stop everything. It would make it hard on Princess."

I looked up at Tony and laid it on the line. "I'm going to come right out and say it. I love Jeff and I want to be with him and we can't go out together, not yet. My parents won't have it. They think Jeff is not good enough for me, but I don't care. I want to be with him. Can you two help us?"

Tony and Michelle looking at each other and then back at Jeff. "If you don't want to double date with us, then how can we help you?"

Jeff said, "You could let Princess go with you guys to the skating rink and I'd be in my car out back where nobody could see us. Then she and I could have time together while you're skating. That's what we're thinking right now. Her parents would let her go with you and Michelle, but if they knew I was going, they would never let us double date. We just want to see each other, Tony. Could you help us?"

And then I asked, "Michelle, you wouldn't mind, would you?"

Tony sat back from the table and we all looked at each other before he answered, "What do you think, Michelle, do you want to help them out? Jeff, this is strange, but if Michelle doesn't mind, then we'll do it."

Michelle looked at us and said, "Princess, you know I'll do it for you and I've got something else to say. Jeff, I've been wrong to make fun of you and I don't hate you. I was just wrong."

Jeff with his mouth open. "Ok, thank you for helping us."

We finished lunch. Jeff and Tony got up to go, then Jeff turned around and told me, "I'll see you in the library after school."

When the boys walked out, I ask Michelle again. "What do you think?"

"I think it will work. Your mom will let you go out with me and Tony and maybe this coming Friday night we'll go to the roller rink. But you know something, Princess? I've got a feeling Tony and I will be in the car with you guys before this is over. I sort of hope so."

I smiled at Michelle and said, "Not too fast. Jeff and I get pretty intense and I don't want to have an audience."

"What's it like? I mean, do you really enjoy having sex?"

"Michelle, I'm not going to get into it. That's something you have to decide. I can't tell you anything about it."

"Tony is already playing around. I'm trying to stop him, but at the same time, I like it."

"I can't give you much help, but it's too late for me to turn back now. My mom's having a fit, that's the reason I need your help so bad." We got up from the table to go to the next class. I was waiting impatiently until after school to see Jeff in the library.

When I walked in, Jeff was there waiting on me over at the window where we always sat. "How did it go with Tony?"

"I guess it's on for Friday night at Red's. He said you guys would be there about seven."

"This is going to be amazing. I can sit with you in your car. I'm getting horny just thinking about it."

"If you're getting horny, then when everybody leaves, let's go to the broom closet."

"I'm ready!"

"You are? I've created a monster." We both were laughing, but I was ready. I wanted him and I was willing to take a chance. We sat around for a little while. There were only a few people in and out of the hallway so we took off to the broom closet. It was exciting and good and we got out of there as quick as we could. The few minutes we were in there, Jeff was so sweet to me, from the way he would kiss my nipples and the way he did everything. We went back to the library and nobody was in there but us. We held each other's hands, and I told him how much I loved him. And then the mood changed.

"Princess, I've got something to tell you," he said in a low, serious voice. "What's wrong?" I asked.

"I wish I had never started this with you because now I know I'm not good enough for you, but it's too late and I am in love with you."

"Then what's wrong, what's the matter?"

"Princess, I only passed two classes this year. They're holding me back. The whole time you told me you guys were laughing behind my back, now here I am with you, knowing I'm not good enough for you. Look what I've done to you. I don't know what I was thinking."

"You stop that right now! I'm here with you because I want to be here with you. Now listen, Jeff, you told me from the beginning we only had these moments, these precious moments. Now, damn it, you stop that. We've got summer in front of us and I'm going to enjoy every precious moment. Do you think I'd be fucking you if I didn't love you? Now we've got a chance with Tony and Michelle to meet this coming Friday and I'm going to be there and you better be there."

"I'm trying to be real, baby, that's all."

"Here is the reality of it. You can show me the best summer I'll ever experience. You showed me everything else. Let's go places, let's do things, let's slip away and find a way, Jeff. I'll do what I have to do to be there. Please don't talk like this anymore. It will all be behind us, whatever you have to do for the next year, we'll face it then. Now I'm calling Mom to come and get me and I want you to come down with me until she gets here. I want you to stand with me, Jeff. I don't care what she says. Stand with me until she picks me up?"

"Are you sure?"

"Yes, I am. Please stand with me until she comes.

I called Mom, she's on her way. Jeff and I walked in front of the school and waited. He was really nervous and anxious. I could tell he didn't want to do this. I insisted, and Jeff listened to me.

Mom drove up, rolled down her window and said, "Hello, Jeff. Did you guys get anything done today?"

"Yes, ma'am. Thank you for letting Princess help me. I need a lot of help and she's a really good teacher."

"Oh, that's good. We're proud of her. She's a giving person."

I turned and looked at Jeff. “I'll see you tomorrow in class. Just go ahead and read where I showed you and you’ll be ready for your test,” I told him, putting on a front for Mom.

“Thank you, Princess. I appreciate it.”

We drove off. “Mom, he asked me if he could take me home and I had to say no. Why couldn't Jeff bring me home?”

“He’s got a car now?” Mom asked.

“Yes, he's got a car, but I'll never be in it, that’s for sure.”

“Princess, are we going through this again? You know your dad is not going to let that happen. So, we need to drop this. You are not going out with Jeff Gray. That’s the end of it.”

“I don't understand, Anyway, I’ve got good news.”

“Oh, you've got good news?”

“Yes, I was asked out Friday night to go skating.”

“See, I told you. Who is he?”

“It's not a he, it's Tony and Michelle. They asked me to go skating with them Friday night at Reds. Now I've got to be a tagalong just to go out.”

“Well, that's good. Go with your friends.”

“You mean I can go?”

“Not if you start getting smart-mouthed with me!”

“I'm not getting smart-mouthed with you. I can't even tell Jeff I like him. He thinks I'm a snob. He wouldn’t sit beside me today in the cafeteria. He thinks that I think I’m better than everybody else.”

"What is so special about Jeff Gray all of a sudden?"

"Mama, what did you tell your parents about that boy you liked that they hated? Think about it. Are you telling me exactly what your mom and daddy told you? I don't understand. Jeff Gray is a decent kind of guy. He's just got a bad home life and he can't read or write."

"Princess, that's nothing to you. You can't help everybody that comes along and feel sorry for them. You're not going to be able to help everybody!"

"I don't feel sorry for Jeff, I..."

"That's enough! I don't want to hear anything else about Jeff Gray. What's so special about him anyway?"

"If I told you, Mom, you wouldn't believe me."

"Princess, I don't want to hear anything else about him. Now you go ahead and go with Michelle and Tony Friday night and go skating, but that's enough."

When I got home, I went straight to my room. I couldn't stop crying. The only thing I had to look forward to was Friday night. I was looking forward to seeing Jeff that night away from school. Tomorrow was Thursday. I lay in bed, and I didn't want to get up. Then Mom knocked on my door.

"Princess, it's time for you to eat supper. Come on down."

"I'm not hungry."

Mom opened the door and came in. "What's wrong with you? Are you crying?"

"No, I'm just mad. I'm mad because... Mama, please leave me alone. I don't want to come down. I'll see you in the morning."

"Princess, we need to talk. You're telling me a whole lot without saying anything. Baby, are you crying over that boy?"

"I don't want to talk about it, Mama. You don't understand."

"I'll tell your father you're not feeling well and you don't want anything to eat."

"Mama, tell me what happened to that boy your parents hated."

"Princess, I'm not ready to talk about that. I shouldn't have told you anything. But baby, you remind me so much of myself right now, and I'm really afraid for you. I know something is going on between you and that boy, and you won't tell me. I remember God help me, I remember exactly what went on in my life, you've got to snap out of this. I'm going to leave you alone and let you think about things. You get your homework done. Maybe I can tell you, father, you're working on your homework and you're not hungry, but he will be asking what's wrong with you. What am I going to tell him, that you are lovesick over some crazy boy?"

"Mama, Jeff's not crazy."

"What's he done to you?"

"It's not what he's done to me; it's what you're doing to me. I'm not allowed to choose my own friends. Why am I not allowed to see whomever I want?"

"Princess, think about things. Think about where you are and think about your future. Right now, you can't afford to be mixed up with a failure like Jeff Gray. He's a nobody and he's going nowhere, and you know that deep down. You can't be pulled down with him. Now, Princess, you and I've got to have a long talk. I'm going back downstairs. If you're hungry, come and get something to eat."

Mom shut the door and I heard her walk down the steps. Now I'm really crying. She kept saying Jeff was never going to be anything. If she only knew he was everything to me.

The next morning, she and I didn't speak at breakfast. Dad had already gone to work. She drove me to school, and as I got out of the car, she did have something to say. "Princess, baby, all this will pass. You'll look back one day and see it wasn't your time. You're too young to think about any young man. Live your life; think about your future"

"Mama, that's exactly what I'd like to do, but you won't let me." I shut the door and went to the school to meet Michelle. She told me Tony and she would pick me up about 6: 30 and we'd go to the skating rink. I couldn't wait to tell Jeff, but I was sure Tony already told him. I should be happy, but I just couldn't get it together. On the way to homeroom, I saw the two of them talking in the hall so I was sure Tony was telling him we were on for Friday night.

All-day long I couldn't get it together. My mind kept wandering back to Mom talking about Jeff. She was so adamant about me not seeing him. I don't understand why things had to be so complicated. I just knew I would have a great summer and I would do everything I could to make sure that happened.

When I sat with Jeff in class, he kept asking me what was wrong. "Princess, you seem down. I'm excited about seeing you tomorrow night, and you don't seem to be happy."

"Jeff, look at me. Look me right in the eyes."

Jeff put his hands on the side of my head and looked at me. "Now tell me, Princess, what is bothering you?"

"Make me a promise, Jeff. Promise me that this summer is going to be the best summer I'll ever spend in my entire life. If I live to be a hundred years old, promise me that this summer is going to be one that neither one of us will ever forget, and no matter what happens afterward, we'll always have this summer. Promise me!"

"Princess, what happened to make you talk like this. you've got me, I'm at a loss for words."

"Jeff you kept saying from the beginning that we only have a moment with each other. I'm asking you to make this coming summer, the whole summer, that special moment. Please promise me we'll have a summer together that neither one of us will ever forget. Make it magical. Let this be our magical summer!"

"Princess, I don't know what brought this on, but I don't care. I promise you we'll make this summer so magical in every way I can. I want to make love to you. I've got all kinds of ideas I told you about. I want to take you skinny-dipping in New River. I want to make love to you in the hot summer sun. If I can make it magical for you, I'm going to do that. I promise you, whatever it takes, this will be our moment. The whole summer is ours, is that good enough?"

"I promise you, Jeff, I'll do whatever it takes to be with you. Whatever it takes, I don't care if I have to lie, cheat, and steal from my parents. I'm going to make every moment of the summer one that we will never forget. Oh, Jeff, let's make it happen and not give a damn about tomorrow. Every moment of the entire summer will be our moment."

I'm crying, I was so excited looking at Jeff and making those promises to each another. Jeff reached up and wiped away my tears. I kept crying. I knew that this was going to be a great summer, but I think deep down I knew, in the end, anything could happen.

We didn't meet under the stairwell that day. We did meet in the library after school. We both looked forward to Friday night at Roller Rink. Michelle and I made the plans, it was almost time.

I was getting ready to get in the shower, and when I lowered my panties, they were spotty. I couldn't believe this. I looked at the blood and thought, *Not now. Oh no! Not now. How am I going to tell Jeff*? I hadn't been thinking about the time of the month. I just completely forgot about it. I got in the shower and got myself ready for the night, but I was so disappointed.

Right before Tony and Michelle came to pick me up, Mom and I weren't talking. We both moped around. I knew deep down Mom had a secret and I certainly wasn't going to tell her mine. Normally we're very close, but now I feel I couldn't trust her with my secrets.

When Michelle and Tony pulled up, I told Mom they were here. Just as I opened the door to leave, she called out to me. "Princess, enjoy yourself." When she said that for some reason I felt guilty. I was lying to her, but I didn't care. I loved her, but I had to see Jeff and this was what it took. I tried to blame her for my behavior. I was sneaking and lying, but I felt like I had no choice. The guilt made me feel sad. I just had a feeling she knew what I was up to.

"I will, Mom." She came to the door and hugged me, I turned and walked to get in Tony's car.

Michelle said, "I bet you're excited. This will be the first time that you'll be out with Jeff."

"Yes, I am excited."

Then Tony joined in the conversation. "Jeff's not a bad guy. Some of the things he's told me that he had to go through at home, none of us would want."

"The stories Jeff told me. I really hurt for him," I answered Tony.

We turned on Pipers Gap Road and drove up to the twisty, rocky road to the Roller Rink on the left. Red's was a favorite place for all of us to go, but when you got to the top of the hill it was a big building and you could see all the way back to Galax. It was getting dark when Tony parked, he and Michelle went in the front door to pay to get in. I went to the right of the building and peeked around the corner. There stood Jeff in front of his car. I ran towards him and jumped into his arms. I couldn't believe it; we were together away from school and we had at least two hours, if not more.

"Let's get in the car," Jeff said.
We got in the front seat
Jeff turned on the radio.
"Jeff, I've got some bad news for you."
"How could it be bad news?
I couldn't be happier."
"It's my time of the month."
"What do you mean?"
"I'm on my period."
"Oh! Ha! Ha! Ha!
Oh, this is hilarious!"
"What's so funny?"
Jeff couldn't stop laughing,
I wasn't laughing.
"This is so funny.
Here we are in my car,
and you're on your period."
"I don't think it's funny.
I was looking forward to this."
"Yes, I want to have sex with you,
but we're together.
I'm not disappointed."
Jeff and I started making out,
and I could tell he was getting horny.

I decided to jack him off.
"Thanks, baby, that relieved me.
By the way, I love you."
All the windows were steamed up in the car.
I thought that was funny.
I knew it was my time of the month,
but I still wanted to have sex.
I was afraid to.

"Jeff, I want to ask you something."

"Ok, what do you want to know?"

"Tell me about her."

"You want to waste time talking about her? She's gone and you're here. This is one of our moments, don't waste it, talking about her."

"I want to know what happened I know you're here with me, but what happened to her?"

He didn't want to talk about her. I could see it in the way he looked down and shrugged his shoulders. I could feel his mood change from laughing at me to being sad about her. I wished I hadn't asked. This was not the time to ask these questions to bring her up I don't know why asking this, first time out in Jeff's car. I ruined it. I ruined it by being jealous.

He looked at me and asked, "Do I really have to talk about her? What on earth do you want to know about her?"

"I'm sorry, I wish I never brought her up. I've ruined this whole night for you. I can't have sex and I'm talking about her. You don't have to tell me if you don't want to."

Jeff sat there silently and then he pleased me so by taking me in his arms and saying, "Ok, but please don't ever ask me about her again. I'm sorry to say I did her just like I did you right here in front of this roller rink. One night she and I were sitting in a friend's car and I forced myself on her just like I did you. She held me back, but then I got my hand in her panties and started fingering her, she relaxed and I asked her how it felt. She said it felt like heaven. After that, I had no problem getting my hand in her panties, even in the Rex Theater or when we came up here roller skating. We'd go out and sit in friend's car and have sex. Princess, I'm afraid I was introduced to sex at a very young age by my cousin. I was having sex with her before I could get off. That's how young I started. So, when I got with that girl, I kept trying because I knew what I wanted. I forced my hands in her panties. Of course, you know what happened after that. That was in the seventh grade. I was one year older than her, just like I am with you. But we got a little bit older and my family life was awful, so she became a place where I could have some peace and sex. It was my hiding place. I don't know if you call it love. I mean, look how young we were. We started double dating with a friend of mine. She went to Woodlawn and I came to Galax. I heard through other people she was sneaking away with other boys in the woods. So, I guess I turned her into a monster because she liked having sex. So do I, but I only wanted one girl. I didn't want anybody else but her. After a while, she knew more about the things that I did, and I couldn't read or write. She didn't want to be around somebody like me. Then one night at the bowling alley, we were sitting in the parking lot out in a car and I was whining and carrying on, just being jealous as hell. I didn't have a driver's license so I couldn't take her out. And then she looked at me, and just came out and said it: "Why can't you be like everybody else?" I got out of the car and left her sitting there. She went back inside. I kept walking, screaming and hurting inside. I'm ashamed to say I started with her just like I did you. I guess you could say I raped her, too."

He paused for a moment. "Now, did you want to hear all of that? Did you want to hear how weak I am? That I'm convinced I'm no damn good? Why did you want to know all the stuff about her? Just tell me why."

"Because I wanted to be here for you. That's how much I love you. I guess I'm so jealous. I know I'm not as pretty as she is, and I know I can't please you the way you want to be pleased."

"I want somebody to love me for who I am. I don't know how to be anybody else."

"If you were somebody else, I couldn't love you. It's one thing for sure, Jeff, you're not like everybody else. You've got to believe me. I love you just like you are."

He looked at me like he didn't know what to say next, then he spoke. "Look, if I were your daddy and I caught you out with me, I'd shoot me. Princess, I'm no good. I'm never going to be anybody or anything worth being with, that's the reason we have just this moment, and sooner or later there'll be no more moments." Jeff took me in his arms and held me really close. I laid my head on his shoulder and I wanted to cry. We made out the rest the evening. Time went so damn fast, and I didn't want to go home. Tony walked around the corner, pecked on the window and told us it was time to go, before going back to his car.

It was time to say goodbye. We kissed. Now that I think about it, this was funny. Jeff was waiting for this moment, my time of the month. We laughed about this a lot. There was only another month left in the school year. I sure hoped I could go with Tony and Michelle to meet him again soon.

"Jeff, this was wonderful," I said. "I love you." I turned and walked away.

Then he shouted, "I promise you, Princess, we're going to have the summer of our lives. I promise you!"

I got in the car, we drove back to Galax. On the way home, Michelle asked, "How did it go?"

"Thank you, guys. It went very well. I got to talk to Jeff about everything, but I want to ask you something. We've only got a month left in the school year. Tony, what do you plan to do this summer? Are you and Michelle going to be able to go out and do things?"

Tony answered me. "I haven't told Michelle yet, but there's a lot of things I'd like to do this summer, like go to Delp's Beach, maybe drive down to Claytor Lake and take a picnic to the Parkway. There are all kinds of things we can do this summer, if it's all right with Michelle, we would love for you to come with us so you can meet up with Jeff. We can arrange something. Maybe the four of us can spend a day on New River."

And then Michelle added, "Always yes, Princess. The four of us can have a great summer if we get Jeff to go."

"I'm sure I can get him to go, and you two are telling me everything I want to hear. I want this to be the best summer that we all will never forget. I really want that to happen."

"We're going to do it," Tony said.

"Yes, Princess. If Tony wants to take me out this summer, that gives a good excuse for your mama to let you go with me. We'll get together every chance. God, I never thought about it, I'm excited."

We got to my house and I got out. Mom asked me if I had a good time. I forgot I'd left my skates in Tony's car, but I went on to my room and went to sleep thinking about what a great summer we were going to have. In spite of everything, I was going to have the summer of my life.

Chapter 7

The following weekend I didn't get to go out with Michelle and Tony. Jeff came by the barn one Saturday morning and had enough time to hold me and tell me that he loved me. We didn't have sex at that time. I think Jeff saw me as more than just somebody to have sex with. I really believed he actually loves me for who I am. I couldn't have been more pleased, two weeks before school would be over for the year.

Friday night, springtime, and the weather was getting warmer. We were behind Red's Roller Rink in Jeff's car. The lovemaking was sweet and so satisfying. I was comfortable in Jeff's arms. We talked about what we were going to do when school was out. Jeff had all kinds of plans. I was excited to go to Delp's Beach, Whitetop Mountain, picnic on the Parkway. One special place he was going to take me. He knew a place up behind the Fries Dam with a sandy beach, he was going to take me there in the middle of the week when everybody else would be at work. We would have that part of the river to ourselves. He told me he wanted to go skinny dipping with me. He had to work his schedule around his part-time job. Things seemed so right and everything was going smoothly until it was time to go home.

We saw Tony come to the corner of the building and motion for me to come on. Jeff walked with me. On the way, we heard a loud voice.

"Hey! Jeff Gray! I've been looking for you, you son-of-a-bitch!" By the sound of his voice, you could tell the person was very angry.

"Who is that?" I asked Jeff.

"Get in the car. Quick!"

"What's going on, Jeff who is that?"

"Get in the car, Princess!"

I got in the car, and I asked, "Who is that, Tony? What's going on?"

"That's one mean guy right there, I don't know what Jeff did to this guy, but Jeff's got his hands full."

"Tony, what's going to happen? What are they going to do?"

"They're going to fight!"

Jeff went over to the guy, I couldn't hear what they were saying. Then all of a sudden, the older guy pushed Jeff. Jeff said something, turned around and came walking back to our car. The other guy with his friends got in his car and left. I rolled the window down.

"What's going on, please tell me what are you're going to do?"

Jeff looked over at Tony and told him, "Take everybody home. I've got to take care of this."

We watched Jeff get in his car and drive down to the bottom of the hill. We followed when Jeff turned into a used car lot. There were a lot of people there. We pulled up to where we could see what was going on.

Then Tony explained, "Looks like everybody's here. There's Lee, Benny, and there's HR."

"Tony, what's going to happen?" I asked. "What are they going to do?"

Jeff got out of his car where the older guy was waiting on him, leaning up against his car. Jeff tore his shirt off and went running towards the man, who was smoking a cigarette. Just before Jeff got to him, he flipped the cigarette at Jeff's chest. Sparks flew everywhere, but Jeff kept going until he got his hands on that guy.

I watched Jeff beat him. He was on top of him and they were wrestling around. I'd never seen anything like that in my life. Jeff didn't know that we were watching. I was afraid for him. Then things got really quiet, and I heard the older guy say, "You get up and you get up easy."

Jeff looked up at another guy and asked him. "Lee, does he have a gun?"

Lee said, "You better get up."

Jeff got up, the older guy pointed the gun in Jeff's face. I heard Jeff say, "You going to shoot me, man?" I was amazed Jeff didn't run. He didn't do anything. "Are you going to shoot me, man?"

We heard four shots. I just knew Jeff was shot. My heart stopped. I knew the guy had killed Jeff, but when I uncovered my eyes, Jeff was still standing there. The guys named Lee and Benny got between Jeff and the older guy. Then the older guy shot again over Jeff's head, Jeff never moved. Everyone left, I was scared to death. I didn't know what happened, but I saw Jeff get in his car, as we drove away.

I was afraid after witnessing that, I couldn't believe it. When Tony and Michelle dropped me off at home, I was shaking. I'd never been around stuff like that. Now I knew why everyone was afraid of Jeff. I couldn't believe it, Jeff had a gun in his face, but he never moved. He acted like he was not afraid. On the way home, I couldn't believe what I just saw. Jeff was fighting a full-grown man who had a gun. He could've killed him. For some reason, it made me love Jeff more.

Mom asked if I had a good time and I told her yes. No way was I going to tell her what happened. I tried to keep my cool in front of her. I got myself a snack before I went to my room. I wanted to call Jeff so bad to find out what happened. I wanted to know why it happened and what Jeff did to make this guy mad at him. Instead, I took a shower and went to bed. I had a sleepless night thinking about what I saw. The next day, I went by the barn long enough to take care of my horse and make sure she was fed. After that, I came back home and called Michelle.

"I can't believe what I saw last night, Michelle. Jeff stood there in front of that guy. He had a gun in Jeff's face and Jeff just stood there. What did Tony say about it?"

"He told me Jeff had bullied that guy's cousin or something like that, and the older guy was getting revenge."

"I can't wait to talk to Jeff to see how he is."

"Tony called me this morning; he went back to see Jeff. Jeff looked like a mess. Tony said he had a black eye and one of his eyes was bloodshot where the older guy put his finger in it. Both of Jeff's knuckles were bloodied where he scraped them on the asphalt when Jeff had the guy down. Tony told me some of the other guys said the older guy had never been beat like that before. They think Jeff was the first one ever to knock him off his feet. It surprised him so, that's the reason he pulled a gun on Jeff."

"I can't wait to talk to him. I'd never been so afraid in my life to actually see somebody pull a gun out and shoot it. I just knew Jeff had been shot." I heard my mother come up the steps. "I've got to go, Michelle. I'll talk to you later."

"Were you talking to Michelle?" Mom asked.

"Yes, we were talking about what a good time we had last night."

"What are you going to do the rest of the weekend, Princess?"

"I don't really have anything to do. I need to clean my room up and help you do my laundry."

I stayed home all day and did my laundry. Late that afternoon, Dad came home. While we were sitting at the supper table, he asked, "Did you see anything out of the ordinary last night at the skating rink, Princess?"

I looked at him and replied, "No, not really."

"Everybody in town is talking. They say that Jeff Gray came close to getting shot last night. I know that boy he was fighting. You didn't see anything? It happened in a car lot down below the skating rink where you turn up to go to Piper's Gap."

"No, Dad. When we left, there was a bunch of people in that car lot. I didn't know what was going on. Did you say somebody was fighting Jeff?"

"I saw him down at the gas station. He's got a black eye."

Then Mom asked, "You didn't see Jeff Gray at the skating rink last night?"

"No, Mom, I didn't."

Dad kept on. "The talk is that Jeff came close to getting shot. I know that guy he was fighting. He's got a mean reputation. I wonder what it's all about?"

"I don't know, Dad. I didn't know anything was going on."

My mother looked at me suspiciously as if she knew I was lying. I guess my conscience was bothering me. I had to lie to her. I couldn't tell them. After supper, I knew what was coming. I knew the questions were going to start, but I didn't know how I was going to handle it.

"Princess, help me get the dishes to the sink, you dry while I wash."

Dad went to the living room like he usually does. Mom looked at me. "You didn't see anything last night?"

"No, Mom, I didn't see anything."

"Baby, it's too late, Michelle's mother told me what happened. You and Michelle saw everything. I believe Jeff was at the skating rink, but you said you didn't see anything."

"Mom, I didn't want to say anything in front of Dad. You know what he would say. We drove down the hill, and Tony saw all those people over there. We stopped to see what was going on and I saw Jeff fighting. That's all I saw, I didn't say anything in front of Dad."

"That was a good idea, Princess. It's just I knew you wouldn't tell the truth."

"I didn't want to say anything in front of him."

"Ok, I'll let you get by this time, but don't lie to me again."

We finished the dishes, I'm going to have to have a talk with Michelle, She got me in trouble by talking too much. I hope that wouldn't happen this coming summer. That would ruin everything between me and Jeff.

In church Sunday morning, I got Michelle aside. " "Please don't say anything to your parents about seeing Jeff in a fight. My parents asked me about it, Mom caught me in a lie."

"I'm sorry, I wasn't thinking. The whole town is talking about it. When something like that happens in a small town, you can't keep it quiet."

"Please, Michelle, please don't volunteer information to your parents."

"There was so much talk about it. They asked me. What was I going to tell them? I mean we were leaving the skating rink. I didn't say anything about you being with Jeff. I wasn't thinking, I told mama what we saw."

"I understand."

Everybody at the church is talking about what happened. People were saying all kinds of crazy things, that Jeff had a gun, that he asked for what he got, they were saying things that's not true. All the adults hated him and I didn't know why they made up silly stuff about him. They even said that he got shot. I wanted to tell them all to shut up, but I couldn't.

That afternoon when we got home from having lunch, I did the best I could do to stay away from Mom and Dad. I didn't want to answer any more questions about Jeff.

Monday when I got to school, I was looking for him. He was nowhere to be seen in the hallway and I thought he might not be at school. All morning long I was wondering where he was, and if he was ok. When I walked in civics class, he was sitting there waiting for me. He had a black eye and scraped knuckles. I sat beside him. I couldn't help it, I was crying.

Jeff looked at me and asked, "Why are you crying?"

"Because I'm afraid."

"You have no reason to be afraid for me, I got through it."

" I saw him pull a gun on you, I knew you were gone."

"You were there? I didn't see you."

"When you left the skating rink we came down, We saw all the people there in the car lot. Tony pulled up above and we saw everything. I can't believe you stood there. He had a gun in your face."

"I remembered what my dad told me."

"What did your dad tell you?"

"My daddy said if a man pulls a gun on you and he doesn't shoot you right from the beginning, he doesn't intend to shoot you. I knew better than to show fear. If I had, he might have shot me. I guess I was too stupid to be afraid."

"I thought you were gone when I heard the gun go off."

Jeff was smiling.

"Why are you smiling? It scared me. It scared me so bad. Why are you smiling?"

"Because you really care for me. Nobody's cared for me like that before."

"I love you; you're part of my world now."

Jeff shook his head and looked to the front of the room. Then he looked over at me and said, "Oh, Princess, what have I done to you? You know this is hopeless I'm not going to pass this year. I can't read or write. I have nothing and you're telling me I'm part of your world? Your world is bigger than this."

"We only have our moments together. You kept telling it's just a moment and I told you I'd settle for that! You can't read, you can't write, you're not going to pass and I don't care about those things. It's not important to me! So please, make every moment when we're together the best."

"Ok, Princess, but be prepared because each moment can end. We never know when we spend one more moment together if there will be another one."

"All right. So, when we are together, we're going to make the best of that moment and not worry about another one. We're both too young to worry. If it does come, enjoy it as long as it lasts."

We sat through the class to the end. I followed Jeff under the stairwell, but this time we just held each other for the five minutes we had together. We never let go of each other. I held onto him and laid my head on his shoulder, and he stroked my hair while I cried. I just wanted to hold him and he held me until we had to go to class.

The last day of school and I was glad, summertime, but the only bad thing, I would not see Jeff every day. I decided to ask him to come down to the barn Saturday morning and talk about what we were going to do this summer. We only had a few months and I hoped to make every day count. He agreed to come to the barn, he had an hour for lunch. I wanted more time with him, but I had to settle for what I could get.

Our time together had changed some. We didn't have sex every time. Jeff had changed. He became more caring, he asks me how I was feeling. Instead of jumping right into sex, he would hold me and kiss me on my forehead, he asks if there was anything he could do for me. He spoke to me softly and treated me as though I were a piece of glass that would break at the slightest touch. I liked that, but I loved it when he was rough with me having sex.

When he came in the barn and to the horse stall, I wanted to make plans for the summer. But this time I really wanted to figure out how to get in his car. Tony was taking Michelle to the drive-in. Michelle and I had talked about it on the last day of school.

"Do you have anything planned for tonight?" I asked.

"No, just get off work and go home. You got something in mind?"

"Tony is taking Michelle to the Star Drive-in tonight; do you want to go?"

Jeff's eyes lit up. "How can we go to the drive-in with them and not be seen?"

I smiled and said, "I don't want to go to the drive-in. I want to meet you, I can go wherever you want to go until the movie is over, Tony and Michelle can come and pick me up, take me home."

Jeff smiled. "I'll tell you what, when I get off work about 5:30 I'll have to go home and shower, we can meet at the Allen graveyard, it's my family cemetery. It's in town, but it's behind the Pentecostal church on Gillespie Lane. I bet Tony knows where it is."

"You've got a family graveyard?" I asked.

"Yes, on my daddy's side. My grandmother was Allen. Years ago, the Allens were a very prominent family. They used to own a lot of land in Galax and they kept enough land for a family graveyard. I go there sometimes to be alone. That's where I'll be. Ask Michelle to tell Tony will meet their, about six-thirty tonight and we'll make plans about what time we have to be back. You and I will slip away for the first time. Now I've got to go to get back to work."

"I can't wait. It's a dream come true for me. I'm going to be with you tonight, just me and you, and I don't care where we go."

He kissed me on the side of my neck and whispered in my ear. "You be ready tonight and I hope it's not your time of the month." We both laughed and I told him whatever he wanted tonight, that's what I was going to do for him. I was walking on a cloud. I didn't know it was a cloud of uncertainty, I didn't care. I was going to be with him away from everything and everybody.

I hadn't to asked Mom about going to the movies that night, but I didn't think I'd have much trouble. After all, I was going with Michelle and Tony. When Mom picked me up I casually said, "If it's ok with you, I'm going to go with Michelle and Tony to the drive-in tonight."

Mom asked me an unexpected question. "It's ok with me, but aren't you going to be a third wheel? You don't have a date?"

She surprised me with that question "No, no one's asked me, Mom. Michelle's my best friend and Tony doesn't seem to mind. As a matter of fact, we've talked about doing a lot of things together this summer. I hope you let me go with them."

"What sort of things? Have you thought about getting a summer job?"

That threw me off guard. She'd never asked me that before. "Do you know somewhere where I can get a summer job?"

Mom kept her eyes on the road, but I saw her look over at me slightly. "I'll ask around. Maybe Dad has something you can do to pick up a little extra money."

"Ok, then. Can I go with Tony and Michelle tonight?"

"I don't care, but aren't you going to be a wet blanket going on a double date without a date?"

"Mom, nobody at school asked me out. I think it's because – I don't know – they're afraid to ask. Besides, I'm not that pretty and you know it!"

"I don't think you've noticed, Princess you're becoming a young woman. We've had that talk about sex before. Why do you think I'm so guarded about you being around certain people? You're becoming a woman and you're going to have all the temptations and desires of a young woman. So don't sell yourself short, baby. You're growing up and it scares me. Now, what are some of the things that you want to do this summer with Tony and Michelle? How long do you think that's going to last between them?"

"Michelle mentioned something about Claytor Lake, Delp's Beach and Mount Rogers hiking. Are we going on vacation this summer?"

"I'm sure we are, but I don't know when. Your dad hasn't said anything about it. He's really busy with everything at work. But from what you telling me, you're going to stay busy this summer. You should look for a job. I don't see a reason why you can't go tonight, just be home by midnight."

"Thanks, Mom."

I called Michelle to tail her the good news I could go and found out what time I should be ready. I was excited and a nervous wreck the rest of the day. Finally, it was time for her and Tony to pick me up. I was sitting on the front porch with Mom when they pulled in front of the house. Mom told me to have a good time. I have to admit I sniggered to myself and thought, *you better believe I am*.

"Are you excited about this?" Michelle asked.

"You know I am." And then Tony asked me where we were going to pick up Jeff.

"Do you know where the Allen graveyard is on Gillespie Lane?"

"I'm not sure."

"It's behind that Pentecostal church on top of the hill. You pull in the church parking lot and go to the left. It's behind the church and that's where he'll be waiting for us."

"Gillespie Lane's across from the bowling alley. I think I know where it is. I go on that road all the time. I didn't pay any attention to the name of it. But I do know where that church is. It shouldn't be hard to find."

We turned around and went to the bowling alley parking lot and made that trip twice as everybody else does on the weekend, just checking out who's in town. I was getting so damn anxious and finally Tony said it was time. On our last trip through town instead of going in the bowling alley lot, we went across the street and turned on Gillespie Lane. The church was on the right on top of the hill, and behind it was Jeff's car sitting there. He was walking around looking at the tombstones until he saw us and came to the gate. I got out of the car, I ran to him. We walked back to ask Tony what the plan was and what time we should be back. Everyone agreed to be back by eleven-thirty. Tony and Michelle left and Jeff turned and looked at me. We leaned up against his car and he wasted no time. I was wrapped in his arms. It was heaven to me. We drove down Gillespie Lane and took a left to Cliff View Road. We were on our way to Iron Ridge. I sat very close to Jeff and slumped down in the seat so no one could see me. It broke my heart that I couldn't be seen in public with him, but I didn't want anything to mess this up because we had a whole summer in front of us. We didn't talk much on the way to Iron Ridge. Jeff had his right hand between my legs, rubbing them. My head was on his shoulder. We drove out the crooked road. Jeff found a place and took a right so we were back in the woods and couldn't be seen from the main road. We wasted no time talking and started making out. How soft and gentle he was to me. I guess you could say this was my first real car data and the more we made out, the more my body wanted him.

Without a word, Jeff got out of the car
and came around and opened the door.
He reached in and took me by the hand
I stepped out.
We stood there facing each other.
I was burning with lust.
I wanted him, all of him.

God help me, I wanted all of him.
I could hear the cool breeze
rustling the leaves in the trees.
We were looking eye to eye.
I pulled his shirt up over his head
and dropped it to the ground.
He unbuttoned my blouse
one button at a time.
I loosened his belt and unzipped his pants
and they dropped to the ground.
He reached around behind me
and unhooked my bra.
I shrugged my shoulders to help him pull it off
I put my fingers in his underwear
and slid them over his hips.
He unbuttoned my jeans and slid them down
He caught my panties with his fingers
as he went down.
We stood there naked and neither of us spoke.
I took a step back
and looked at his broad shoulders.
His penis was hard and firm. I wanted him.
Jeff opened the back door.
He took me by the hand and I followed him
in the back seat in his car.
"Straddle me, Princess, and put it in," he said.
I stepped my leg across his body and
as I sat down, he guided his penis in me.
The sensation was unbelievable.
I hugged him while he pushed my breasts

away from his body and sucked my nipples.
I threw my head back with pleasure.
I couldn't help it, I was screaming.
He stiffened his body and thrust upward
I worked my body in rhythm with his.
Without saying a word, he picked me up
and turned me over in his soft back seat
my legs were straight up in the air.
with every stroke of Jeff's body
I begin to feel climax, an orgasm
I begged him not to stop and he didn't.
He took a few more strokes
and then he said,
"I've got to quit. I don't want to
I just got off. I got to quit."

We both sat up in the seat.
We had worked so hard
the sweat was running down our faces
"Why are you looking at me?" I asked.
"You're so beautiful," he said.
"I've never really seen you completely naked before.
You're beautiful, you're so beautiful."
I was breathing hard, sweat was in my eyes.
"You make me feel beautiful, but I know I'm not."
"You will never have to ask me if I love you again.
I didn't think I could love anymore.
My family took all the love out of me."
"What about her?
Are you sure you really love me?"
"Please don't ever talk about her.

She is one of the reasons
I didn't think I could love again.
As much as I tried not to, yes, I love you
I didn't want to love you.
Honestly, Princess, all I wanted to do
was fuck you and hurt you.
You told me once when we were having sex
that I took you to heaven,
tonight, you are my angel.
You mean everything to me
that makes me afraid."
"Why does that make you afraid?"
"Because I know how it's going to end."
"Don't let it end right now.
You've always told me there's no tomorrow
there's no yesterday, there's just right now.
So, fuck me right now and don't stop."

We both stretched out in the back seat
I was on top, kissing his chest.
I kissed around his neck and sucked it a little bit.
I could feel him get hard again.
He rolled over on me
and for the first time
I realized we were not having sex,
we were making love.

This experience changed me. It was beyond anything we had done together before. Time was moving and I did not want it to end. Jeff held me and made me feel secure, at peace. We put our clothes back on and drove to the cemetery to wait for Tony to come and pick me up. Jeff showed me his grandmother's grave. It was peaceful to be in this graveyard.

We walked to the foot of his grandmother's grave and he began to talk to her. "Grandmother, you see this girl with me? She's not supposed to be here. She gave me the most wonderful night of my life and I couldn't think of a better place to be after being with her, just to talk to you. What would you tell her if you were here, Grandmother?" I stood beside Jeff as he talked to her. I could feel his emotions in the words he was saying. "Would you tell her how beautiful she is? Would you ask her who her parents are? You probably would know her grandparents. If you did, you'd know it's a miracle that she's here with me, Grandmother, I know."

Before Jeff could finish his talk with his grandmother, Tony pulled up. As we were walking towards Tony's car, I stopped Jeff and asked, "What were you going to say to your grandmother before you stopped?"

Jeff lowered his head and said, "That's ok, Princess, it can wait."

"Please tell me. What were you going to say to her?"

"I was going to tell her that I believed that you would be the last thing I would love before I die."

My heart sank when Jeff said that. "Please don't talk like that. Oh my God, please don't talk that way.

Right now, if anything happened to you, I would want to die."

We walked hand-in-hand to Tony's car. Before we got there, Jeff turned me around and said, "Princess."

"What, Jeff?"

He just looked at me sadly, but I didn't understand why. We had such a wonderful night and the summer was just beginning I was looking forward to more nights with him and whatever was in front of us. But I kept thinking even after I got home what was Jeff talking about that I would be the last thing he would love before he died?

I almost got in trouble when Mom asked me about the movie, and I didn't have a clue. I said it was some Western, and I don't like Westerns. I sure hope Mom didn't check after me but I had a feeling she did.

The next day I was a little bit sore. The sex was rough. I had more on my mind than sex, how much Jeff meant to me. He was really becoming everything to me. Once school was out, I could ride my horse. I had plenty of time and my parents never required me to get a summer job. I did help Mom around the house.

When I talked to Michelle on the phone, we tried to figure out what we were going to do next. She told me Tony wanted to go hiking up to Mount Rogers. Mount Rogers had a spectacular view, the highest peak in Southwest Virginia. We could take a picnic lunch. I hoped Jeff could go. It would be a great day away from Galax in the middle of the week. Nobody would be there but us.

Later Michelle called and told me Tony went by Higgins' Garage to see if Jeff could go with us hiking, and to my delight, he was ready. He and Tony made plans to pick him up in Baywood. Jeff could leave his car there. The plan was they would pick me up about nine-thirty Thursday morning. I'd bring a picnic lunch for everybody, and Michelle would bring drinks.

I asked Mom to help me get the picnic together that morning. When I started making sandwiches, she asked, "Princess, how many people are going to be there? You made eight sandwiches. I hope that's enough for the three of you."

"I forgot to tell you, Tony's cousin is going to go with us. We're going to pick him up in Baywood on the way."

"Tony's cousin, where is he from?"

"He's up for the summer. He lives in North Carolina somewhere. I agreed to make the sandwiches and I just want to make sure we have enough."

"Well, I'm glad someone else is going with you."

"Don't make a big deal out of it, Mom. I never met him before, and I don't know if I'll like him or not."

"Baby, I'm just glad you're going to meet somebody new. All this talk about Jeff Gray, I told you that would pass."

"I know, Mom, I know." She was eager to help me now that she thought I was going to be seeing someone else. Every time I went out of the house, I had to tell her a lie. I didn't like lying to my mother, but I did what I had to do to see Jeff. I wished it wasn't that way because I love my mother and it hurt me. Jeff was taking up my whole world and I couldn't help myself.

Once I was ready, I looked out the front window, waiting for Tony and Michelle to pull up. When they did, I went out and off we went. I couldn't get to Jeff fast enough. When I did, we embraced in front of everybody and Jeff cautioned me.

"Princess, please, people will see us!"

"I don't care. I'm so glad to see you. We've got the whole day together." We got in the back seat of Tony's car, sitting close. I was so excited. We all laughed and talked and everyone was in such a good mood. The feeling was adventurous and exciting. To me, everything was perfect. From Baywood, we drove to Independence on Highway 58 right through the Mouth of Wilson and Rugby before we started up the mountain. The day was perfect. The sun was shining and there was not a cloud in the sky. We were together and it was like we were the only ones in the world just for that moment. I realized this was another moment with Jeff I was going to make the most of. On the way there, he had his hand on my leg. This day was not about sex, this was about being together. Having time together was so important in making the summer truly magical.

We were almost in a community called White Top. Right before we got there, we took a right where you turn left to go up Whitetop Mountain. Down from there, we parked at the foot of the walking trail to go up Mount Rogers.

We locked the car and walked across the road to hit the trail. Tony had brought a canteen full of water. I'm glad he did we didn't think about that. It sure would come in handy halfway up the trail. He took the lead and set a fast pace. Jeff and I lagged behind. We were in no hurry. We had the whole day. The scenery was beautiful. There were a couple of places that you couldn't see any signs of life, no houses no radio towers, just mountains as far as you could see. Tony and Michelle went on ahead of us on the trail and waited on us to catch up. Jeff told him to keep going. We finally caught up with them again and Jeff told him he and I were going to talk and to go ahead and not worry about us. I wasn't sure what Jeff had on his mind; you never know with him. Just like a few nights ago the lovemaking was wonderful, but Jeff ended the night talking about dying. We came to a place on the trail that was open. The view was spectacular and we sat on a log, hand in hand.

"Princess, we need to talk."

I let him know quickly I wasn't going talk about anything that was sad. "Don't you start, Jeff Gray. I don't want to hear you say that you're not good enough or that you're going to die. I'm not going to hear that any more from you now that we're having a good time. Please don't mess it up"

"Princess, you don't understand."

"What do you mean I don't understand? Let me tell you what I do understand! This is one of those moments and that's all you promised me. Now, this is my moment, and I'm not going to let you mess it up by talking crazy. I chose to be here with you this moment. Isn't that good enough for you? You have to keep putting yourself down, talking like there's no tomorrow!" I was raising my voice. I was so aggravated. Things were perfect but Jeff didn't see it that way.

"Princess, you know what I think?"

"What!"

"You're the crazy one. You're crazy enough to be here with me on this mountain. What have I done to you?"

"I'll tell you what you've done to me, you took my virginity so now take the rest of me with it!"

"If you put it that way, I want all of you then. I want all of you, Princess, and I mean more than just your pussy. I want all of you." Jeff finally said the words I wanted to hear.

He settled down. I wanted him to enjoy the rest of the day. I tried to make it clear to him. "This is another one of our moments, don't spoil it."

We walked on up the trail, almost on top. We were the only ones there that day. When we reached the top, we noticed some movement in the bushes off the main trail. Jeff turned to me and put his finger to his lips as though he were saying be quiet. We tiptoed over and pulled the bushes back. Tony and Michelle were having sex. Jeff and I backed up without disturbing them and when they came back on the trail, we acted like we didn't know anything about it. I was about to burst. I didn't know when all that started. I knew she told me before that he was having trouble keeping his hands to himself.

When they came back up the trail, I couldn't help but notice Michelle's face was red. So, to open up a conversation I asked her about it. "Michelle your face is so red. Is something wrong?"

"No, I'm just exercising walking this trail, that's all."

Jeff and I grinned and tried to keep from laughing. He would turn his head away from me so he wouldn't burst out. The four of us got to the top and decided to sit down on a log to rest. That's when Michelle came up with an idea that shocked me.

"Listen, guys, Saturday night Princess can spend the night with me and we can camp out in my backyard. We'll sleep in my tent all night. You guys can show up about 12 o'clock, maybe a little earlier, but make sure that my mom and dad have gone to bed. You could come and spend the night with us."

I looked at Jeff and he looked at Tony. Before we could say anything, Tony responded, "Hell yes! How about you, Jeff? Are you up for it?"

Jeff looked at me and said, "I'd better not."

I smacked him on the head while he was laughing. "What do you mean, you better not!"

"Because I can't stay with somebody else, I mean the four of us!"

"Why?" I asked.

Then Jeff grinned at me, "Because I'm going to be fucking you."

And Tony said, "If Michelle doesn't mind, then I don't mind."

Michelle said, "I think Tony and I can find something to do to keep us busy if you guys decide to."

We all burst out laughing and I asked, "You don't mind, Michelle? You really don't mind, because Jeff really gets intense with me and I love it."

"I believe I can keep Tony busy," she said, "and we won't even know you're there."

"Then we're on for this Saturday night," Tony asked.

"Ok, I'll be there," Jeff agreed. "Tony, what are we going to do? Can we get together for sure Saturday night?"

"Wait a minute, I think I have to work until at least until nine. That will give me enough time to go home and shower. We'll figure out something."

Michelle and Tony started walking back down the trail. We laid back and let them go on. I whispered to Jeff, "Watching them have sex got me hot. Take me to the bushes and fuck me."

Jeff never said a word. We walked a little ways off the trail, he looked around and told me, "Right here is fine, Princess. Pull your pants down."

"There's no place to lie down here," I said.

"Drop your pants and turn around and bend over and we'll do it dog style."

"Dog style? What do you mean?"

"That means we're going to have sex, dog style and I'll come in from behind. All you've got to do is bend over and I'll put it in you and we'll have sex."

I did what Jeff told me, not knowing what to expect and then he put it in me. This was very pleasurable. It was funny in the end. Jeff got faster and my butt smacking against his body making a funny sound. I hadn't planned on having sex that day, but surprises are wonderful. We all walked back to the car and tried to figure out where we were going to have lunch. It was about one in the afternoon.

That's when Jeff said, "On top of Whitetop Mountain would be a good place to sit and have lunch.

This was my first time on Whitetop Mountain and my first time hiking Mount Rogers. We drove up to the road a little way and took the turn to go up on top of the mountain. I loved the fact you could drive up there. We got out of the car with the picnic basket and had lunch. Jeff was telling me how much he loved this part of the country, and how much he loved these mountains. I told him how much I loved him in these mountains.

We stayed there for an hour or two and started back toward Galax. Jeff wanted to stop under the bridge at the Mouth of Wilson at the boat launch. That was a really nice place.

"Next Wednesday, let's take the whole day and drive down to Claytor Lake," Tony suggested. "We'll spend the day there and take a picnic lunch. They've got a nice beach and shower houses. What you say?"

Jeff looked at me and asked, "You want to go, Princess?"

Michelle jumped up and said, "Yes, I'm ready, Princess. Let's go with them.

"Ok, I'm ready. We're going to go on Wednesday morning and spend all day there?"

"Yes, we'll go through the details Saturday night in the tent," Tony answered. "By the way, Michelle, are you sure your parents won't come out and check on you and catch us there?"

"Princess and I have camped out there before. Most of the time, Mom will just holler from the back door to check on us. She never comes out and looks in the tent. As long as we are quiet, I think we can get away with it."

We sat under the bridge at the boat launch at Mouth of Wilson. A nice quiet place. We had a few minutes before we had to start back home. We were talking and making out and everybody was laughing and having a good time. Jeff came up with another idea I liked.

"So, let me make sure I got my schedule right," said Jeff. "Saturday night we're going camping in Michelle's backyard?"

"Yes," she answered.

Jeff continued, "And next Wednesday, we're going to Claytor Lake."

"Yes," I answered.

"Then I suggest the following Wednesday we go to Delp's Beach."

"That's a great idea," Tony agreed. "If we go to Delp's Beach early, nobody else will be there. Because it's the middle of the week, everybody will be at work and we'll have the place to ourselves."

"Maybe. Sometimes there'll be a few people there," Jeff said. "It's such a popular place, but I'd like to go and spend the day. We can take another picnic, are you girls ready for that?"

Michelle said, "Princess, I'm ready for it if you are."

"Yes, I like that idea. Let's do it."

With a big grin, Jeff said, "I have a full schedule. That's what we'll do." We sat under the bridge in the sand for a little while longer, then the sad part of the day came when we had to go home. I snuggled in Jeff's arms on the way back to his car. At the car, I didn't want him to leave.

We kissed passionately and he whispered in my ear, "Damn you, Princess. Look what you've done to me now. I'm in love with you and I see another broken heart coming."

"Please, Jeff, you know I'm in love with you. You're my first and I would hope you'll be my last for the rest of our lives."

"You know that's not realistic We'll have this summer, but for now, everything we do together let's do it hard. When we're having sex, my passion for you will be strong and hard."

"Jeff, I'm going to ride it and I pray the end is a long way off. We've only been in summer for a few weeks. It's been more than magical for me. Damn you, Jeff. You've matured me before my time. Please don't talk about the end ever again. If it happens, it happens. Let's just be together as long as we can. Please, just ride it to whatever the end is."

"Ok, Princess. We're going to ride to the end, whatever that is." Jeff got in his car and we followed him back to Galax. Tony took me home. I was walking in the clouds in my mind. The summer had a good start and was more than magical to me.

Mom was waiting for me and asked if I had a good time. "So how was your day, Princess? Was Tony's cousin a nice guy?"

I was almost caught off guard. Then I remembered telling her I was going to meet a new guy today. I took a moment before I answered her, trying to think of something to say. "He was ok. He was sort of silly, quite honestly."

"Well, that was the first time you met him. Is he going to be here for a while?"

"I don't know, but if you don't care, Mom, Michelle's asked me to spend the night with her next Saturday. Is it ok if I go? I think she wants to sleep in her tent-like we used to."

"When you girls were younger, you'd sleep in her father's tent all the time. You haven't done that in a while. You don't think you're getting too old to sleep in a tent when you're at home?"

"We thought it would be fun. We can talk about girl things and stay up as long as we want to and not bother her parents. If we don't have anything planned for that day, I'll probably ride my horse Saturday morning. And one other thing, Tony has asked Michelle next Wednesday to go down to Claytor Lake and spend the day. They asked me to go with them, will it be all right with you?"

"It sounds like fun, no problem with me."

"Tony told Michelle that he'd like to do something once a week. They are talking about going to the river at Delp's Beach."

"That's a pretty place on the river, and there's a nice beach, you'll enjoy that. That's fine with me, but be careful on that river," Mom said.

I got through that all right. I had gotten Mom's permission for the next couple of weeks. This was working out so well. This summer is working out better than I imagined.

Saturday morning, I called Michelle and asked her if she would go to the barn with me. We picked her up on the way. Mom dropped us off and said she'd be back later. This gave me and Michelle a chance to talk about what we had gotten ourselves into with these boys. I was anxious to find out how Tony and she starting having sex and I'm sure she would ask me all about how it happened between me and Jeff.

Michelle helped me clean out the stable. I was waiting for the question, and then Michelle found her opening to ask me. "Why didn't you tell me about Jeff in the beginning?"

I stood up straight and leaned on the shovel I was using to clean the stall and I answered her. "I was afraid you wouldn't understand. We made fun of him all the time. I was sure you would laugh at me over it."

Then she asked me the question "When did you start having sex with him?"

"I can ask you the same about Tony."

"How do you know we are having sex?"

"Jeff and I saw you when we were on the mountain, Wednesday. We looked through the bushes and he was on top of you. I could tell you were liking it."

Michelle's face turned red. She didn't know Jeff and I caught them. "You saw me and Tony on the mountain?"

"Yes, but we didn't say anything. Honestly, I was sort of relieved."

"Relieved?"

"Yes, I didn't know how to tell you that Jeff and I were having sex."

"When did you start having sex with Jeff?"

"It's a long story. It started in school."

"You were having sex in school!"

"That's another story, but anyway, Jeff kissed me in civics class. He kissed me, I really liked it, I started meeting him under the stairwell in school to make out every day. I invited him to the barn, and just like Tony, his hand started to roam. I fought him off at first and then one thing led to another. I let him go too far and I didn't want him to stop. I lost my virginity; I blame myself for part of it."

"Why would you blame yourself?"

"Because I invited him here and I laid with him in the hayloft"

"What did you do after that?"

"When I got through crying, he was sorry for doing it."

" You didn't tell me what did you do after that?"

"After a little time went by, I let him fuck me again and we've been having sex ever since. Michelle, I'm in love with him. I don't know what to do. I know it's crazy. I know it has no future, but he's giving me the time of my young life. He's teaching me things that I love doing with him. I don't know what I'm going to do. I don't know how this is going to end. I know I'm just a lovesick girl having sex before my time, but it's too late, Michelle. I feel helpless. My mom is giving me a fit over him and my dad hates him, so thank you for helping me see him. I've decided to let whatever happens, happen, I'm trying to keep from getting pregnant. Most of the time Jeff uses a rubber, but sometimes he doesn't. Sometimes I just don't care. Michelle, every time I think it's the best, he does something different to make it even better. When Tony took me to the graveyard to meet Jeff, we went to Iron Ridge and parked in the woods and I've never experienced anything like it. Ok, I've told you everything about me and Jeff. What about you and Tony?"

"The night we dropped you off we went to the movies. The movie just had started and we were making out and Tony started rubbing my breasts. He got under my bra and flipped my nipples. I pushed him away, but the more we made out, the more I liked it. He was sucking on my neck and then unbuttoned my blouse. I let him suck one of my breasts and he put his hand between my legs and before I knew it, he had his hands in my panties and put a finger in me. It was over then, and I gave up. Now when we get a chance, we're having sex."

Then I asked, "So when we're in the tent tonight and you look over and see me and Jeff having sex, you don't mind?"

"No, I won't mind because I'm sure Tony will be on top of me and I'll be too busy to have time watching you and Jeff."

I felt better after we had that talk. We knew what to expect. We finished cleaning the stall and feeding my horse. Mom came back and picked us up. We went back to my house and I picked up some clothes before Mom took us to Michelle's that afternoon. Mom stayed a while talking to her mom, and her dad got the tent set up in the backyard. It was a nice backyard and we asked her dad to set it up away from the house, back close to the fence. There was a big field behind her house so no one could see the boys come in at night. Everything was ready and so was I.

Chapter 8

Michelle's parents took us to play miniature golf. We stayed there and played long after dark. We watched TV when we came back home, and around 10 o'clock we decided to go to the tent. I think Michelle's parents were glad to have the house to themselves. One good thing about that night, no moon so the boys could sneak in easily without anyone seeing them. Michelle and I lay in the tent, waiting.

Giggling and laughing like little girls. I looked at my watch and it was about 11:30 PM. Then we heard some scraping against the fence, and sure enough, it was the boys. When they got to the tent, they were afraid to come inside. They were afraid of getting caught, but I insisted they come in and stay with us. We looked at Michelle's house where all the lights were off.

When the boys finally came inside, Jeff took his shoes off and crawled into the sleeping bag with me. We never spoke. He took his clothes off. I don't know what Michelle and Tony were doing. I didn't care.

Then all of a sudden, Michelle's mama called out. "Are you all right? The dog wants to come to stay with you, Michelle!"

Everybody froze in place. Michelle looked out of the tent flap and yelled back. "Ok Mom, we're fine. Let the dog come on out."

Jeff whispered in my ear, "I hope she's not coming out here. And I hope that dog doesn't get upset and bark at us."

Michelle opened the tent door and the dog came inside and lay down. Everybody was relieved. All through the night, we were having sex. I was in heaven again. We stayed awake all night long. I was in Jeff's arms and that was heaven to me.

Tony looked at his watch and whispered to Jeff, "It's almost five in the morning, we'd better go."

Jeff and I rolled over and kissed. We had sex one more time before they had to leave. It was a night in the tent that I'll never forget.

The next morning in Sunday school we both fell asleep, but Michelle's parents didn't say anything. They knew we were up all night. If they just knew what kept us up all night! That was the first time we stayed all night in the tent. We did that a couple of more times before the summer was over, and every time was better than the first.

Wednesday morning, I was getting ready to go to Claytor Lake. I had no idea where Jeff was. I wondered if he was going to come down or if we were going to pick him up. While I was having breakfast, Mom didn't say much to me. She didn't talk about Jeff, but she did notice I was in a good mood.

After breakfast, I showered and got ready, and Mom helped me pack a lunch for us. I was patiently waiting, looking out the window for Tony to pull up. I was glad when he did. Mom hugged me and told me to have a good time. I was thinking to myself, *if Jeff shows up, I know I will.*

As soon as I got in Tony's car, I asked, "Did you talk to Jeff? Is he going to come?"

"We'll pick him up in Hillsville behind the courthouse, then drive down 52 and go the back way to Claytor," Tony answered "I was worried. I didn't know if he would be able to come or not. I wasn't sure about his work schedule."

"Looks like it's going to be a pretty day," Michelle said. "I've been waiting for this."

We all made small talk on the way to Hillsville. When we pulled behind the courthouse, Jeff was waiting. We pulled up beside his car and I got out. Jeff was in a good mood. He took me in his arms and squeezed me real tight, kissed me and told me he was glad to see me. We got in the back seat of Tony's car and drove down 52.

On the way down the mountain, I could sense something different about Jeff. It was like he'd forgotten all the bad times behind him. Forgotten about his family life and I thought maybe I was a joy in his life. I really hoped so. He was such a joy to me. It was just the two of us. With the help of Tony and Michelle, we were going to have a wonderful day together.

We drove all around the lake to come to the main gate to pay our way in, and then to the shower houses to change into our swimsuits. Michelle and I both had bikinis. When we walked out and met the guys, Jeff looked at me. "You're beautiful," he said with a real low voice so Tony and Michelle couldn't hear him, and then he whispered again. "How am I going to keep my hands off of you? God, you're so sexy."

I was all smiles for Jeff to talk to me that way. It made me feel good inside. We walked down to the sand and found a place to spread out towels to sit before getting into the water.

Jeff and I tiptoed to the lake and went in about waist deep. It was cold at first, but the sun was hot. It was one of those perfect days that couldn't have been better. We all played in the water and splashed each other as though there was no tomorrow. Jeff and I were having one of our moments together, and I was doing my best to take advantage of it. The morning passed quickly and we decided to find a picnic table to have lunch.

Michelle brought a few things to go with the lunch Mom and I packed. Everything was going really smoothly. After we ate Tony and Jeff carried the picnic basket back to the car and locked it up in the trunk. We went back down to the beach. Although the sun was hot and the air was humid, staying in the water felt so good. Tony and Michelle went their own way, while Jeff and I walked back to the towels to sit down and watch everybody.

He started to talk, "This is one of those moments, Princess, one of those precious moments with you, but it scares me." I looked at him. I was worried he was going to start telling me he wasn't good enough to be with me.

"Don't you start. It's a perfect day, don't ruin it, listen to me."

Jeff looked me right in the eyes. I had a serious look on my face and so did he. "I'm here with you because I love you. I don't care what everybody says about us. I don't care what my mama and daddy say about you or about me, about how young we are. I don't care. Jeff, I love you and it's too late for me to turn back. So, don't you start telling me you're not good enough! I don't want to hear it anymore. I gave you all of me. Let me talk plain to you. When you want pussy from me you get it! When you want to talk to me, I listen! You have all of me, everything that I can give you, my body, my love, everything! Stop it, stop talking crazy! This is one moment. I realize that but just live this moment. The rest of the time we're together I don't want to hear you're not good enough for me! I'll hear none of that! How many times do I have to tell you that I love you for who you are! Have I asked you to change? Have I asked you to be somebody else? I love you for who you are!"

Jeff just sat for a moment. He never said a word but kept mumbling to himself. "I love you, don't you understand? I love you. I didn't mean for this to happen to you, Princess I didn't mean to get you involved with me. I don't know how this happened to us. I never expected you to end up loving me and now I'm in love with you. This is hopeless, I just know deep down this cannot last. I know I'm headed for disappointment in the end. I'm telling you, Princess, when this ends, it will be the end of me. I will have nothing to live for, nothing to look forward to without you in my world. I'll have no world. I'll have nothing and no reason for living."

"I told you not to talk that way! How many times do I have to say it?"

Tony and Michelle came back to the towels and sat down. She said, "Don't look over there, Princess, but there are some people who know our parents, and they're watching us."

"They'll certainly tell your parents you've been here with me, Princess," Jeff said. "This may be the end of it. You know they are going to tell your parents." The four of us never let on that we saw them.

Then I said, "I don't care. I don't care if they go back and tell my mom and dad that they saw me here with you. I don't give a damn anymore. Have a good time and ignore them."

"Are we going to speak to them?" Michelle asked. "Are we going to say anything?"

"No," I said. "Just be polite. If they speak, speak back." I could tell Jeff was uncomfortable, but I made sure everybody kept on enjoying the beach and the water. The afternoon went by, the people who knew our parents left.

We were there for a little bit longer. It was 5:30 PM when we walked back to the car and decided to go and shower off the lake water and change clothes. We met back in Tony's car. left the lake to go the way we came.

When we drove through Poplar Camp, Tony had a suggestion. "Next Wednesday, let's go to Delp's Beach if it's not raining or storming."

"That's a great idea," Michelle said.

"I'm ready. Are you, Jeff?"

"Yes," Jeff answered. "I would love to go there. That's one of my favorite places. I used to camp out there with Carty Phillips."

I turned around in my seat facing Jeff's arms. He was holding me so tenderly, play with my legs and came to the bottom of my shorts. I helped him. Everyone was quiet because I was busy with Jeff. He was rubbing his hand back and forth in the hair and sticking his finger in me without saying a word. I looked at him and sat up. I unzipped his pants and pulled his dick out. I pushed my panties and shorts to the side of my crotch, straddled him and he stuck it in. I sat there on him going up the mountain. He kissed me with his tongue in my mouth and his dick in me. I certainly was in heaven. The pleasure of having him in me, I can't explain. And as we were going around the curves I slid back and forth until we both got off. I don't know what Tony and Michelle were doing and I didn't care. I had gone all day long wanting to fuck Jeff and this was the only chance I got.

Before we got to his car, I turned and sat back down and asked him, "Will you come by the barn Saturday morning?"

Jeff shook his head yes and pulled me close to him again as though he would never let me go. This was a great way to finish up a wonderful day. When we got to Hillsville, Jeff kissed me goodbye, got in his car, we followed him back to Galax. I wished I was in his car with him. I didn't know what the people would say who saw us at the lake, but I didn't care anymore. Nothing was going to stop me from seeing him now. I didn't care what they would try to do to me, I was going to see him every chance I got.

When Tony and Michelle dropped me off at home, Mom asked me to go to Roanoke the next morning to do some shopping. I was afraid she would start questioning me about Jeff and she did. "I spoke with the Williamses this afternoon. They said they saw you and Tony and Michelle, but one other guy was there, too. You didn't tell me about him."

I was waiting on this "Mom, Jeff Gray was there with some friends. He came over to talk to Tony. I can't control that. So, you think what you want to. Tony and Jeff Gray are friends, what am I supposed to do?"

"Ok, don't get huffy."

"Mom, am I going to have to go all summer with you worrying about Jeff Gray? Can't you just let me have a good summer and not worry about those things?"

Mom hung her head and never brought it up again that evening. We drove to Roanoke the next morning. I was trying to be pleasant and give her the impression that my summer was going very well and I was enjoying myself with Tony and Michelle.

"I guess Tony is taking both you girls out now," she laughed.

"What do you mean? Tony doesn't seem to mind."

"I didn't mean anything, don't get touchy."

"I'm not touchy, Mom, but I enjoyed going to the lake and we're going to Delp's Beach next Wednesday. Remember me asking you before?"

"I remember. You'll enjoy that place. We always did. Just be careful. That river can be dangerous."

"We're going to stay all day. And by the way, Mom, I want to spend the day at the barn Saturday."

"That's the reason you have a horse, to enjoy it." We had a good time shopping together. On the way back home, I bought some clothes for school for the coming year. But for sure, I didn't have my mind on school. I had my mind on the few weeks we had left this summer. I was going to make sure I enjoyed every day, every moment. I intended to do everything I could to live every moment with Jeff.

Friday was a long day. I stayed around the house and helped Mom clean the place up, just waiting to go to the barn Saturday morning. When I got there, Jeff was too. I know Mom saw his car but she didn't say anything. She dropped me off, said she'd be back later on in the afternoon, to take my time. Jeff was there so I certainly was going to enjoy myself.

I walked into the barn, but he was nowhere to be seen. I knew he was in the hayloft. I started working on my horse and cleaned up the stall. I let my horse in the corral and then went back into the barn. Jeff was waiting for me. He said he was going to help me shovel out my stall. Before I could do anything, I had to hug and kiss him. “You know how glad I am to see you?” I said.

He smiled, “Not as glad as I am to see you.” He took a deep breath.

“Are you ok?” I asked.

“If it wasn’t for you, I wouldn’t be ok.”

“What’s wrong?”

“My family is fighting, and I can’t take it anymore. If it wasn’t for you, I’d go crazy.”

I took Jeff in my arms. He was almost crying on my shoulder and I felt bad for him because he never cried. He got mad and aggravated, that’s the reason he fought all the time. This time he was not taking it out on me. I asked him, “Do you want to go up in the hayloft?”

“Ok,” he answered. Jeff sat me down against a bale of hay and he lay back in my arms. We sat there, and he never made a move for sex. He just lay in my arms and I stroked the hair on his forehead. It’s like he had a moment of peace. Honestly, I was surprised. I was ready to have sex with him, but he wasn’t in the mood. So I held him. I could feel him hurting. I never felt that from him before. Normally he was angry when he was hurting.

We talked and made plans for Delp’s Beach. Now I was really worried about him. This was a different Jeff that I was used to. We stood up, Jeff kissed me and told me how much he loved me and appreciated me. Being with me made a difference in his life. Then he left. He didn’t want sex. I was surprised and disappointed and happy all at the same time. He really loved me and I felt like he needed me. I know how much I needed him, but everything had changed. We'd come a long way in our relationship. After he left, I took my horse out for a ride. I was doing a lot of thinking. Crazy thoughts ran through my mind. I was thinking about running away with Jeff, but I knew that really was crazy.

Chapter 9

Everything was closing in on me. My life was getting so complicated all of a sudden. When I looked back, I don't know how it happened. I shouldn't have been involved in such things with a boy like Jeff or with anybody, for that matter. I should have been enjoying high school and getting ready for college, but I wasn't. I was busy having sex with a boy who showed me attention, and I was hopelessly in love. I didn't realize love could be so complicated. I was lying to my parents and doing everything I should not be doing, and I couldn't stop myself. I knew my mother loved me, and when I would lie to her, I felt so ashamed. But the lure of Jeff would overtake me, and I resorted to lying to a loving mother. I realized how out-of-control I was over him. I was sacrificing my relationship with my mom for him. I was torn between trying to do right by my mother or seeing Jeff. At times, it was agonizing. Jeff was winning, he had control of me.

At church, I got a chance to talk to Michelle after the service. While we were waiting on our parents I stood beside our car and told her, " I'm in trouble, I'm not having second thoughts about Jeff I'm so far away from who I used to be." I said with a serious voice.

"What!"

"I'm so in love with Jeff and I can't stop. I'm having crazy thoughts about running away with him."

Michelle quickly turned around and looked at me. "Are you crazy! You know you can't do that. Why can't you just see him? You're not supposed to think about doing something stupid like that, you know better, Princess!"

"I don't know what to do, I want to keep seeing him and I don't want it to end."

"I don't know what to tell you, Princess. Are you still going to Delp's Beach with us?"

"Yes, I'm going, I'm having a ball experiencing things, and you and Tony are great. I'm just confused, Michelle. Jeff keeps saying it's not going to end up well and now I believe him. It can't keep on going this way."

She was silent for a moment and then said, "Why do you have to complicate everything? Just live each day as it comes. We'll all be going back to school soon. I mean, what else is there to do, Princess?"

"I know, I'm just worried. I want to be with him every chance I get and now I'm afraid. I'm just afraid."

Our parents showed up and I told Michelle I would see her and Tony Wednesday morning to go to the river. Then I thought to myself the plans had been made. I was sure Jeff and Tony would work out what they would do to meet up with us for a day at the river. On the way home from church, Mom asked what Michelle and I were talking about.

"We were talking about Wednesday at the river what to bring to eat and drink, that's all.

And then Dad asked, "Are you going to the river?"

"They're going to Delp's Beach," Mom told him.

"That's a beautiful place, probably the best place on New River around here. You be careful, Princess. Don't get too far out in the river."

"I won't. We don't usually get deep to start with."

"Who are you going with?"

I got nervous, looking for the words to answer him. "I'm going with Tony and Michelle. We've been going to Claytor Lake and different places. It's good to have something to do during the hot summer days. We're having a good time."

"Ok, baby, enjoy yourself and be very careful around that river. I'll worry about you." Dad and Mom talked about things around Galax the rest of the way home. We had lunch and Dad sat around reading the paper and watching the news. I went out to sit on the porch. It was a beautiful day for a summer afternoon.

Mom came out, asking, "Is everything ok with you? Sometimes you seem so moody. What are you not telling me?"

"Mom, I'm not doing anything different than I normally do."

" I can tell you've changed."

"Mom, I'm fifteen now. I thought I was supposed to change?"

"Ok, I'm just saying I'm watching you change before my very eyes and it bothers me. It makes me feel old."

"I don't know what to tell you, Mom."

"Baby, don't get mad, but I know what's going on. It's about Jeff Gray."

" Can't you leave this alone? I'm already confused about the whole world and you're making it worse on me."

"I don't mean to, but I'm afraid you don't trust me anymore. You're not telling me the truth. Remember, I was your age once and I know things can get confusing."

"You've always known about Jeff. Why haven't you stopped me from seeing him? You knew I've been seeing him and you didn't stop me, why?"

"You tell me how I'm going to stop you? I'm trying to keep this from your father. I don't know what he would do if he found out. He would kill Jeff and you know that. What do you want me to do, send you away to another school? What would you do then? How can I convince you that you're really messing up your life? You tell me what I can do to stop you from seeing this boy. You don't have a damn clue about love!"

She was raising her voice to me, she scared me. She talking about sending me away. That would truly kill me for sure. Then I answered her. "What am I supposed to do, Mom? You tell me I don't know anything about love. If I don't, then why does it hurt so bad?"

"Let me ask you this, Princess. When you go away with Michelle and Tony, is Jeff anywhere to be seen?"

I was thinking to myself now I've really messed up. She knew too much about me and I didn't know what I was going to tell her. It took me a moment before I answered. "No, no not every time."

"Then how many times have you seen him and what do you do with him when you do see him? Don't you think I know what's going on, Princess? What am I going to do? Please, Princess. I can't stop this. If your father finds this out, you're as good as gone and you know it!"

I kept my composure. "Please don't send me away. Please, let me work this out. Mama please, please let me work this out."

"What are you going to do to work it out? How far is this going? What's made you fall so much for this boy that you think you're in love with him? Am I supposed to let you go with Tony and Michelle now? Would I be a good mother and let you do that?"

"Mom, I love you, but I'm hurting so bad right now. I'm trying to make the right decision and if you don't let me do it on my own, I'll find a way."

" Are you telling me that you're going to go against my authority as your mother? You're putting me in a bad spot here."

"Can I ask you one question then? You just got through telling me you were my age once, what did you do?" I got up and left Mom sitting there. I looked back and she was almost in tears. I went too far. That's how confused I was, but I was still going to see Jeff. I couldn't stop loving him even if I didn't know what love was. There was something inside me that wanted him and I was out of control.

I went back to where Mom was sitting and she stood up, I hugged her. She held me while we cried. She loved me and she just didn't want to see me hurt or mess up my life. *What am I going to do*? I thought over and over in my mind. *What am I going to do*?

Monday and Tuesday were very slow for me. Wednesday morning, I had breakfast with my parents. Mom was busy frying bacon and eggs, I could tell she wasn't her happy self. She hadn't looked at me. Dad didn't seem to notice. Mom always made breakfast, but it was Wednesday morning and she knew where I was going.

Then Dad asked me a question that scared me to death. "Princess, how would you like to go to a private school?"

Mom stopped, turned and looked at him. It caught me off guard. "Is there a reason you'd want to send me to a private school?"

"No, I just thought maybe you would get a better education than public schools. It would prepare you for college better."

Mom spoke up. "What brought that on? She's doing ok in Galax High School. She's got good grades."

"I know. It was just a thought."

"Dad, I'm ok. Like Mom said, I've got good grades, and all my friends are here. And I would miss you and Mom if you send me away to school."

"I can afford to send you to a private school. As long as you're happy here and you're making good grades, and you're doing the right things in life, you'll stay. But always keep that in the back of your mind.

You must be better than everybody else. You've got to work hard and respect yourself. That's all I'm asking you to do," Dad said, firmly.

Mom had that look on her face and I knew why. Dad got up from the table, kissed me on my forehead and told me to be careful on New River before he said goodbye.

Afterward, I asked Mom, "Did you say something to Dad about me?"

"No, I didn't. But always remember, Princess, if he finds out about Jeff Gray, I don't know what he would do. Always remember that."

After breakfast, I showered and came back to the kitchen. I made some sandwiches for the day to take with us. Michelle told me she would bring the drinks. We had everything worked out. At 9:30, Tony and Michelle were in front of my house.

Before I walked out the door, Mom took me by the hand, we walked out on the porch. As she turned to look at me, she said, "Princess, you don't understand. I want you to have a good time, be careful. You told me yesterday you are in love with Jeff Gray. It worries me to think what you're doing with him," she paused. "I can see in your face you've lost your innocence. I feel like I have failed you as your mother."

I hugged my mother's neck and said, "You've not failed me, Mom. I've told you the truth about Jeff. You said I can trust you, and to tell you the truth. I took a chance and told you I'm in love with him. Mom, you're not telling me the truth, and I'm not sure what it's all about, but when you talk about your past, I can see the sadness in your eyes. I can see the pain from your past, Mom. You're not telling me the truth, are you?"

She shook her head and turned her back on me. "It's not time to talk about me. My time has come and gone, but your time is in front of you. Go on now, enjoy yourself because you'll never have another time like right now, you've got to be careful."

I got in the back seat of Tony's car. I was going to see Jeff, Mom almost ruined everything for me. I had the whole day, I was going to enjoy it and try not to think about anything else. Just to have our moments together. I was trying to be happy, it was so damn complicated.

Michelle knew something was bothering me and she asked me about Mom.

"Were you and your mom arguing?"

"No, but I told her something she didn't want to hear."

"Oh, what could that be?"

"I told her I was in love with Jeff."

"You didn't! What did she say?"

"I don't know, but since I started seeing Jeff, it's like Mom always knew. There's something in my mother's past she's not telling me. I can't figure out what it is."

Tony didn't get involved in the conversation until finally, he told me, "Princess, I've got some news for you."

"Don't tell me, Jeff, not going to come with us today, please don't tell me that."

"No, it's something else. I've never seen Jeff like this before. He's completely in love with you. I'm surprised because that other girl he was seeing, you know she was his first love and it's been hard for him. For a long time, he didn't care about anything. Jeff has talked crazy a few times with me, especially if he's drinking. He told me he didn't want to live. That's why he was fighting all the time. I hope maybe you've changed that for him."

It made me feel good to think that Jeff was in love with me, but when Tony told me he didn't want to live anymore, that bothered me. "Are we going to pick Jeff up today?" I asked.

"He's going to meet us at the river. He should be there when we get there," Tony told me. I didn't talk anymore on the way to the river. There were a lot of things going through my mind like, what was Mom keeping from me? Crossing the low-water bridge, we drove through Fries, turned by the diner and down the dirt road, we went until we went through the gates and pulled around to see the sand. I didn't see Jeff's car anywhere. Maybe he's not here yet.

After we parked, I could see Jeff lying on the beach. As he came walking towards us, I jumped out and hugged his neck. He helped us get everything out of Tony's car, we all went back to the beach and spread the towels out to sit down.

Michelle and I had our swimsuits on under our clothes, so we stripped them off and were ready for the water.

Jeff took me by my hand, we walked into the water waist-deep. I put my arms around him. Jeff turned me around with his back to the beach. Tony and Michelle couldn't see him. He told to put my hands in his pants, and I smiled at him. Then he whispered in my ear, "You want to go up in the woods and have sex?"

"I thought you'd never ask." We walked out of the water and into the woods. That's where he had his car parked. Once we were out of sight, he untied the bottom of my bikini. I got in his back seat and we had wonderful sex. The whole time he was on top of me he was telling me how good I was. I told him to turn over and I got on top of him. He stiffened his body as I was working him. He was so beautiful to me. I could tell he was pleased.

Jeff got off and we sat in the back seat almost completely naked. He asked me to get out and we came around with the back door open. I bent over and he fucked me from behind. This was a lot of fun. I got off this time, and we both put our swimsuits back on and went back to the beach. Tony asked Jeff if they could sit in his car. While they were gone, Jeff and I waded out into the water.

In the river, the hot sun was bearing down on us, the water was cool. It was one of those special summer days. "Do your parents know you're seeing me?" I asked.

"No," Jeff said quickly.

"Why not?"

"It's none of their business."

"Looks like the shoe's on the other foot now," I smiled.

"What do you mean?"

"The whole time that you and I've been seeing each other, all I hear from you is that you're not good enough for me. Now I find out you didn't tell your parents about me. Are you ashamed of me?"

"You know better. I didn't want anybody to talk. If my mom or dad said something it could get back to your parents, Princess. I don't want anything to happen to us now." " You know damn well I'm proud to be with you. I never dreamed in a million years somebody like you would be with me."

"Do you mean that? That you're proud to be with me?" Jeff excitedly said.

"Yes" "You make me want to go back to school. Maybe I could learn, better myself, to have somebody like you to be proud of me."

I pulled Jeff close to me and hugged and I kissed him. I nibbled on his ear and told him how proud I was of him, but to think that he would change for me, I never saw that coming. I pushed him away so I could look at him, put my head on his shoulder and held him. I just wanted to hold him. We walked back to the sand and sat down. In a few minutes, Tony and Michelle came back. The morning was passing quickly so we decided to eat.

Later the three of us were sitting there looking at the river while Jeff was relieving himself in the woods when we heard a car coming. Michelle jumped up, looked around, "My God, Princess! Here comes your mother! My mom is with her!"

They pulled to the edge of the sand and got out of the car. I sure hoped Jeff would see this and stay in the woods.

"Hello, Helen and I were just riding around and decided to check on you," Mom said. She kept looking around. I knew what she was looking for and I couldn't say anything. She knew I would be mad. I was praying that Jeff could see her. I was sure if he did, he wouldn't come out of the woods, my mom checks up on me. She could tell by looking at my expression I wasn't happy.

"You're checking on us," I said. "Why would you do that?"

"Now Princess, don't get upset. We haven't been to Delp's Beach in a while. We thought we would come by and say hello."

Michelle's mom asked, "Are you enjoying yourself, Michelle?"

"Yes, Mom, we are. Matter-of-fact, we were talking about going back to Claytor Lake next week and taking advantage of the summer sun while we can."

"I think you should enjoy every minute of the summer," Mom agreed. "School will start back before you know it and then winter will be here."

I knew Mom had come to see if Jeff was here. She wouldn't come for any other reason. I couldn't say a word in front of Michelle's mother, but now I was mad at my mom.

"We just got through with lunch and now we're resting before we go back in the water like you're supposed to," I told her.

Then Tony spoke up, "Mrs. Sutherland, I'd like to take the girls to Claytor Lake next Wednesday. Would that be ok?"

"If that's what you want to do, it's fine with me," she said. I could tell my mother hadn't said a word to her about Jeff and me. My mother didn't want it to get out that I was seeing a boy everybody in town hated. At least, the parents hated him. They didn't know the Jeff I knew.

"You don't mind if I go, Mom?" I asked.

"If that's what you want to do, baby, that's fine with me. Helen, I guess we'd better go, and leave these young people alone."

We walked them back to the car and watched them leave. Jeff came walking out of the woods. "That was a close one," Jeff said. "I almost got caught."

"I think she was checking to see if you were here."

"What made her think I would be here? Doesn't she doesn't trust you?"

"I've got to confess something. I told my mom I was in love with you."

"You did what! How could you, Princess? She'll check on you all the time now. What did she say when you told her that?"

Michelle and Tony decided to go walking in the water to leave us by ourselves so we could talk. "I had to tell her. I'm so sick and tired of telling her lies so I can see you. This is not right. I'm just tired of it. I want to be with you. There's no reason why you can't come to my house and pick me up. She knows I'm in love with you and she's not going to let it rest."

"You told your mom you are in love with me? I don't know what to say! You love me enough to tell your mother, knowing that she hates me?"

"Yes, I did, and I'm not sorry I told her."

Tony and Michelle come back and sat down with us. Tony said, "We're going back to Claytor Lake next Wednesday. Do you two want to go?"

I spoke up first. "I do."

Then Jeff looks at me and replied, "Tony, I need a favor next Wednesday. When you guys go to Claytor Lake, will you bring Princess to Fries? Meet me somewhere where I can pick her up. I'm going to take her to a special place and spend the day, just the two of us. Would you go with me, Princess?"

"You know I will. What do you have planned?"

"If we meet somewhere, I'll have my dad's boat. We'll go up behind the Fries dam. There's a private beach up there, and it'll be just me and you. If you bring something to eat, I'll bring something to drink. We can spend the day just me and you behind the Fries dam."

Turning to Tony, he asked, "Would you two help us out? Then you and Michelle can be by yourself."

"We can do that. We won't go to Claytor Lake either. We might take a ride to the mountains and spend the day there. That way we can come back through Fries and pick Princess up. Does that sound ok to you, Michelle?"

Michelle nodded, and we all agreed. We stayed at Delp's Beach the rest the day and made plans where to meet the following Wednesday. I asked Jeff to come by the barn Saturday. I couldn't go two days without seeing him.

Chapter 10

The day at Delp's Beach was over. I knew when I got home I had to ask Mom why she was checking up on me. When I walked in the door, she knew I was not happy. I went straight to my room and she followed me.

"May I come in?"

"Yes."

"I want to talk to you."

"What about? I know you were checking to see if Jeff was with me."

" That's not true."

"You're not being truthful with me, You were there to see if Jeff was with me, What would you have done if he'd been there?"

"I never gave it a thought. Honestly, I don't know. I'd probably be nice and polite. While we're talking about Jeff Gray, let me ask you when you go to Claytor Lake this coming Wednesday, is he going to be there?"

"No! I wish he could. Why would it be a problem if he was?"

"You listen to me, Princess! Now that you told me how you feel about him and the way you're talking, you're doing more than just seeing him."

"What do you mean doing more? Come out and say it!"

"You know what I'm talking about without me saying it."

"Mama, you stop this talk right now. Please stop and let me tell you. Jeff Gray is not going to be at Claytor Lake with me next Wednesday. You came by the river today to check on me. Be honest with me and tell me the truth!"

"Watch your tone, Princess! Yes, I was checking on you. Where was he?"

"I don't know."

"What happened to make you fall in love with him?"

"Mom, I'm not going to talk about it. Please leave me alone."

"All right then. Clean up and come down for dinner. when your father gets home, I'm not going to say a word about this"

"Please leave me alone." Tears rolling down my cheeks. Mom went back downstairs. I sat on the edge of my bed, took off my clothes and got in the shower.

After Dad came home, I went down and had dinner with them. Mama kept her promise and never talked about the beach at the river today. Dad asked me if I had a good time, but he never said too much. He went through his regular routine of getting a beer and going into the living room to watch the evening news. Mom asked me to do the dishes, and I knew what was coming.

Mom started washing. She handed me a plate to rinse and dry. "I'm sorry, Princess. I'm so worried about you. I see trouble coming, and you're not ready for it."

"The only trouble I've got, Mom, is that you won't let me be myself. You won't let me see Jeff. Why can't he come by and pick me up? Why can't I date like everybody else?"

We both whisperings so Dad couldn't hear us. "Because of this girl, he was seeing in Woodlawn. The rumors about her and him," She paused. "Her parents must be having nightmares about him. What happened to her, and why is he seeing you? Because you are having sex with him, aren't you?"

I put the dishes down, went to my room and didn't answer her. She knew I was having sex. I didn't know what to expect or what was coming next. What would she try to do? Would she stop me from going out with Tony and Michelle? I did the wrong thing by telling her I was in love. I messed up. My mind was racing, my heart pounding, crying. After a few minutes, there was a knock at my door.

"May I come in?" Mom asked.

I had no choice but to say yes.

Now I was sniffling back the tears. Mom sat on the foot of my bed. "Baby, how long have you been having sex with him?"

"Please don't ask me that."

She was silent as though she didn't know what to say next. I looked up at her and there were a few tears running down her cheek. "Oh, Princess, my baby. I don't know what to say to you now. Is that the reason you think you're in love with him?"

"I know I'm in love with him, Mom. I know I am." I said.

"I'm going to ask you this. When you have sex with him, are you protecting yourself? I mean are you using a condom or something to make sure you don't get pregnant?"

"Yes. I've got something to say to you. I love having sex with him. He takes me places that I've never been to before. It's wonderful, and I'm trying to keep my head about myself. I remembered everything you told me about sex, but there's one thing you didn't teach me."

"What's that?"

"How wonderful it can be."

"But Princess, you're supposed to wait. It's too soon for you. You're only fifteen; that's way too young."

"I've got to ask you something. How old were you when you started having sex?"

Mom stood up and looked back at me. She closed her eyes, turned around, and walked out of the room without answering.

The next two days, I moped around the house. Mom and I never talked much. I was looking forward to Saturday. Friday was slow, but Michelle and I went to the bowling alley. Friday night, she wanted to know what my mom said when I got home after Delp's Beach.

"Princess, you've not been very talkative, what's wrong?"

"I really messed up, Mom knows Jeff and I are having sex. She doesn't know what to do, and I don't either."

"You told your mother that you're having sex! I hope she doesn't say anything to my mother."

"I don't think she'll say anything to anybody about it. She's too embarrassed."

There was nothing to do in the bowling alley but play pinball, and watch people from school. Then the word got out that Jeff Gray and some guy from Independence were having a fight at the rock quarry. It was a big buzz. Everybody was going out there to watch it. That's all the boys had to do on a Friday night is fight. I would have to wait until Saturday morning to see Jeff, find out what it was all about. Michelle's mother came to take us home. When they dropped me off, there wasn't much going on until the phone rang.

"Princess," said Michelle. "Tony called me. Jeff got into a pretty bad fight with some guy from Independence I don't know what happened. He said it started before we got there."

"Did Tony say Jeff was all right?"

"He told me that Jeff was the same. It didn't take long for the fight to be over."

"He's supposed to meet me at the barn tomorrow. I hope he does. Do you want to go with me in the morning?"

"Don't you and Jeff want to be alone?"

"I thought you could ride my horse while Jeff and I stay in the barn and talk."

"If you don't mind, I'll go."

"I'll have Mom pick you up tomorrow, say about 10 o'clock?"

"Ok, I'll be ready." I lay back in my bed with all kinds of thoughts going through my mind. I couldn't help it. I wished Jeff was a better student and that he had a better home life. Not that it made any difference to me. I loved him, but it would make it easier if he didn't have a bad reputation and if he wasn't fighting all the time. If he did, I was sure Mom and Dad would let me go out with him. My mind was racing until I fell asleep.

The next morning, I woke up from a nightmare. The dream was about Jeff. I could feel my heart pounding Jeff was dead. It took me a moment to realize it was only a dream, but it was so real. Jeff and I were in the hayloft at the barn. We were both naked and making love. Then my dad came up and caught us. When Jeff jumped up, my dad shot him, in front of me.

It was daybreak. The sun was shining through my window. I lay back until I had to get up to go to the bathroom. All I could think was something was going to happen to Jeff, and I was afraid. I heard Mom in the kitchen. I went down to sit at the kitchen table.

"What time do you want to go to the barn?" she asked.

"I talked to Michelle last night. She's going with me. I told her we'd pick her up about 10."

"Your father's already gone out this morning. Princess, don't get mad at me because I'm worried about you. You know I love you. I see no good coming out of this, Princess. You're headed for a long heartbreak, you don't see it coming. And nothing I can do or say is going to make you see that. Right now, you're so involved in this world that Jeff put you in, that you're not thinking in reality. So please, baby, don't get mad at me. I'm your mother. I've been through this in my life."

"You've been through a lot mother? What have you been through that you're not telling me?"

"Listen, Princess, when it comes time to tell you, I'll tell you, but this is not the time. This is not about me; this is about you and your future. You don't realize how easy it is to mess up your future."

"Is it my future, or are you worried about what people may think? You're worried that I will bring a bad name on the family just because I love Jeff!"

"Don't you understand, Princess? We're talking about the rest of your life. If something goes wrong, we're talking about you being a mother before your time. You are still a child. Get that through your head. You may be enjoying what you're doing with him, but do you think he can support you if you got pregnant? Where would he work? Who will take care of your baby? He can't take care of himself."

I went back to my room and put my head on my pillow. I knew everything my mom was telling me was the truth. We were just too young, but it was too late. I was doing it and I was in love with him and I didn't want to stop.

It was time to pick up Michelle. Mom didn't talk much. The silence between us was loud and the tension between us was bad. I didn't like this feeling. She loved me and I loved her. She loved me enough to talk to me about what I was going through instead of just trying to stop me from seeing Jeff. There was something Mom was not telling me, but she seemed to understand me.

At the barn, I told Mom I loved her and that I was glad she was my mother. She let me and Michelle out and told us she'd be back in a couple of hours. I knew I would never know when she was coming back. She would try to surprise us and see if Jeff was here, but when we got there Jeff was not there. We cleaned up the stall, but Jeff didn't show up. I was worried he wasn't coming.

"Where do you think he is?" Michelle asked.

I walked out of the stall and sat down, crying. "I don't know Michelle. It's becoming impossible. I've been on top of the world to this point. I just don't know what's going to happen, and I'm afraid. When we went by the old rock quarry, all I could think was Jeff there last night fighting. He's fighting the world, Michelle, and I can't stop him.

"He'll probably show up in a minute, It'll be all right."

"Did you hear any more from Tony on what the fight was about last night?"

"No, but Tony and I are supposed to go to the movies tonight. I guess I'll hear something then. If he tells me anything, I'll call you. Or I'll tell you Sunday when I see you in church."

We sat there for a moment, Michelle with her arm around me, trying to console me because I was crying. And then I just gave up.

"He's not coming today. He's not going to show up. Now I have to worry about what happened to him."

"I'm sorry, Princess. There's nothing I can do and nothing I can say. I feel helpless. There's just nothing I can do."

"I know. Thanks for being here. It's good to have somebody to talk to. That means a lot to me."

We finished everything we needed to do with the horse and took a ride. Michelle sat behind me, we let my horse walk. We didn't say a whole lot until we got back to the stall and rubbed the horse down. Mom came and took us home.

Saturday night I stayed home. Michelle and Tony went to the movies. All I wanted was for Jeff to come by and pick me up. It was not going to happen. I had to live with it, and that's just the way it was.

I'm in the living room with Mom and Dad, trying to read, but there was nothing that would take my mind off of Jeff and what happened to him in that fight. I had to wait.

At church Sunday morning, I finally had a chance to take Michelle aside. During Sunday school, we were sitting in the back, whispering. "Did you and Tony have a good time last night?"

"Yes, Tony brought a blanket with him we both got naked. Tony did things to me that drove me crazy," she whispered.

"What did he do? What was so great? I mean, I know I love having sex with Jeff, but what did Tony do differently?"

"You're not gonna believe this, Tony stuck his tongue in my pussy. It drove me crazy!"

"Really? He did that?"

"Oh yes. He was kissing down my stomach and the further he went down... it was unbelievable."

"What did you do then?"

"I'm not going to tell you."

"You've got to tell me now. What did you do?"

"I went down on him."

"I did that once to Jeff."

"We had a good time, but when I got home, my mom asked me why my face was so red. I didn't know what to tell her. I hope when we go to the mountains on Wednesday, we'll find a place to spend the day and do crazy things to each other."

"Did Tony say anything about Jeff and the fight he got into?"

"No. The only thing Tony told me when we picked you up Wednesday, we will meet Jeff the other side of the low-water bridge, For A moment, we all can talk before we go our separate ways. Tony wants to get started early, be there about 9:30. I think Jeff's got a big surprise for you, and I know Tony has a surprise for me. I'm ready for it."

"I'm looking forward to spending the day on the river with Jeff. My mom's giving me a hard time now that she knows everything."

"She knows everything!"

"Yes, I told her everything. I've got to have a talk with Jeff Wednesday. Michelle, I want to run away with him."

"You can't be serious, you're in high school, what are you thinking, you can't be serious!" The Sunday school teacher told us to be quiet. We stopped talking and waited until after church to talk again. While we waited on our parents in the car, I told Michelle, "I don't know what to do. I just don't know what to do. I've told my mother everything. I want Jeff to be able to come by my house and pick me up so we can go out together like you and Tony, but my mother is not going to let it happen."

" Princess, you know you can't run away with him. What would you do, where would you go? You are not thinking straight."

"I know I'm not. I'm dreaming, but I'll tell you one thing, if everything works out Wednesday, I'm going to show Jeff a great day. I'm going to do anything he wants to do to me and what he wants me to do to him. I intend to take advantage of every precious moment because I know it can end at any time. I'm going to make memories with him.

On the way home from church, my parents stopped and we ate out. My mom kept asking me why I was moping. I couldn't help myself. Jeff didn't show up at the barn Saturday and I didn't know why. I'd never been above the Fries dam before, I knew it had to be a special place. The next two days I helped Mom around the house. We talked, but she kept looking at me. I could feel something from her. It was like she was thinking back on her own life. I don't know why, but I just had a feeling that something was going to happen. She was going to tell me something one day that I wouldn't understand.

The day I had been waiting on to be with Jeff was here, Wednesday morning. I was ready. The sandwiches were packed and I had my swimsuit on. I waited for Tony and Michelle to pick me up.

Dad already left for the day, and Mom had one more thing to tell me before I left. “Princess, I want you to have a good time today. You told me Jeff is not going to be at Claytor Lake today, I believe you.”

“No, you don't, Mom. You don't believe me, but this time I'm not telling you a lie. He’s not going to be at the lake with me. Although, I wish he could. I wish you would accept him. Mama, it’s gotten so complicated and it hurts me that I can't share my happiness with you as my mother. It hurts me that Jeff can’t come to my house and come in and talk to you and Dad, he and I could go out together. It hurts me, Mom.”

“I know, it hurts me when that boy in my life would come to my house and my mother and father would have a fit, but they let me go anyway. I never understood why they let me go. I guess they knew what I know now.”

“What's that, Mom?”

"They knew they couldn't stop me. I know if you really want to see him, I can't stop you. You will find a way, I realize that. You're telling me he's not going to be at Claytor Lake today. I'm glad that he's not. When are you going to see him again? I shouldn't ask you that because I know you're going to see him, and whatever I do, I can't stop you, no matter how hard I try. It scares me to think about all the things that could happen to you and the mistakes you could make with this guy, it worries me."

Tony and Michelle were in front of the house. Mom and I stood up, she hugged me and told me she loved me. I didn't feel too guilty. I didn't tell her a lie. Jeff was not going to be at Claytor Lake today – and neither was I. She was right, I'd find a way to be with him and she knew it, just like she found a way to be with the guy that she was talking about. I wondered if that guy was as wild as Jeff.

I got in the car with Tony and Michelle I waved as we left to mom. When we got to the other side of the low-water bridge, Jeff was standing beside a truck. I was thrilled to see him. It was his father's truck with a John boat in the back.

The very minute the car stopped, I ran to him. He told me how glad he was to see me. If he only knew how ready I was to see him. The four of us set for a moment and looked at the low-water bridge. Tony and Jeff talked for a moment and we told each other to have a good time. They planned to be back around four or five o'clock. I got in the truck with Jeff. He drove through fries up the road and took a left over

the bank behind the Fries dam where there was a swinging rope.

Jeff got the boat off the back of the truck and we slid into the water. I got the picnic basket I had gotten together for our lunch, and Jeff had a cooler. The boat had a battery-powered trolling motor.

"Why didn't you show up at the barn Saturday?"

"I had to work."

"Why were you in a fight on Friday night?"

"why are you asking questions about Friday night and Saturday? I told you I had to work Saturday morning and I couldn't get to the barn."

" I was disappointed. I didn't know whether you were all right, how did you come out of the fight and what was it about?"

"What is life about, Princess? Drop it, it doesn't matter now. I'm here with you, just let it go."

"I can't help it. I worry about you. I'm disappointed when I can't see you."

It was such a beautiful day riding up the river. We had that section to ourselves. There was not another person to be seen. A little way upriver we came around some curves. There was a sandy beach and that's where we stopped.

We pulled the boat up on the sand and left the cooler and the picnic basket in it, we spread a couple of towels out so we could sit. The sun was shining hot and it was a little humid, but the birds were singing a perfect day.

"You want a beer?" Jeff asked.

"I don't know. I've never drunk a beer before. How did you get beer? I thought you were too young to buy beer."

"I drove across the Carolina line last night, went to Jimmy Atwood's and bought a 12 pack of Falstaff. Do you want one? I'm going to have one."

"I don't see why not." Jeff handed me a cold beer.

I took my first drink. "This is funny. Will I get drunk?"

"I hope so, then I can take advantage of you."

We both laughed. "I don't have to get drunk for you to take advantage of me. You've already done that. Today I'm ready to do anything you want to do. You show me you'll see I'm a fast learner."

"Let's sit here and drink a couple of beers. It's early in the morning. The birds are singing, the sun is shining, and there's nobody here but me and you."

I drank that beer and asked Jeff for another one. I belched loudly and laughed. I was getting silly and enjoying it. Once I got halfway through my second beer, I started a serious talk with him. I looked over at him and giggled

"Let's run away together."

"You've only had two beers
and you're having a silly talk," said Jeff.

"I'm serious.
Let's run away together."

"Princess, that's crazy."

"Don't you want to run away with me?"

"You're not drinking any more beer," he said.

"You are being completely silly."
I was giggling as I took another drink of beer
"You hurt my feelings; I'm going to cry."
"Let's get in the water," Jeff said.
"I've got my swimsuit on under my clothes
let me take them off."
"You don't need a swimsuit here.
Take them all off."
"Nobody will see us?"
"We're going skinny-dipping."
I took off all my clothes and then my swimsuit.
There I stood in front of Jeff naked.
Lust was taking over.
"Time for you to take yours off," I said.
I watched him pull off his shirt.
When he dropped his pants, his dick was straight.
He was ready and so was I.
I took another drink of beer and hugged him.
His dick was rubbing across my body.
It made me want him.
I put everything out of my mind
I didn't think about Mom
all I thought about was me and Jeff.
This was one of our days,
one of our moments,
that's all that mattered.
"Michelle told me that Tony did something
special for her," I said
"What, did he do something we're not doing?"
"She told me Tony stuck his tongue in her "
"Is that something you want me to do to you?"

"I want to experience everything with you"
"Ok, then. Let's do something special"
"Are you going to stick your tongue in me?"
"Yes, lay back "
I did. Jeff was kissing me.
He kissed my lips and sucked my nipples.
he went down my stomach.
My eyes were closed.
The sensation was unbelievable.
When he got between my legs,
I opened them wide.
When he licked up, I moaned with pleasure
he went deeper and begin to suck
I was getting off not once but three times.
Then Jeff said, "I'm going to fuck you. Lie back."
I did. He stuck it in me and got off.
I was pleased, we got up.

Jeff said, "Let's go in the water." We walked into the water about waist deep
I took another big drink of beer and asked for another one. There both of us stood naked in the river.

"I've got to pee," I said.

Jeff laughed and said, "Go ahead and pee."

"Right here in the river?"

Jeff was laughing at me and took a drink of beer. "Yes, right here in the river." This was so funny to me. I was peeing in front of Jeff. I guess it didn't make any difference. He just got through sucking my pussy, why should I care if he saw me peeing?

Jeff handed me his beer. "Hold this." He took

both hands and splashed river water on his face.

"What are you doing?" I asked him.

He laughed and said, "Washing your pussy off my face."

I laughed and handed his beer back to him. We both took a big drink.

We walked back up to the towels and sat down. The sun was burning and drying us off. I could feel my skin burning so I took another beer. We sat there a minute I looked at him, reached over and started playing with him, He lay back. I got him hard and straddled him, we had sex again.

He got off in me this time and I never gave it a thought. We did things together that day I never dreamed of.

"You say you love me, don't you, Jeff?"

"More than I thought was possible."

"I'm ready to leave with you if you say so."

Jeff turned to the side and stared at the river. He got up and walked back in the water. I followed him.

"Did I say something wrong? That's how much I love you."

Jeff stood there staring out at the middle of the river. I walked behind him and grabbed him around his waist. I laid my head on the back of his shoulders. I'm sure he could feel the tears I was crying. This was such a wonderful day. I didn't want it to end.

"Princess, you've had too much to drink. You don't understand, we're having a good time here, but it's not reality. I know enough. If we ran away together, could you really leave everything behind? Could you live in an old run-down mobile home in a trailer park somewhere? you don't know what you're saying. I love you too much to let you do something stupid like that. You've got your education to finish. I'm a nobody, I have nothing. Today is a good time, but you can't live on good times. Stop and think for a minute. I'm sixteen and you're only fifteen. This is just one of our moments. I know it's a very special moment that we will never forget, but you're not being realistic. You're drinking too much beer and you're having too much fun, but that can't last forever. Real-life is working every day. Real-life in the real world is just something you're not used to. So let's stop this crazy talk and think."

I stood beside him in the river. I loved him, but I knew he was right. We couldn't live like this forever. After refreshing ourselves in the water, I took a drink of beer, swished it around and spit it out. The taste of Jeff was still in my mouth, but it was a good taste.

Jeff started laughing again and said, "I've created a monster. Look at you, girl. You're beautiful and you've got that curvy butt, firm breasts sticking way out. Just look at you!"

I smiled and asked, "Are you hungry?"

"Yes, I could eat a sandwich." I dried off and put on my shorts. Jeff asked me to leave my top off. He put his shorts on and we sat to eat. I was surprised to find he had a bottle of wine in the cooler for us to share. After one glass, my head was really spinning. The songbirds were getting louder in my ears and I was in heaven. When finished eating and drinking, we got naked again and waded into the water. I was in Jeff's arms and getting a little bit sleepy from all of the drinking. We got out, spread the towels and lay on our stomachs. Before I knew it, I fell asleep.

I woke up with a sharp sting on my butt. I looked over Jeff was sound asleep. I shook him and we both sat up. There was a hard rain coming down and there was nowhere to go to get out of it, sharp and stinging our sunburned bodies. It seemed to come down harder with every drop.

"Jeff, it hurts!"

He got over the top of me to block the rain from hitting me. The big raindrops were cold and felt sharp when it hit my body. Jeff lay on top of me. He looked in my eyes with a very serious look. Without saying a word, he spread my legs and stuck his dick in me and fucked me while the rain was coming down. I forgot about the hard raindrops. He made me feel so alive.

"I need to ask you something, Princess. How many times did you get off to today? I mean how many times did you come?"

"I guess every time we've had sex, why?"

"Because we're taking a big chance! If I get you pregnant, I don't know what in hell I'll do?"

"I don't care anymore."

"You better care! I don't want to get you in trouble. I don't want to be the one who ruins your life." I felt Jeff spoke those words from his heart. he didn't want to hurt me anymore. I didn't know how to answer him.

"This is a wonderful day and it's not over yet. I've been so lost in you, I never thought about getting pregnant. I feel good right now, and I'm on top of the world. You've brought me here to this place. This day will be forever in my heart. God, I feel like I have to grow up all of a sudden."

"I know in the end I will never have you."

"Please stop talking that way. Please don't ruin it. Don't think about anything else right now. What time is it?"

Jeff went to his pants pocket and pulled out a watch. "1:30. We still have some time."

"Is there any beer left?"

Jeff opened the cooler and looked. "Yes," he answered.

We both put our shorts back on and sat down to eat. It was the first time that day we didn't say much. We ate a sandwich, drank another beer and watched the river go by. I knew the day was going to be over. I was really sunburned and we had no lotion to put on. Jeff came up behind me. I leaned back against his chest and we sat there. He was holding me close to his body. My imagination went wild, thinking about everything we did. We both felt like we'd had enough sex for the day and honestly, I was tired. I couldn't quite finish that last beer and had enough. Jeff told me we drank six apiece. I guess that's the reason it hit me so hard. I'd never drunk before. I'm pretty sure that's why I didn't care what Jeff did to me. It was all good and sweet.

Jeff's mood changed. "I want to ask you something, Princess. Why are you ready to run away all of a sudden?"

"I don't want this to stop. I know I'm not being realistic, but I just don't want to stop."

"I've got some news for you I haven't told you yet."

I stood up and looked back at him. "What haven't you told me? Is something wrong?"

"I'm not going back to school this year. I found out my parents are moving to Richmond. We're leaving Galax."

I got on my knees and took him by his hand. "You can't leave me. You can't leave me here. I'll follow you."

"You know better than that. This is probably the best thing that could happen to you."

"What do you mean the best thing that could happen to me? After everything we've been doing together, you can't sit there and tell me this is the best thing that could happen to me. I thought you told me you didn't want to hurt me anymore? You waited till the end of the day to tell me this?"

"What am I going to do, Princess? I'm sixteen, I have to go with them. I've got no choice."

"Yes, you do. We can run away together this weekend. We can leave together. Let's run away."

"As much as I would like to do that, it's not going to happen. You would be sorry you did it when you realize every day is not like today."

"You took the breath out of me. You could've waited to tell me this. Now, what am I going to do?"

"I'll tell you what you're going to do. When I'm gone, I will be nothing but a memory. You will meet someone else, maybe not in Galax, but you'll go to college and you'll start a whole new life. You'll look back on this day and say I had a wonderful time with a crazy boy."

Jeff ran out of words to say to me. I couldn't help it. I started crying. Jeff stood up, took me in his arms and I cried on his shoulder. I couldn't help it. He spoiled a wonderful day for me. He could've waited to tell me this. I knew it wasn't going to last forever, but at least we had the rest of the summer.

"Why did you have to tell me this now? You could've waited."

We sat down and I leaned back in Jeff's arms. The day was gone. I couldn't stop crying. Jeff looked at his watch. It was 4 o'clock, time to get the boat loaded and start back down the river. We put on our clothes; Jeff picked up all the empty beer bottles and put them back in the cooler. I got in the boat, Jeff pushed it off the bank, we floated back down to the dock. I couldn't talk anymore. Jeff ruined a good day for me after all.

At the dock, Jeff pulled the boat out of the water and put it in the truck. We drove back on the road overlooking the cotton mill and waited on Tony and Michelle. While we were sitting there, Jeff had his arm around me.

"I was only telling you the truth," he said.

"Why did you have to tell me today? I went beyond going all the way with you. I did things today I never dreamed I'd ever do. I love you so much, I didn't care. I want to please you and be with you."

"I didn't know how else to do it. I came really close disappearing without saying a word, but I couldn't do that."

"You would do me that way, You'd leave without telling me?"

"I love you too much to do you that way. Do you think I want to go? Do you think I want this to stop? I'm not going because I want to. It's because I have to and when I think about it, it's the best thing that could happen for you before I get you in trouble."

"I'm already in trouble. When do you have to leave?"

"The middle of August, before school starts in Richmond. I know I'm not going to stay in school."

"You've got to, you've got to stay in school."

"For what reason? I can't read or write. I can't get a decent job with no education. That's the reason this is good for you that I'm gone."

I turned around in Jeff's arms. Tony and Michelle pulled in beside the truck. Jeff kissed me and whispered in my ear. "When will I see you again?"

"Why do you want to see me again?"

"You better call me when you get a chance."

I got in the back seat of Tony's car. I had forgotten my picnic basket in Jeff's truck, but my mind was racing as we started back towards the low-water bridge.

Michelle turned around and asked me. "Did you have a good time today? You sure are sunburned. Why are you crying, what happened?"

"I had a wonderful day, then Jeff ruined it."

Michelle looked back at me. "How did he ruin it this time?"

"His family is moving to Richmond in August and I'll probably never see him again."

"He told me something about that," Tony said, "but he acted like he didn't want to go."

"We had a wonderful day and now I am mad at him. He could've waited to tell me. He didn't have to ruin the whole day we had together." I tried to wipe the tears out of my eyes before I got home. I knew as soon as I walked in the front door my mother would be all over me. I was sunburned, my eyes were red from crying, and I had to ask Michelle for some chewing gum in case my breath still smelled like beer. If Mom smelled beer I'd be in trouble for sure.

Chapter 11

As we crossed the low-water bridge, I looked upriver, thinking what a day I just had. I was burning from head to toe. My butt was so blistered, it hurt to sit down. We got to the turn where you go to Iron Ridge and kept going straight through Hickory Flat and down Fries Hill into Galax. I was dreading getting home, knowing I had to face Mom.

When Tony pulled up in front of my house, Michelle turned around and said, "Good luck, Princess."

I smiled at her and went to the front door. Mom and Dad were getting ready to eat supper. I asked her to let me shower before I ate. Mom followed me to my room and came in.

"Did you have a good time?"

"I had a wonderful time. It was a hot day."

"Your eyes are so red. What's wrong?"

"I'm sunburnt, Mom."

"I can see that. I'll get some lotion and rub you down after your shower."

"Ok, I'll be down in a minute." The shower was refreshing, but my skin was burning. When I got downstairs, they had already finished eating. After I ate my supper, I asked to go back to my room.

Mom said she'd be up in a moment to rub my back with lotion to help the sunburn. I felt a little bit better because she didn't ask me to help her wash the dishes. I knew if she did, she would want to talk to me about the day. Later, she came in with a bottle of lotion and I laid on my belly while she rubbed lotion on my shoulders. That felt so good.

"So, you had a great day?" she asked.

"I had a wonderful day, Mom, probably one of the best days I've had all summer."

"Jeff Gray must've been there today."

"Mom, he was not at the lake today."

"Ok, don't get angry. What made it so special?"

"Just being with friends. It's been a great summer so far."

"I'm glad you're having a good time. Are you coming downstairs now?"

"If you don't mind, Mom, I'm so tired I just want to lie back in my bed. I'll probably fall asleep pretty soon."

"It's still early. If you feel like it coming down, we can talk." She got up and walked to the door.

Before she left, I told her, "I love you, thank you."

"I love you too, baby. What brought that on?"

"Because you're a good mother. I just wanted to tell you that."

"Thank you, baby. We'll talk later."

I was biding my time. I wanted to call Jeff. I was mad at him. I believed I was in paradise today and he had to tell me he's leaving. I wanted to go with him so bad.

I didn't know what time it was, I dialed Jeff's number. His mother answered the phone. I asked to speak with him. By the time he came to the phone I was almost crying again. When he answered, I said in a low voice. “Hello, how are you feeling?”

“I was hoping you would call me. Are you ok?”

“No, I’m not. In spite of the wonderful day we had together, I’m not ok. I’m almost crying right now, but I wanted to call you. When are we going to see each other again?”

“When can you get away?”

“I don’t know. Maybe Friday night. I have to see if Tony and Michelle are going skating. Maybe we can meet behind Red’s as we did before.”

“I’ll try to see Tony and to find out if he is taking Michelle out Friday night. He will probably come by the filling station. You stay in touch with Michelle, then we’ll know for sure. I do want to see you.”

“I don’t know why you had to tell me bad news today. It was going so good. I had the time of my life. Now I wish you never kissed me that first day because this is the way it’s going to end.”

“I told you, Princess, we need to live in the moment because that’s all we’ve got. That’s all we’ve ever had.”

“I’ll be in touch, Jeff. I am burned up. I’ve got a bad sunburn.”

“I do too, I’ll never forget today. I’ll never forget it.” Jeff hung up, and I listened to the silence.

I slept solid all night long, I was so tired. The beer and all the sex and the excitement with Jeff wiped me out. I didn’t know what time it was when I got up the next morning, Dad had already gone to work. By the time I got myself together and went downstairs

Mom had breakfast on the table for me. I thought everything was fine until she sat down across the table and watched me eat.

"You really enjoyed yourself yesterday,"
she said.
"Yes, it was a lot of fun."
"You are really sunburned from head to toe.
I didn't know they had a nude beach at Claytor Lake."
It took me a minute to realize what she said.
"Claytor Lake doesn't have a nude beach,
you know that."
"They must have."
"What makes you say that?"
"Don't take your mother for a fool
I put lotion on your back last night.
There were no lines where your top was
and your butt was red as a beet!"
I didn't think about Mom seeing me naked.
"You didn't go to Claytor Lake yesterday did you?"
What was I going to say to her? She had caught me.
"Mama, I'm not going to lie,
you know I didn't go to the lake"
"Were you with Jeff Gray!"
She caught me in a lie
nothing to lose now.
"Yes, we were together all day yesterday on the river."
Mom shook her head and looked down at the table.
"Where were Tony and Michelle?"
"I don't know.
They went off to be by themselves."
Mother stared at me

as if she didn't know what to say next.
"I had the most wonderful time yesterday
I'm telling you because I'm so tired
of trying to keep it from you
I love him. Why can't I be with him?
I'm going to tell you everything.
I asked him to run away with me.
He told me I was crazy,
that I couldn't give up what you and Dad gave me.
He said I couldn't live without as he does.
Mama, he's not crazy."
"You were skinny-dipping in New River!
I'm sure you had sex all day long, didn't you?
I can imagine you put everything out of your mind
but the moment you were in, didn't you?
I can imagine you tried new things with him.
I noticed when you came home
your eyes were bloodshot.
You were drinking yesterday.
Whatever he asked you to do you did it
to the point, the pleasure was so overcoming.
You wanted to leave with him, thinking
that was real life."
Mom was telling me things as though she was there
everything she was telling me,
that's the way it was.
Jeff was teaching me
and I wanted more of him
surely my mother had been through this,
and I didn't realize it.
"Mom, everything you just said

is exactly what happened.
It was all new to me, and it was exciting.
I lost myself in the moment,
and nothing else mattered.
Mama, how did you know that's what I did."
"So, you had sex all day.
Did you protect yourself?
Did you use a condom?
Did you ever think
about getting pregnant yesterday?"
"Believe it or not,
Jeff brought it up about getting pregnant.
But you're right,
we didn't use any protection
I got so into it I didn't care anymore."
Mother stood up and walked back and forth
as though she were trying to think of what to say.
I could sense that I'd hurt her.
She stopped in front of me and looked down at me
"Princess, it's time I told you something.
You forced me to.
I knew this day was coming
and I tried to put it off,
but now I don't have any choice.
You remember me telling you
about a wild and crazy boy?
We met at the Pocahontas State Park
in Chesterfield County,
they've got a beautiful lake there.
That summer was hot and humid.
I was there with some girlfriends from school.

I watching him lie in the sand.
He was handsome
When he got up to go in the water,
I decided to go in behind him
I wanted to get his attention.
So, I pretended to accidentally bump into him.
He was charming and he had a beautiful tan body
We begin to talk.
His name was Jim, and he asked me out.
The following weekend
he came to the house and picked me up
and we went to the drive-in.
He was pleasant to be with,
so, we kept seeing each other
He was nineteen, I was seventeen.
I had just graduated from high school
and he was getting ready to go to college
at VCU in Richmond.
He would take me over there
and we would go to places like Luigi's
and the village places where all the kids went.
He would sneak me a beer.
I loved drinking draft beer
We got to see each other regularly
I guess you could say we became a couple.
I looked forward to being with him.
When I introduced him to my parents,
they hated him.
The more I saw him,
the more they hated him.
Your grandmother kept telling me

she didn't trust him.
I guess because she could see in me
what I see in you,
a lovesick girl headed for trouble.
That's why I'm so worried about you.
Jim made plans for a Saturday morning.
We were going to the James River.
There big boulders
in the middle of the river.
He picked me up very early that morning.
My mother tried to stop me from going,
But I went anyway.
When we got to the river,
he had a blowup raft
a cooler full of iced beer
and a few sandwiches.
we stayed the whole day.
We were above everybody else
that was on the river that day.
We were alone.
The sun was hot, the beer was cold
The summer heat and humidity could be unbearable
and thunderstorms would sneak up on you.
He talked me into going skinny-dipping.
So, I took off my swimsuit
I had just enough beer in me that I didn't care.
we were hugging and kissing and
I let him put his hands wherever he wanted to.
When the storm came, there was really no place to go.
The summer was almost over
and we were supposed to meet

at Pocahontas State Park.
He was going to take me to meet his parents,
But he never showed up.
I waited and waited.
I was going crazy with worry.
He told me he loved me
and that he had a surprise for me
I finally went home, and your grandmother knew
something was wrong with me.
Days passed,
and then months.
I never saw him again.
I don't know what happened,
he just disappeared.
He did leave me two things, Princess."
"What did he leave you with?"
"Memories." She paused.
"And you."
"What did you say? Me!"
"Doug is not your real father."
You could hear a pin drop in the room.
"You kept this from me all these years? "
"I was going to wait until you were older.
I probably would've never told you.
I didn't have to.
When I found out I was pregnant
I was afraid to tell my mother.
Princess, I can't express to you the anguish
I was going through. What was I going to do?
You've got to believe me.
You don't want to go through what I went through,

knowing you're pregnant with nowhere to turn
nobody to talk to.
I was alone, Princess.
I'm going to tell you something, baby
I thought about ending my life and yours with me.
I had to do something to take care of you.
I got a job in a grocery store,
and one day Doug walked in.
I still wasn't showing and I wore loose clothes.
Doug was in his senior year at the University of Richmond,
and he asked me out.
I was afraid he wouldn't want me
because I was pregnant;
nobody wants to take out a pregnant girl,
but he kept coming back
until I went out with him to dinner.
I waited at the end of the dinner
to tell him I was pregnant.
I braced myself for rejection and I wouldn't blame him.
I didn't want to deceive him,
and the worry was unbearable.
I finally got brave enough to tell him
the baby's father had disappeared.
He didn't say much,
he looked at me
and told me he felt like
I was the one for him regardless.
He would stay in Richmond if I would marry him.
He said he would take the baby
and raise it like it was his own.

He told me he'd fallen in love with me
and that it didn't matter.
When he introduced me to his parents,
he told them the baby I was carrying was his
and he was going to marry me
your grandparents took me in
and treated you like their granddaughter
no one in Galax ever knew the difference,
not to this day
not until I just told you what happened.
Princess, Doug loves you.
He loves both of us and he's taking care of us
and made sure we had anything we needed or wanted
I don't know what happened to your real father.
In time I learned to love Doug"
"Mother I need to know one thing
would you have married Jim?"
"Yes.
He took me places that I've never been to.
He taught me what he wanted from me
I wanted more from him.
But it was a fantasy, Princess. It wasn't real.
Can you see why I'm worried about you
Can you understand
why I don't want you to see Jeff again?
If something happened to you, Princess
you might not be as fortunate as I was
to have somebody come and take care of you
Please stop seeing him, Princess.
Before it's too late."
"Mama, in spite of everything you just told me

I'm afraid it's too late.
I'm hopelessly in love with him.
You just got through telling me
that you loved my real father
so much you would've married him.
If I could marry Jeff, I would."
"Princess, that's blind love
you will regret it one day.
It's important that you get your education
and plan your future.
You can't blindly go through life,
you'll end up miserable.
It will be a life full of regret
and pain and disappointment.
I can't let you do that.
You've got to stop seeing him."
"Mama, it's going to take care of itself.
Jeff's family is moving
to Richmond in the middle of August.
If I could go with him I would.
I know I can't, so your problem is taken care of.
My heart will be broken
for the rest of my life when he leaves.
So please, let me see him until he leaves.
I know you won't let him come to the house.
You know if I go out,
I'm going to see him whenever I can.
It will end because when the summer is over,
he will be gone."
"Do you expect me to agree to that knowing
what you're doing

and the chances you're taking?
How can I do that, Princess?"
"Would you have snuck out to see Jim
no matter what your mother told you?
Trust me on this, Mom.
I know I'm only fifteen, but it's too late.
I've had sex, drunk beer and if I'm with him,
I can be careful.
I just want to see him before he leaves,
then it will all be over."
"This will drive me crazy

I just can't do that, Princess."
"Then you better lock me in my room and tie me to my bed
Because I'm going to see him
whatever it takes until he leaves."
Mom walked around the room shaking her head and wringing her hands.
"Ok then. On one condition."
"Ok, Mom. What is it?"
"You never let Doug know that you know
he's not your father.
You do nothing to hurt him.
He loves us. We can't do anything to hurt him.
He's provided and taken care of us, Princess
you respect him as your father and you call him dad
you make sure you respect him.
I'll turn my head to know what you're doing.
I shouldn't do this.
I'm responsible for you.

And if you get pregnant,
you don't have to marry that boy.
If you get pregnant, I don't know what I'll do.
Princess, I don't know what I'll do
because it will be my fault for letting you do this.
God help me, Princess
I'm not a good mother, I guess,
because I know how you feel inside.
I felt that way for years not knowing what happened
Promise me you'll take care of yourself."
"Mama, I'm afraid."
We got up together and cried
I couldn't stop crying.
Mama whispered in my ear while hugging me
"I love you, baby. You're growing up
and I know I'm not doing the right thing,
but please keep your word to me
you'll never let Doug know."

It took a little bit for it to sink in what Mom just told me. That the father I've known all my life is not really my father. Now I had more questions than answers. What was my real father like? What kind of personality did he have? Did Mom love him as much as I loved Jeff? Was I going to end up as she did? If she had the chance, would she have married him? I'm not sure that I'm glad she told me. I went to my room after breakfast but then went back downstairs.

"Mom, you've got to tell me about him. I want to know more about my real father. I need to know more about him. Mom, please tell me."

"Princess, he's the reason that Jeff Gray scares me. I can see in your face what I was feeling back when I was your age, the good times, the sex, the partying everything was a fantasy world. I couldn't see reality and I can see you're not in reality. You're talking about running away with him, but you don't know what you're saying."

"Tell me, Mom, if you had the chance back then, would you have married him?"

My mother shook her head and grimaced. She didn't want to answer me. "Please, don't ask me questions like that, Princess."

"I've got to know, Mama. Would you have married him if you had the chance?"

My mom looked down at the floor and in a low voice answered, "Yes." I walked to the front porch and sat down looking towards the mountains. My heart was thumping. Mama came out and sat down beside me. She put her arm around me. "Baby, please listen to me. When I found out I was pregnant with you, I didn't know what to do. I had nobody. I was afraid to tell my parents. I had no idea what I was going to do. I knew I had a baby coming and I had to take care of it. I was not making much money, and then Doug came along. We dated a couple of times before I told him I was pregnant. Doug fell in love with me to the point he didn't care that I was pregnant. He asked me how long it would be before I would give birth. Doug took me in, he got a job right out the college and it was a good job. When he got settled in, he asked me to move in with him, and then he asked me to marry him. I don't know why baby. It took me a long time. I still had the memory of your real father, and that was fifteen years ago and you're doing the same thing that I was doing. It worries me to the point I can't sleep at night. The same anguish, the same worry I went through has come back to me because I can see what's coming to you. Princess, please don't make the mistake I did."

"I'm not going to make a mistake. I want to see Jeff. He's leaving, and I know he's leaving. My father wasn't a bad guy. He didn't know you were pregnant with me. He just left."

"Princess, he left me without saying a word. If he had loved me, why did he leave me? Don't you understand? He walked out on me, and now I'll never know what happened!" Mother said loudly.

"I'm not going to let Jeff just leave. Please, Mom, don't interfere. Let me work this out with Jeff. Please, trust me to make the right decision."

"Do you know what the right decision is? You are blinded by the good times, Princess. Do you know what the right decision is?"

"No, I don't, Mom, but I'm going to see him again as much as I can before he leaves because I know I have no other choice." I got up to go back into the house. Before I went through the door, I looked back at my mother. She was openly crying and I didn't know what to do for her. She still had a broken heart over my real father and now I couldn't say a word to anyone about it. I went back to my room and I lay face down on my bed. All I could see was Jeff leaving. I was in a situation. I didn't know who my real father was and I was losing Jeff at the same time. Everything had gone from bad to worse.

I stayed in my room staring at the wall. My mind was so jumbled up I couldn't think straight and my mother was right. I didn't know what the right decision is. I knew deep down it had to come to an end. But I was not going to give up. I wondered if Jeff would marry me? My dad could give him a job. I had to shake myself when I realized I was talking silly again. Jeff was not going to marry me. I was living in fantasy land as Mom said. I decided I had to get out of my room before I went completely crazy, mumbling to myself.

Mom looked at me differently, as though she felt sorry for me. I guess in a way she did feel very sorry for me because she recalled her own life. I was so glad that my dad was not at home. I didn't know how to act when I had to sit across the table from him or have a conversation. I couldn't let him know that I knew he was not my real father. There were too many secrets to keep and I was about to burst.

Later, Michelle gave me a call and told me she and Tony were going to the roller rink Friday night and invited me to go. When I told Mom about it, she said it was ok. She knew I was going to see him, but she never tried to stop me.

I got myself together and tried to show her that I understood what she was going through, watching me destroy my own life. Of course, I didn't think I was, but she knew where I was going and how this was going to end. At dinner that night, Dad didn't notice I wasn't myself. He was preoccupied with his own business.

Friday, all I could think about was seeing Jeff that night. Michelle called and said Tony had spoken with Jeff and he was going to be at the roller rink waiting for me. I hadn't talked to him since we spent the day on the river. Should I tell him about my father? I decided to keep it to myself.

At the end of the day, Tony and Michelle picked me up. Mom watched me go out the door. She knew where I was going, straight to Jeff's arms. Michelle kept asking me on the way if I was ok, I couldn't tell her. I sat in the back seat watched them, they were the happiest people in the world. Their relationship was growing. I envied both of them. I imagined in my mind if only my mom and dad would let Jeff come and pick me up.

When we got to the roller rink, I got out of the car and didn't take time to say anything to Michelle. I went to the corner of the building and looked. Jeff was standing in front of his car. When he saw me, he put out his arms inviting me to come. I rushed to him and hugged him tightly. I sensed something different about him. He pressed me to his shoulder like he was protecting me.

I could feel his heartbeat against my body and I asked him, "Is there something wrong?"

His voice was soft. "Everything's wrong. Everything that I hoped and dreamed for has gone wrong."

With my head on his shoulder, his hand stroking my forehead, I asked, "Have I gone wrong for you?"

Without hesitation, he answered me. "That's my problem, Princess, you've become everything that I hoped for. I never had anybody to love me, nobody I could trust to love me. I look back at what I thought of you before I kissed you that day, and now you've shown me how much you love me. Yes, baby, you have gone wrong but it's not your fault, it's all me. I'm thinking about running away, not going with my parents, just leaving and I don't care where I go. If I can't have you then I don't want to live. I'm just going to leave."

I pushed myself out of his arms, looked him straight in the eyes and said, "You're not leaving without me! Hear me? You're not leaving without me!" I was screaming in Jeff's face. I burst out in tears. "You will not leave without me. I will go with you anywhere you want to go!"

Jeff put his hand over my mouth. "You're getting too loud. People will hear us. I can't take you, and if I decide to leave you can't go with me."

I took a step back and turned my back to him.

He came up behind me, pulled me back into his arms and whispered in my ear. "Are you telling me you would give up everything just to leave with me? This is not going to last forever. I'd never let you do that, never."

I regained my composure and calmed down. "Are you really going to leave? Would you really just get up and leave and not go with your parents to Richmond?"

Jeff shook his head. "I don't know if I've got the courage. I've not gone yet and I'm already lonesome for you."

I didn't like this mood. It was not like when we were on the river when things were happy. Now Jeff was so solemn and I didn't like this. He made me so happy, and somehow, I felt so hurt. We stood in front of Jeff's car holding each other, and it felt so good to me.

Finally, night fell, it was dark. I could hear people skating inside the building when we went to Jeff's car. We stopped talking and he laid me down easy in the back seat, I looked up at him. We kissed passionately, and my body was responding to every touch. I wanted him. He started pulling my pants down and I raised my butt to get them off. We both were completely naked and the lovemaking begins. We never spoke, we made love, we knew what each other wanted. While Jeff was on top of me and I looked over his shoulder I couldn't imagine him leaving. I couldn't imagine being without him. I couldn't imagine this ending. Without a word, we got up, put on our clothes, got out of the car and walked to the front of the building. It was a warm night and while we were waiting on Tony and Michelle, I was in Jeff's arms. There was nothing else to be said. I had no idea where this was going, but I knew it was coming to an end. I didn't want to think about it but, I knew it was coming.

In a few minutes, they came walking around the corner and back to the car with us. Tony said he had an idea that comes Monday morning, we should all go to Buffalo Mountain in Floyd County and spend the day. Jeff agreed to go so the plans were made and I told Michelle I would see her in church Sunday. It was time to leave. Jeff turned me around in his arms, put his hands on each side of my face, brushed my hair back and kissed me like it was the last kiss I would get from him. He whispered in my ear, "I love you, Princess." I turned and walked away with Tony and Michelle who took me home.

When I got there, my mother was sitting in the living room with my father. I went to the kitchen to get a bite to eat. Mom came in and sat at the table with me. Dad was watching TV and never gave us a thought. Then she asked her usual question, "Did you have a good time tonight?"

"Yes, I did and no I didn't."

"What do you mean by that?"

"Let me finish my sandwich, Mom, and let's go to my room."

"Ok, I'll go tell your father that we're going to have girl talk. No, maybe I better not. I'll come up in a minute. Is there something you want to talk to me about?"

"Yes, I do."

"Ok then. I'll be there in a few moments."

I finished my sandwich and went on to my room. In a little while, Mom knocked and I told her to come in.

She shut the door behind her and sat in the chair beside my bed. “Did you see Jeff tonight?”

“Yes, I did. I didn’t like the way he was talking. He told me tonight he’s thinking about running away and leaving everything.”

“Did he ask you to go with him?”

“No, he didn’t. I told him I would go anywhere with him.”

“What did he say?”

“Mom, he told me no. He loved me too much to put me through that. Mom, I want to go with him. Mama, please let him come by the house and pick me up. You already know I’m seeing him. I’m telling you the truth. What time we’ve got together, Mom, please let me go out with him without aggravation or worry.”

“You know I can’t do that. Your father would never allow that to happen and you know it. But I’m willing to keep your secret. I’m willing to let you go without interfering with what you think you have to do.”

I looked down at the floor at my feet and shook my head yes. Then she asked, “Did you use protection? Are you doing everything you can do to keep from getting pregnant?”

“He was different tonight. He was so down. It’s not just having sex, Mom. Don’t you understand I love him and he loves me? Now I’m in a hopeless situation. He’s leaving and I can’t go with him.”

“When are you going to see him again? I know you are.”

"Tony and Michelle are going to Buffalo Mountain in Floyd County Monday. Jeff and I are going with them. Mama, time is running out and I know that. Please let me enjoy what little time I have left with him."

"Princess, I know I can't stop you. I know you will go to extremes to see him. But if you keep on asking him to leave with you, I'm afraid he will give in to you and I'll lose you forever. Princess, you've got me in a bad situation. It's damned if I do and damned if I don't, so I'm not going to try to stop you."

We were both crying. She was trying to clean herself up before she went back to sit with Dad. She wiped the tears from her eyes, and I turned over in my bed, sobbing until I fell asleep.

Saturday morning, I got up and went downstairs, to my surprise, Dad was still home, sitting at the breakfast table. I didn't know what to expect. Usually, he was out playing golf or at the filling station talking to the guys. The mood between Mom and Dad seemed to be pleasant, I felt relieved.

"Good morning, Princess," he said.

"Good morning, Dad. I thought you'd be playing golf this morning?"

"I thought maybe I would stay around the house today. I haven't seen much of you lately. I thought maybe we could have breakfast, and you and I could sit on the porch."

Then Mom spoke up. "I think that would be a great idea, Princess. You've been gone all summer and both of you have been so busy. Usually, you two do a lot together on mornings like this. It's been a while."

I was nervous about what Dad wanted to talk about. Surely Mom hadn't told him what's been going on. We finished breakfast and I went back upstairs telling him I would be on the front porch in a few minutes. I wanted to take a shower first.

I knew Mom promised me she wouldn't say a word about Jeff to him but didn't know how I was going to keep a secret that I knew he was not my real father. I nervously took a shower and went back to the front porch where Dad was sitting. I sat down beside him. It was a beautiful sunny morning.

"Princess, we haven't talked for a while," he said.

"What is there to talk about, Dad? Is something wrong?"

"I need to ask you some questions. I'm worried about your mom. Is something going on I should know about? She seems worried, and she's not sleeping very well. I'm concerned about her. Is everything all right in your world?"

"Things are ok. It's a good summer, and I've been having a really good time with my friends."

"I can't figure out what's bothering your mother. When you're not home she walks the floor, wringing her hands. I noticed a difference in her mood. Are you and she getting along?"

"I guess so."

"Princess, I'm going to ask you a question and I want an honest answer. I've not seen much of you this summer. I've been so busy with work, and you've been busy with your friends, but while I'm at the filling station sometimes, I'm hearing rumors. I don't like what I'm hearing, Princess."

"What kind of rumors, Dad?"

"You know how I feel about Jeff Gray. The rumors I'm hearing are that you have been seen with him. That you and he have something going on and I want to know what that's all about."

"There's nothing going on between me and Jeff Gray. What are the rumors saying?"

"It's that you, Michelle, Tony, and Jeff have been seen together."

I had to be quick and think on my feet. I had to tell him outright lie. I didn't know what else to do. "Is that all that makes you think I'm with Jeff Gray? Don't forget he and Tony are friends, and sometimes when we're out, Jeff shows up and there's nothing I can do about that. Do you want me to stop going out with Michelle and Tony?"

"I guess that explains it, but I was wondering if that's what's bothering your mother when you're not in the house. She is just beside herself. She's not at peace, and she's not talking to me. Is that what's bothering your mother?"

"Have you asked Mom what is bothering her?"

"I have, and she's not given me a good answer. I think something is going on. You're growing up right before my very eyes. You're becoming a young woman. A father doesn't know what to do, especially when he has a daughter. I want you to know, Princess, how much I love you, how much I love you and your mother."

"Dad, you've asked me all kinds of questions, can I ask you something?"

"Of course."

"When you first met Mom, what made you fall in love with her? Did you know she was the one for you?"

"That's a funny question, Princess. Why would you ask me that? I loved your mother the first day I laid eyes on her. I can't explain it. There's something called chemistry between two people. I just felt that she was the one. She's beautiful, and she is a loving and caring person."

"I'm going to ask you one more question, Dad, and I want an honest answer from you. Did you get my mother pregnant before you got married?"

He looked at me with surprise. "Princess, that's not a fair question."

"I was just wondering. I'm fifteen years old, and you guys have been married for fifteen years. So, you either got Mom pregnant on the honeymoon night or you got her pregnant before you got married."

"Baby, I don't know how to answer you, but I'm going to tell you the truth. I love your mother so much that she moved in with me before we got married and yes, I got her pregnant before we got married. I will let you know you came out of that and I love you and I love your mother."

Now I knew I wasn't the only one telling a lie. Mom already told me that he was not my real father, but what was I going to say? He took very good care of me and Mom and he showed nothing but love all these years. Now I wished I could ask him about Jeff.

“You have surprised me, young lady, with your questions I was supposed to ask you questions to find out what’s wrong with your mother, to see if you’re ok. I feel like I have neglected you this summer; I’ve been so busy with my work, but I wanted to let you know I’m still watching you. I’m watching you grow up and I’m wondering, Princess what’s going on in your life now? Don’t take your father for a fool, something is bothering your mother to the point she can’t sleep at night. I’m asking you again what is going on that I need to know?”

“I’m not sure, Dad.”

“Ok, but I feel like you’re not telling me the truth. You’re asking me questions about me and your mother when we first met. I’m not sure what brought these questions on. Why would you ask me such things? Princess, you’re 15. Are you not seeing a young man? You spend a lot of time with your friend Michelle and she’s dating Tony, you seem to be a threesome, and then I hear rumors about Jeff Gray.”

“Dad, I need to know something from you, what is it about Jeff Gray that you dislike? If he would ask me out would you let him come by here and pick me up and take me out?”

“No!”

“Just no? Why can’t you tell me why?”

“Princess, that boy stays in trouble all the time. The only reason he’s going to Galax High School is that the Carroll County school system wanted to get rid of him, and Coach Lindsay wanted to build a good high school football team. Jeff Gray is big and tough, and he has no future. I understand that he can't read or write, and there's no way he's going to finish high school. You are better than that! I forbid you to ever see him for any reason. I can't stop him from showing up with Tony and Michelle, but at least he's not taking you out."

"Now I want to know one more thing before I leave this morning. Has he asked you out? You are asking some funny questions that I didn't expect. I have great hopes for you. Remember, Princess, you are our only child and we want you to be well educated and choose the right man to marry because you will inherit everything we've got. You will be responsible. In my will, you and your mother will have complete control over my business and you need to be educated and use wisdom to run a business. Jeff Gray is not that boy. Now, Princess, I'll be honest with you, if I find out that he's bothered you in any way, I don't know what I will do! That's how much I love you. I don't want to see you mess up and I want you to tell me you're not seeing that boy!"

I was heartbroken to hear him talk like that. There was no way he would ever accept Jeff. The only father I'd ever known had just lied to me and I lied to him. I couldn't tell him how much I loved Jeff; he would never accept it. After our morning talk, Dad left and I went back to the kitchen. Mom was sitting at the kitchen table and I sat down across from her.

"Did you and your father have a good talk?" she asked.

"Mom, he lied to me and I lied to him, but I kept my promise. I'll never tell him that I knew he was not my real father."

"Thank you, Princess. I never want to hurt Doug."

"Mom, I think he knows about Jeff. He kept talking about you and he asked me about you because when I leave the house, you walk the floor wringing your hands and you're not sleeping very well at night. Am I doing that to you, Mom?"

"I can't help it, Princess. You're out there at 15 years old having sex like a grown married woman, and that's going to worry me. I made a bargain with you not to let your father know so that you would handle this with Jeff and break this off before it's too late. What am I supposed to do, Princess? Be glad that my daughter is out there having sex and she can come home pregnant at any time? Princess, you're headed for trouble, more than you ever realized, more than you've ever experienced in your life. Real grown-up trouble. You're getting a taste of the real world, I'm helpless to stop you."

I sat across the table looking down. Saturday morning started out really bad. Mother told me everything about her past, the only dad I'd ever known just lied to me. How did I get in a hopeless situation like this? Mother was right, I was too young for this kind of worry. I kept thinking I'd run away with Jeff if he would just take me, damn the consequences.

Chapter 12

Saturday morning, I asked Mom to take me to the barn. I wanted to get out of the house. I didn't tell Jeff I was going to be there. I just decided I wanted to go that morning. On the way, Mom and I didn't say a word to each other. There were some stress and tension between us. When we got to the barn, Mom came in with me. I went through the routine cleaning out the horse stall while she got some hay to feed the horse. Then out of nowhere, Jeff came in.

When Mom looked up and saw it was Jeff, my heart stopped. I took a deep breath and looked at her. She was red in the face, and I didn't know what to expect. What brought this on, I wondered. There he stood in front of us, and he was shaking.

"Hello, Mrs. Grant," he said.

My mother looked at me, then turned to Jeff. "Hello, Jeff."

Then Jeff looked at me. "Hello, Princess."

"What are you doing here?" My voice cracked.

"I saw your mother's car, and I wanted to speak to her."

"You want to speak to me, what about?"

Jeff looked at me and then back at Mom. I took a step toward him, kissed him on the cheek and stood beside him while he tried to talk to her. "Mrs. Grant, I know you know everything about me. I just want to let you know I didn't mean to get your daughter involved with me, but I fell in love with her and I want to come and take her out."

I couldn't believe what he was saying to my mother, but I was so proud of him. I was beside myself. I turned and looked at Mom. She was looking down at the floor shaking her head, and then she sat down on a bale of hay.

"You've taken me by surprise," she said. "I didn't expect this to come from you."

And then I spoke to Mom. "Why can't he come and pick me up? He's doing the right thing and asking your permission. Why can't he do that?"

"Princess, you know why. It's more than just me. How are you going to convince your father? Jeff, I hope you understand. We have great hopes for Princess. She's too young to be going out. Yes, she's told me everything about you and it worries me sick."

"I know, Mrs. Grant. I guess... I guess I'm not good enough for her. I know I'm not. I'd better go. Please forgive me, Mrs. Grant. I'm not good enough for anybody.

"Jeff, wait a minute," Mom said. "It's not that you're not good enough. Both of you are so young. As a parent, do you think I can feel comfortable about this knowing, you're having sex with my daughter? What am I supposed to feel? She's only fifteen. Ask yourself, what would you do? How would you feel knowing your daughter is going out with someone so young? You put me in a bad place and I wish you had not done it."

"Mrs. Grant, I just want to let you know I'm trying to do the right thing. I love your daughter that much to do the right thing, I can't win."

"Jeff, I appreciate you trying to do the right thing, but we both know that my daughter will do everything she needs to do to see you and I'm not going to try to stop that. But I cannot go to her father and tell him that you are coming by to pick up his daughter. Here's what I suggest, I know when she leaves to go with her friends you're going to show up, I can't stop that. I can only pray that things don't go wrong. That's the best I can do. I'm doing this much because I love you, Princess, and I know it hurts. But you've got to understand what you are doing and the consequences of it. This can affect you for the rest of your lives. Jeff, I've got nothing else to say to you. I do appreciate you coming and asking me, but I must say no."

I looked at my mother and I walked over and hugged her while Jeff was watching. He turned to walk out the door. I went with him and when we stepped outside, I hugged him and I was crying.

He kissed me and then he said, "I tried, Princess. I don't know what got into me, but I tried."

"This doesn't change anything Jeff. I'll see you on Monday and we'll have the day together now that my mother knows. I love you. Thank you for trying."

I watched Jeff go to his car and drive off. I went back to the barn and my mother was crying uncontrollably. I sat down beside her. We didn't talk.

There was nothing more to say, but I was so glad she wasn't going to stop me from seeing him.

We got back home, I stayed in my room most of the time. I didn't feel like talking to Dad. I didn't tell Michelle that Jeff confronted my mom. All I could think about was going to Buffalo Mountain on Monday.

Monday morning Tony and Michelle were on time. It was almost nine-thirty as I walked out the door with the picnic basket in my hand. Mom stood in the doorway and watched me get into the car. She knew exactly where I wanted to go. We met Jeff in Hillsville, but this time Jeff told Tony he was taking his car and that he and I would follow them, I got to sit in the front seat with Jeff. While he drove, I was on top of him. His 1956 Pontiac was a beautiful car to me.

As we drove down the road I said, "I can't believe you showed up at the barn Saturday and asked Mom if you could come by and get me."

"Why can't you believe that I was willing to take a chance so I could come by and pick you up? What did your mother say after I left?"

"Not much. She was surprised. I was glad, you love me that much."

"I love you that much, but I knew nothing would come of it."

We both laughed a little bit because we were going down the road and I was with him. I laid my head on his shoulder. He put his arm around me and held me close. We drove through the small communities and got to the road to turn up to Buffalo Mountain. It was a mile hike, but beautiful every step of the way. When we got to the top of the mountain the view was awesome. We all sat down on a rock looking at North Carolina in the far mountain ranges. All through the valley, you could see the farms. The wind was blowing, and the view was breathtaking sitting there on a rock against Jeff's chest. The view was too pretty to talk. It's that kind of view. It felt like time was standing still like everything was all right. Now I believed Jeff truly loved me. It's as if he would not let me go and we sat there for hours being together. We decided to walk back down the trail to the parking lot to have our picnic.

We found a nice place to sit and spread a blanket. The four of us sat and shared the picnic. Tony and Michelle were caught up with each other just like me and Jeff, but for some reason, I felt like it was our last time together. I don't know why, but something inside me was tugging at my heart. We made small talk between the four of us, but the mood was solemn and we didn't have the same laughter that we usually did. We were just sharing the moment together.

We finished eating and I asked Jeff, "Do you want to go back to the top of the mountain one more time?" He agreed.

With the picnic basket back in the car, the four of us started up the mountain again. It was getting late in the afternoon, and time was running out. We knew when we got the top we wouldn't be able to stay very long, but I was with Jeff, and I didn't want to let him go. We held hands as we walked towards the top and got to the rocks. The sun was getting low in the sky. I wanted to stay to see the sunset. The sky was beautiful, and two big red tail hawks were flying by. Jeff and I sat down for a moment while Michelle and Tony walked to the edge of the rocks. We looked towards the setting sun. We knew we had to get back down the trail before it got dark. Like every time with Jeff, I never want the day to end.

The closer we got to Hillsville, the loneliness sit in on me. We pulled up in the parking lot waiting on Tony. Jeff and I were standing in front of his car, and I took him in my arms. I didn't say a word and neither did he. We stood there holding each other as though something was going to happen, but neither one of us knew what. Tony finally pulled up. I kissed Jeff and got in the back seat of Tony's car and we drove back to Galax. Twice Michelle turned around and asked me why was I so quiet. I told her I didn't know why, but I just felt like something was going to happen. When I got home, Mom didn't say much but she could tell that I was not happy.

I went to my room and I crawled into bed. I pulled the covers over my head, I started crying. Mom knocked on the door and I invited her in.

"What's wrong, Princess? You've got that look on your face."

I pulled the covers off of my head and sat up. I asked her, "When my dad left you, did you ever get over it?"

She turned her head away from me and looked down at the floor before she answered. “No, Princess, not really, but Doug helped me.”

I sat up beside her and put my arm around her shoulders.

“How long will it take me to get over Jeff?” I asked.

She stood up, looked at me and answered, “Never. You'll go to your grave thinking about Jeff because he’s your first.”

“Mom, why does it hurt so bad, wanting someone you can’t have?”

“Why are you asking me these things, Princess?”

“Believe it or not, Mom, we didn’t have sex today. We just wanted to be together.”

Mom stood there looking at me, not saying a word. I think she could see herself in me. She had experienced these feelings, and she knew what I was going through. She knew she couldn’t help me. I was on my own, and I had to experience life and the pain of living. What a cruel lesson that life gives us. To love someone and realize there’s no hope. Jeff was right, we only had moments together. There was no future, there’s no yesterday, it’s just that one moment we’re together. The moments we’ve had together were not enough for me.

Tuesday morning was a new day, but the pain was still there. I longed to see Jeff, and the pain of not seeing him was real. I wanted to call him so I took a chance and dialed his number. When his mother answered the phone, I could hear screaming in the background. I think it was Jeff's dad. I was so worried about Jeff. He had no peace in his life and neither did I.

I hung up the phone quickly, I knew Jeff was in a mess.

Michelle called me that afternoon. I asked her to come by, we could walk downtown to the drugstore. It was late afternoon when she came by, walking down the street all Michelle could say, "What's wrong, Princess?"

I shook my head and kept walking until we got to the corner where we stopped. I looked at her and said, "Everything is wrong. I'm so worried that something bad is really going to happen, and I don't know what it is. I called Jeff this morning and his family was fighting. I could hear them over the phone, so I hung up." We kept walking down the street by Higgins gas station, Jeff was working. I waved at him as we walked by, as usual, Jeff looked sad. He blew me a kiss. I really wanted to go see him, but I didn't dare. We kept on walking until we got to the drugstore, and sat down in a booth. We ordered something to eat.

I looked around to make sure nobody was listening. Then I asked, "Do you and Tony have any plans to go anywhere for a whole day somewhere we've not been?"

"Yes, as a matter fact Tony mentioned something about Lovers Leap Mountain."

"I haven't been on Route 58 in a long time. Mom and I used to drive to Danville to Dan River Mills and buy clothes."

"I don't know what Tony has planned. Do you want me to ask him if you and Jeff can go with us?"

"No, I want to talk to Jeff first. Michelle, I need a favor."

"Sure, what do you need?"

"I want to make plans to spend the night with Jeff somewhere, and I need you to lie to mom and tell her that I'm staying with you. Do you think you could help me?"

"I don't know, Our parents are really close. Do you think we can get away with that?"

"Would you be willing to try? I'll take the *chance. That means you have to lie for me if our* parents find out."

"I don't know, Princess. It's a big chance."

"Give me a chance to talk to Jeff and see what he thinks. I feel like I've got to do something."

We finished eating and started walking back to my house. On the way, Michelle stopped and asked me again. "Princess, are you sure you want to do this? You and Jeff are going to take off and spend the day and night together. How will you get back home? I mean, how are you going to work this without getting caught?"

"I don't know, I really don't know."

Michelle shook her head and looked back at me and then she said, "You know I'll help you. What's going to happen if you get caught."

"When will you see Tony?"

"Probably Friday night. We're skating if you want to go with us."

"Would you ask Tony to go by and ask Jeff to meet me there Friday night? I can ride with you two. I can talk to everybody about what I want to do and how to get away and spend some time with Jeff. Do you think Tony would mind?"

"We'll just have to see what he says. Tony and Jeff are friends, I'm sure he'll help out.

The rest of the week was long and slow and lonely for me. Michelle called Thursday and said Jeff agreed to meet me at the roller rink Friday night. But in the meantime, Mom and I were not getting along. She kept pressuring me about Jeff, especially after Dad would leave the house. I still called him Dad. He was the only dad I'd ever known, and I still loved him. Thursday morning, I had a chance to talk to Mom again about my real dad.

I was sitting on the front porch after breakfast that morning when she came out and sat on the steps in front of me. If you didn't know the difference, everything was all right in God's world, everything but me.

"Mom."

"Yes, Princess."

"Tell me more about my real dad. How did he treat you before he left? What did he tell you? I don't understand how could he leave if he loved you like you thought he did, without telling you why?"

"Princess, I don't want to talk about your real father. That was over fifteen years ago, and I don't know what to tell you about him."

"Mom, you knew I was going to ask you. Why did you tell me anything about him?"

"Because I went through what you're going through right now. I took a chance to tell you the truth, to let you know you're headed for a real serious heartbreak. Something that's going to change you for the rest of your life, no matter which way this goes with Jeff Gray. Baby, you're not going to be happy in the end."

I stood up, almost screaming at her. "How do you know how it's going to turn out! Just because it didn't work out for you what makes you think it won't work out for me!"

"Calm down, Princess, don't raise your voice out here in the front yard for everybody to hear."

I lowered my voice. "I'm sorry, Mom. You know how I feel, and you know what I'm going through."

"Baby, let's do some work around the house. We can mow the yard for your father and clean out the back building. We need to stay busy, and you need to stay busy and get your mind off of everything, especially Jeff Gray. It's only a few weeks before school starts. You just need to get your mind off of everything."

I agreed with her. I started mowing the yard while Mom was in the back building trying to throw things away and get it straightened out. That's what we did for the rest the day. Mom didn't want to talk anymore about my real father. I could see she never got over him. Not because of me, because he didn't know I existed before he left, so I couldn't hate him for that. I didn't hate him, but I was sorry he left my mother like that. I kept wondering if I would end up like her. When I got older, I wondered if I would take the memory of Jeff Gray to my grave. Would he be a bad memory one day? The thought horrified me. That's the reason I felt like I'd better see him all I could and make more memories, good or bad. Hopefully, I could make good ones while I had a chance to be with him.

Friday morning, Michelle called. She had spoken with Tony who said Jeff would meet me. I was trying to plan it all out. I don't know why, but for some reason, I felt uneasy. I was going to take a chance to stay with Jeff all night, and that excited me. I was willing to take that chance.

Mom let me go with Michelle. She knew where I was going, and she didn't try to stop me. At six-thirty, Tony pulled in front of the house and I told Mom they were having a dance after skating on Friday night. Sometimes they'd have a band, other times they played records. It gave me an excuse to stay out a little bit longer that night.

When we got to the skating rink, Jeff was waiting and I walked around the corner of the building to find him standing in front of his car. I ran to him and he opened his arms and we hugged, "It's been a long day for me waiting to see you."

I kissed him on his ear. "Not as bad as I want to see you. I've got a lot to talk about, Jeff, and I want you to help me to make plans."

He pushed me back so he could look at me. "Plans, what kind of plans?"

"I want to spend the night with you."

"Tonight?"

I shook my head. "No, not tonight. We have to make plans. Tony and Michelle are talking about going to Lovers Leap Mountain. You've been there before, haven't you?"

"Yes, we've had picnics there. It's a nice place. I remember my mom and dad would take me down to my grandmother's house and I would get car sick. I hated that mountain because it's so curvy."

"I want to spend the day on Lovers Leap Mountain and then find a motel somewhere down the mountain away from here and spend the night together."

"That sounds great to me, but how are you going to pull this off. What will you tell your parents?"

"I've asked Michelle to help me lie about it and she agreed. So, I don't know the details, but let's talk about it."

I went around the other side of the car and got in the front seat. Jeff got in the driver's seat. I slid over close to him and we begin to make out. I loved this place. The night was warm. Jeff and I finally got in the back seat and made love lying there, holding each other.

"Jeff, I'm going to ask you again. Runaway with me."

" You can't be serious. You know I'm leaving in a few weeks and you've got to get ready to go back to school. I was supposed to start practicing football in a couple of weeks, but we're leaving. I don't want to leave my hometown. I don't want to go."

"Jeff, I'd do anything if you stayed. I'm already lonely and you haven't left yet. This may be the last night to be at the skating rink and then it's going to be just a memory. Jeff, tell me that we have more than moments. You always said we only had moments, just right now. Tell me that's changed with you."

He got up and started putting his clothes on, and so did I. He got really silent and solemn, and never answered me. I had a feeling he knew this was the last night we'd be at the skating rink, the last time we would meet here and it was only a moment.

"Answer me, Jeff, do we have more than moments now?"

We stepped out of the car leaned up against the side. " No we don't, I've got a feeling this could be one of our last moments together."

I laid my head on his chest, He kissed me on top of my head.

"One of us has got to face reality, Princess, and I'm being honest with you. I don't want to leave here I'd like to be with you forever, but that's not reality. We can't fool ourselves, baby. I'm leaving and you're going back to school, that's the way it's got to be."

Before I could say another word, it took me a moment. "Then tell me that we're going to spend all day and all night somewhere. We'll buy some food and watch the sun go down, then find a motel somewhere and spend the night together. Tell me at least you'll do that, we will have that moment."

"All right, how are we going to do it?"

"We'll have to talk to Tony and Michelle. I'm sure they'll help us." Jeff told me to get into the car we drove around to the front of Tony's car. We waited for them to come out so we could make plans, hoping they would help. I was getting excited just thinking about spending a couple of days with Jeff on the mountain and then somewhere that night. I tried not to think about Jeff leaving. I couldn't imagine he would leave without me.

When Tony and Michelle came outside and saw we were sitting beside his car, they were surprised we didn't try to hide. We got out of Jeff's car and got in Tony's back seat. We told them what we wanted to do.

I asked, "Are you guys still going to Lovers Leap Mountain anytime soon?"

Tony turned around and looked at Michelle while he held her hand and said "I sure hope so"

"When do you plan on doing this?" Jeff asked.

"I don't know yet. We haven't really made plans. When do you want to go, Michelle?"

"I don't have anything planned. You tell me when you want to go and we'll go."

Tony asked, "Are you guys going with us?"

"We want to go, but Jeff and I've got some plans," I told him. "We want to go with you, but we need your help because we're going to stay all night somewhere. Michelle, I need your help."

"Ok, how are you going to do this?"

"I'll tell Mom I'm spending the night with you, so when you and Tony come back, Jeff and I are going to find a place to spend the night, after we leave the mountain."

Jeff interrupted, "What day is good for you, Tony? I've got to see if I can get off work."

"What do you think, Michelle?"

"What day do you have off? Maybe that would be better?" I said to Jeff.

"Let me see, Thursday and Friday. I have to work the weekend. Can you do that, Tony?"

Tony looked up. "I can do that."

"Ok. I'm going to tell Mom we're leaving Thursday morning, and that I'm going to spend the night with you and won't be home until Friday evening."

"Princess, what will I do if your mother calls to talk to my mom? What then?"

"Don't say anything, I don't want to get you in trouble, but I'm going to spend time with Jeff one way or another. I think maybe we can meet in Hillsville and I can ride with Jeff and follow you guys down 58 to the mountain. When you leave, Jeff and I will do something else. Is that ok with everybody?"

Jeff almost backed out right then. "Princess, I don't want to get you in trouble. What do you think your daddy will do if he finds out that you spent the night with me? We will never see each other again. I don't want to get you in trouble. I don't think we should do this."

"You listen to me, you've got two or three weeks before you have to leave, maybe forever. I may not ever see you again. We're going to do this! Are you going to see me or not? I've done everything you asked me and I want to hear you say it, right here in front of my friends. Do you love me?"

Jeff looked at all three of us. He was silent and then he answered, " I love you enough to know this is not going to end well for either one of us. I love you enough not to get you in trouble and we've pushed it all summer long. I'm afraid that you would mess your life up over me. But yes, Princess, I love you. I wish I didn't. I didn't intend to love you. I love you."

"Give me this moment, give me these two days and let me worry about getting caught."

"You two have got me in tears. Is it really that bad, I mean, really?" Tony said.

Michelle looked at Tony and said, "I wish I had somebody love me like that." Tony shook his head and smiled.

As Jeff got out of the car, he asked, "So we're going to meet in Hillsville, right?"

"I guess we are, say about ten o'clock on Thursday morning. We'll meet up behind the library and you and Princess can follow us down 58."

Jeff and I embraced, kissed and he whispered in my ear, "You're crazy, Princess. God, I hope I don't get you in trouble."

"I don't care, Jeff. Let's make this moment, a wonderful moment. This has been the most exciting summer of my young life. Please, Jeff, don't let it stop now." Jeff told everyone goodbye, got in his car, and drove off.

Chapter 13

When I got home, Mom was waiting for me. She put me through the third-degree, trying to find out if I saw Jeff that night. She followed me to my room. I decided to be honest with her. She knew everything.

"Did Jeff go to the skating rink, did y'all skate?"

"No, Mom. We sat in Jeff's car. We talked and made out."

"That's all you did is talk and kissed?"

"Mom, do I have to go through this every time I go out? Look, I'm seeing Jeff and I told you I would. I told you I'll see him every chance I get. He's leaving, and then all this is going to be over. The end of summer is almost here. Please, please leave me alone. I'm already heartbroken. You're asking me questions you already know the answer. You might as well know, we're going to Lovers Leap Mountain next Thursday. After that, I'm spending the night with Michelle. Now I'm being honest with you, are you going to let me go?"

"Lovers Leap Mountain! Princess, you're not getting stupid are you?"

"What do you mean?"

"Jeff is going to be there?"

"I hope so. We don't have much time left for the summer. He's leaving, and your worries will be over!"

"My worries will never be over. This is too much for me. I can see in your eyes you think you're in love, but you really don't know what love is!"

"Then you tell me what love is!! You tell me what love is because if this is not love what the hell is it!!"

She smacked me across my face. I fell on the bed crying. "Don't you ever talk to me that way again! I love you, baby, but you're out of control! I'm trying to work with you. I know what you're going through. Princess, you're headed for trouble, how many times do I have to say that! You're only fifteen years old! Don't you raise your voice to me like that your father can hear you!"

I looked up at her with tears running down my face. "Doug is not my father! You've already told me he's not. He can't stop me from doing anything!"

"That's enough! You're not going anywhere Thursday! That's the way it is. You're not going to talk back to me that way. Do you understand me!! You're not going anywhere!"

Mom went out the door and slammed it behind her. I really messed up I'm not going to get to go. I lay back in my bed and closed my eyes. It felt like the whole room was spinning.

It was morning before I woke up, and Dad had gone. When I went downstairs, Mom had breakfast for me. She sat across the table, I didn't talk to her, I didn't want to look at her. The mood was tense.

"Princess, what are you thinking? I give you a lot of leeways, knowing what you're doing, I can't continue to let you do this."

"It's too late, Mom. I'm sorry I raised my voice to you. I don't know what to do." I stared at my plate.

Mom asked me the big questions. "How did all this start? How did you get so involved with this boy? What did he do to you to make you feel this way about him? Tell me, Princess, how did it start?"

"He kissed me in class and I liked it. Nobody's ever paid attention to me, and one thing led to another. We started meeting secretly and then I asked him to come to the barn. It all felt so good I let him do things to me that you wouldn't like, Mom."

"Look at me, Princess. What did he do to you that's got you so involved? What did he do to you?"

"Mama, you know what."

"All of this started just by him kissing you one time, and now here we are. You're having sex. This is serious. Anything could happen."

I stood up, crying. Mom stood up behind me, turned me around and shook me.

"Princess, you've got to stop this before it's too late. You've got to stop it now!"

"Please let me spend the night with Michelle, please. It's all going to be over, and I'll never see him again."

"Do you know what you're asking me to do? Let you go out and have sex with this nobody boy. What kind of mother do you think I am? I'm trying to get you to do the right thing!"

"It'll be the four of us on the mountain, and I'll spend the night with Michelle. What's wrong with that?"

"How can I trust you to do the right thing, knowing your state of mind. Baby, it's not going to end up the way you think, don't you understand that!"

"Did you understand it when you went with my Dad? How old were you? Could anybody tell you anything?"

"That's not fair, Princess. I trusted you enough to tell you what I did, now you are throwing it back in my face. You've got to be honest with me, Princess. Now sit down and finish your breakfast!"

I moved my food around the plate, but I had lost my appetite. I carried the dishes to the sink, where Mom was standing, crying again. When I turned to walk out of the kitchen, she stopped me.

"Ok, promise me you'll stay with Michelle, and don't do anything stupid."

I hugged her tightly and thanked her. I went upstairs and cleaned my room. I tried to do things to pass the rest the week. When Dad came home, we went through the routine of having supper. Mom told him I was going to stay with Michelle on Thursday. I was glad she kept my secret. I'd be afraid he'd shoot Jeff. Now each day was a challenge until Thursday. It seemed like it took forever for that morning to finally get there.

Thursday morning when Tony and Michelle picked me up, Mom looked like she was regretting she let me go. Maybe she remembered how she felt when my real dad was making love to her, how much she loved him.

When I got in the back seat, Michelle immediately asked me how I pulled this off. She was scared to death that my mother would call her and ask to speak to me.

"Don't worry, Michelle," I said.

"How do you plan to get home? Have you thought about that? I'll be going home without you."

As I looked out the window, I told her "I haven't figured out how that's going to work. Right now, I don't care. I'm going to spend the day and night with him somewhere. We don't know where yet. I just don't care, He's going to be leaving soon and I want to take advantage of every second I have with him. I'll get home somehow; we'll figure it out."

Michelle shook her head and turned around to watch where we were going. When we pulled behind the library in Hillsville, Jeff was waiting, but then Tony surprised us. He said he and Michelle were not going to Lovers Leap, and that we were on our own.

"When did you change plans?" Michelle asked.

As the four of us stood in the parking lot, Tony told Jeff, "We'll probably go to the mountain with you two but we're going to keep on moving. Michelle and I are going to ride around, maybe go to some of the creeks in the backwoods and just make a day of it, wherever we go."

"That sounds like a plan to me," said Michelle. "I like to be next to water anywhere, but first let's go to Lovers Leap and check the view out. Jeff and Princess are going somewhere tonight anyway."

We agreed, and it was all settled. I got in the car with Jeff, with Tony and Michelle following us right out Route 58, we got to the mountain and stopped in the picnic area. The four of us walked to the overlook and sat for a few minutes until Tony decided to leave.

I was alone with Jeff. I felt as though I were on the edge. This was a precious time, as Jeff would say. Another moment we had together not knowing what tomorrow would bring. I tried to get in my mind that he was leaving so he could be happy, but for some reason, I could feel Jeff wasn't. We walked around holding hands until we came to a sign that told the history about Lovers Leap Mountain.

"Read that, Jeff, it's about how the mountain got its name."

Jeff stared at the sign and never said a word before I realized he couldn't read it. He looked at me and then said, "This is another reason why you shouldn't be with me." I wondered why he said that. Jeff turned his back on me like he was ashamed, then turned around and asked me, "Read it to me?"

I took a minute for me to collect myself, once I realized I had hurt him. I felt so bad. We faced the sign and I begin to read.

In the 1600s,
the Indians inhabited the Blue Ridge Mountains.
White settlers started arriving
and begin to clear land to farm.
Conflict arose between the Indians and the settlers,
and legend has it that the son of a settler
saw the twinkling in the eye

of the chief's daughter, Morning Flower
and was immediately love-struck.
The couple began to meet secretly,
and their love continued to grow.
The young man and the Indian maiden
were threatened and shunned.
With the beautiful rock and wildflowers
as their backdrop,
they jumped into the wild blue yonder
ensuring they would be together forever.
As you gaze out at Lovers Leap,
you can still see the evidence of their love
in the beautiful view
and hear them whisper
in the cool evening breeze.

I looked at Jeff. "That's just like us," I said. "Nobody wants us to be together, and we have to hide our love. In spite of that, it has grown. At least mine has. I love you so much. If you asked me to, I would take you by the hand today and jump off this mountain with you. I would do that."

I looked in Jeff's eyes. A tear ran down his cheek I pulled him close and kissed him. "Tell me what's wrong, why are you crying?"

LOVERS' LEAP

We walked hand-in-hand to a picnic table and sat down. Jeff sat on the opposite side of the table where we could look at each other face-to-face. He was hanging his head down, and tears were running down his face. "What's wrong? I thought you are glad. We're together today. Why are you crying? Please don't cry. I can't take that from you. Please, tell me what's wrong?"

Jeff looked up and answered me. "Everything's wrong, Everything is wrong. Do you know how I felt when I couldn't read that sign when you asked me to? You shouldn't be here with me, why are you here? I've treated you so bad. I raped you, and you stayed. I just knew that day I kissed you in class I was being spiteful. I wanted to hurt you because I hated you, hated everything you stood for. I thought when I kissed you that day, you would smack me in the face and give me the satisfaction of laughing at you. But you didn't. You wanted me to kiss you again, and I don't know why. Here we sit on this mountain together on a beautiful day. Nothing is right. Why are you here with me after the way I've treated you! I raped you! I wanted to hurt you! Why are you here with me?"

I got up from the table and turned my back on him. I could feel his eyes boring through me, but I never turned around. "Jeff, I don't know how to explain it," I said. "You know you're my first. I would hope you would be with me for the rest of my life, but I know that's not reality. I need you to tell me something here and now and I need to know."

He was silent for a moment, then asked, "What do you need to know?"

"You had been in love before you started seeing me. How do you really feel about me? Not just sex. In other words, do you love me? I keep asking you that, and then you start talking this way. Don't you know this hurts me? I've risked everything for you. I've proven my love over and over. I don't care you can't read. I just want you to love me. That's all I want from you. I told you from the beginning I'll settle for moments, but let's make more moments. Stop talking like you... I don't know. Jeff, stop talking that way to me. It hurts worse than you raping me!" I felt so weak. He was pulling strength out of me, I couldn't help him.

I turned around and saw Jeff had his head down on the table. In a muffled voice he answered, "Yes, I love you, I'm mad at myself for falling in love with you because you're so much better than me."

"Please don't say that. I'm not better than you. I've been told that all my life, I'm sure that's the reason I made fun of other people, but I'm not. After experiencing loving you, I'll never say I'm better than anybody else again. You've shown me so much. Please, Jeff, don't ever say that again. I'm not better than you. I'm not better than anybody. Just because I have more than some people doesn't make me better. You've shown me that. You've helped me grow up some just by you being who you are. It's not your fault that you think you're not good enough. You don't have to prove anything to anybody, especially me

"Sit down, Princess. I've got to tell you something. I just can't stand it anymore. I got in a fight with my father last night. I knocked him down. I can't take it anymore. They're always fighting. There's no peace in my house and I'm sure that's a reason I love you. You bring peace to me. I don't want to go to Richmond with them. I want to leave. I want to get away. I'm going to have to get away from you. We can't be together. It's just like this Indian girl and farm boy. They knew it was never going to be accepted, today is the last time we'll have a moment, the moments are over. I'll be leaving soon and you're going to meet some boy and have a whole new life. You'll meet some guy that at least can read and write, treat you like you should be treated."

"I don't want to hear any more about this," I told him. "You keep saying this is one of our last moments, so then let's enjoy it. Tony and Michelle are probably making love somewhere, and I'm going to make love to you. I'll do anything you ask me to do, but let's be together and forget about what's next. Live the moment like you've always told me. Just live the moment."

We walked together on the mountain and looked at the beautiful view for hours before we decided to move on. Lunch, so we found a place to eat. Every time I was with Jeff, I thought I was in heaven, but I was afraid it was going to turn into a hell of loneliness. I tried my best not to think about him leaving, but I couldn't get away from it.

We went down the mountain on 58 through Stuart and then to Martinsville where we found a motel. I had to go inside with Jeff to check us in and sign the papers. I checked us in as man and wife, and nobody asked us about it. We went to the room.

I opened the door and locked it behind us. I took off all my clothes, so did Jeff. We crawled into bed together and made love as we had never made love before. Whatever he wanted, I would do it, and what I asked him to do to me he did. That was round one.

When we got in the shower together and cleaned up, I told Jeff we had to go somewhere because I needed to buy a toothbrush and toothpaste. We drove to Martinsville, found a restaurant and ate. Then we stopped at the drugstore and bought what we needed. Jeff bought some condoms.

When we got back in the room, it was a little bit after 8 PM. We brushed our teeth, got back in bed and made love again. I wanted him and he wanted me and that's all that mattered. There was no tomorrow, no yesterday, it was just a moment and we had sex as much as we could. Finally, we were lying in bed together. I wasn't sure what time it was, but we started talking about what we're going to do.

"Is this what it feels like being married?" I asked.

He looked at me and sat upon the edge of the bed. I put my head on his back. His body was warm and reassuring and comfortable.

His voice was low when he said, "I wish it was. Then there would never be another divorce. This is not a reality. You and I have each other. We're pleased with each other because we have no responsibilities. I'm saying this because I see my own family. Real-life sets in Princess. You've got to work, and you've got to eat. I used to go to church and I would listen to what they were saying about when you get married, you become one with each other. There's no two anymore. You've got to be together and you've got to go in the same direction. That was a problem with my dad. One woman was never enough for him. He would drink when he would come home, the mood in the house would change. Mama found another woman's man's, shirt one time when she was washing clothes. I don't know why he would do things like that, but I live in a house where there is no peace, and fighting all the time."

Jeff got up and walked around the bed to look at me and asked, "What about your house, Princess? Have you experienced anything like that, your folks fighting? I mean really fighting. I'm talking about fighting to the point they drew blood from each other. Can you imagine that? Have you seen that happen in your family?"

"No, I haven't. They've argued, but I never heard them really raise their voices at each other. Fighting like you're talking about, I haven't been through that."

He came back around the bed and sat down again looking down sadly like he was thinking back. "One time I was sound asleep and I heard a noise downstairs. My parents were screaming at each other. I heard a big crash and I ran downstairs. My mother had her robe tied around her waist and she was naked underneath. My father was lying on the floor. I guess he was knocked out. There was blood running from his shoulder. She'd taken one of those big ashtrays and broke it over his knee and stuck it in his shoulder. She poured a jug of water over his face to wake him up. I was so upset when my father got up, I opened the front door for him and told him to get out. He pulled a knife out of his pocket and told me he'd cut my throat if I ever talked to him like that again. He raped my mother while I was upstairs asleep. I lived in that kind of house, Princess, all my life."

I listened to Jeff tell how he was living with no peace in his life. "I remember when I was three, I think, I was under the back porch playing in the dirt with my truck. I remember I was having a good time by myself, then I heard the door open up and my father said to come out. He stood there in the doorway looking down at me he said, 'I hated my father, and you're going to hate me.' That's all he said and I went back under the porch. Something changed, Princess. Something changed in me. I don't know what it was, but I've never been the same since. My parents managed to get along through the years until it was time for me to start school. When my father sat me down and tried to teach me how to read. He didn't know he was trying to teach me out of a second-grade book. He didn't know the difference. I tried to learn, but he kept telling me I was never going to be anybody or any good and that I'd never been able to learn. Princess, I believe that's the reason I can't read or write today. He kept telling me I was never going to be any good. It's almost like he was speaking a curse on me and now I am in high school and I can't read or write."

"We always had plenty to eat, clothes on our backs, a roof over our heads, but no peace in the house. I hated it when he would come home. Then I had to go to school, but I couldn't keep up with the other kids, because I was bigger than the rest of them, I bullied my way through. I'd always make friends with the smartest kid in class and he would help me get through. I would cheat to pass tests. Then when I got in high school, people made fun of me behind my back."

Jeff stopped talking for a moment and looked at me. I don't know if he was trying to or not, but I felt so guilty. I loved him so much, but I used to laugh at him behind his back. I didn't know about his home life, I didn't care.

Jeff started talking again. "You asked me about the girl. Don't you ever try to be like her! She wanted me to be like everybody else. That's something I can't do, no matter how hard I try. I made myself a promise. If I meet a girl that would take me just like I am and agreed to marry me, I would never put her through what my parents put me through. I'd make sure that there was always peace in my house. I heard a preacher one time. A guy asked what's the best thing a father can do for his children? And the preacher looked him in the eye and replied, 'Love their mother.' The problem with my dad, he loved them all and paid no attention to me. But both of my parents were raised hard. It's obvious my dad fought with his dad. Maybe that's the reason he treats me the way he does. He taught me how to fight. That night that guy put a gun in my face, you asked why I didn't run. I remembered what my dad told me. If a man pulls a gun on you and doesn't shoot you immediately, he doesn't want to shoot you."

"I'm sorry that you had such a hard life. You had to go through all that, I understand why you did some of the things you did. You're fighting the world."

I put my head on Jeff's chest and kissed him. He hugged me tight, pulled me close and kissed me passionately. Then he said something I loved hearing. "Princess, I wish we could run away. I do want to leave, but I don't want to go to Richmond. I'm in love with you and it really hurts to think I'll never see you again."

"We can run away. I'll go if you go with me. I will, Jeff. I'll run away with you right now. We don't have to go back if you don't want to."

"You're talking crazy. We don't have any money. I don't have a job. What would you do about your education? You're not thinking straight. All the sex has gone to your mind and you think this is going to be forever? You've got to go back. I'm uneducated, Princess. I can't read and write and you would quit school? You're only fifteen. You can't do that. You just can't do that; we don't have any money and no future. You're not thinking."

"I have some money in savings. I have over ten thousand dollars in my savings account. I can go take some of it out and we can leave together."

"Where did all that money come from? You saved that much?"

"My parents are rich. They're teaching me to be responsible, handle the money they gave me. Some I earned, and some for college, but I'll take it out when we go back tomorrow night. I can't take all of it out. You can pick me up, and we can leave together. Jeff, you don't have to go to Richmond with your parents. We can leave together. Please think about it. I'll go with you. I'll go with you anywhere you want to go."

"That's tempting, It wouldn't last long. What about your school?"

"I don't care. I'll do it. I love you, and I'd do anything you want me to do. When I get back home, I'll take that money out of the bank and we can leave together."

Jeff rolled me over, got on top and we made love again. We kept making love as long as we could until we both fell asleep.

Chapter 14

When I woke up the next morning, Jeff was in the shower. He told me while I showered he would get us something to eat.

After we ate, Jeff told me he wanted to have sex one more time so we did. We got in his car and drove back up the mountain towards Hillsville. I was dreading it. I didn't know how I was going to get back home without getting caught. When we got back to Galax and stopped at a phone booth, I called Michelle.

"Michelle, it's me. We're back. Did anything happen last night? Did my mom call or anything?"

"No, she didn't. I was worried all night, wondering where you were."

"We're at the bowling alley right now. Do you think you and Tony can come and pick me up?"

"No, he's working remember? I'm sorry."

"I'll get Jeff to drop me off downtown and I'll walk home. Would you walk down to the drugstore and meet me there?"

"Yes, I'll start walking that way. I'll get a head start and you won't have to wait long."

Jeff drove in the back alley in front of the Rex Theater. I sat up, leaned over and kissed him and told him what a wonderful time I had. I didn't want to go, but I got out of his car and walked to the drugstore to wait for Michelle.

When she got there, I was so glad to see her. Now we could walk back together to my house and maybe Mom wouldn't be suspicious.

Michelle was asking me all kinds of questions. “What did you guys do, where did you go?”

“We spent most the day on the mountain and then we drove all the way to Martinsville and got a room. Oh, Michelle, it was wonderful making love, not worrying and being in the bed with him for the first time. I can’t explain it. I don’t know what I’m going to do. I can’t stand the thought of him leaving. It’s a few weeks away, and he’ll be leaving me. What am I going to do?”

“Princess, I never thought I’d see you so in love. I mean it’s true Tony and I are having sex and it’s good, but I’m trying to stay in reality, Princess. You’re not, you’ve gone head over heels, completely nuts. I’m worried about you.”

“I can’t help it. I just can’t help it. I’ve lost my virginity; I love having sex with him. I think I’m addicted to it now, but I can’t imagine having sex with anybody else. Michelle, I want to leave with him and he won’t let me.”

“Do you know what you’re saying? Do you want to leave with him? You're in high school! You are willing to give up everything to leave with him?”

“I would, I’d give up everything if he would take me.”

“You don’t know what you’re saying, you really don’t. You better slow down, this has gotten too serious. You're going to end up pregnant, then what are you going to do?"

"I don't want to get pregnant, but if I do, I'll raise his baby; that's what I'll do! I'll have his baby." We walked on. When I got to my house, I asked Michelle to come in so Mom could see her.

When we walked in, looked relieved. "Did you girls enjoy yourselves? Did you have a good time on Lovers Leap Mountain?"

"Yes, Mom, we did. We're going to go to my room. I'm tired. Are you going to stick around awhile, Michelle?"

"No, I think I'll go back home. I'm tired too. We didn't sleep much last night. I think I'll go home and try to catch up."

I decided to jump in the shower real quick to freshen up. I was afraid to go back downstairs. I knew Mom would ask me, questions and I just didn't feel like putting up with it.

The next day I decided to go to the barn and tend to my horse. I had no idea when I would hear from Jeff again, but I was hoping it would be soon. Several days went by and I never heard a word. I got anxious and just had to call him. I wanted to hear his voice.

Another day went by and I still didn't hear anything. That night I called his house, and it was a mistake. Jeff's mother answered the phone. I asked her. "May I speak to Jeff?"

"Jeff's not here right now. Who is this?"

"I'm a friend of his from school, and my name is Princess."

"Jeff isn't here right now. He's somewhere with his father. Do you want me to have him to call you?"

She put me on the spot. He can't call me; my parents might answer the phone. "No ma'am, just tell him Princess called and I'll talk to him later, maybe I'll go by where he works."

"Are you the girl he's seeing? Are you Jeff's girlfriend?"

I didn't know if I should answer this question, or how to answer. I just blurted out. "Yes ma'am, I've been seeing Jeff for a while."

"Do your father and mother know about you and Jeff?"

I tried to avoid answering her, so I said real quick, "Ok, ma'am, I'll try to get in touch with Jeff later." I hung up before she could say anything else. Now I was worse off than before. Jeff can't call me and it worried me. I wanted to see him, and I was afraid something was wrong.

Something was wrong, I just knew it. It was driving me crazy. Football practice started, the end of summer was upon us. Jeff and his family would be leaving soon, and I hadn't heard from him. Over and over in my mind, I kept asking myself if he was going to leave and not say goodbye. At least he could tell me goodbye.

I went to Michelle's house to spend the day. Her mother made lunch, we ate at the picnic table in her backyard where we could talk in private. "Have you spoken with Tony? Has he seen Jeff?"

"No, Tony hasn't mentioned it. Why, what's going on? Haven't you seen Jeff?"

"No, I haven't since we came back from Lovers Leap. I don't know what's happened. I called his house his mother answered the phone, but she started asking too many questions. I asked her to tell Jeff that I called, I don't know if she did or not, he can't call me. The only way he could get in touch is through Tony. Could you do me a favor, Michelle?"

" Do you want me to ask Tony to go by and see what Jeff is doing?"

"Would you please, I don't know what's happening. Would you have Tony tell him I'm going to be at the barn Saturday morning?"

"I'll tell him, Tony will go by the filling station and see if Jeff is working."

We sat together for a while. I told her what a wonderful time I had with Jeff in the motel room and how exciting it was.

Friday morning, I didn't know if Tony went by to see Jeff or not. I hadn't heard from Michelle, so I didn't know if Jeff would be at the barn the next day. My Friday was miserable just waiting for answers. I didn't go anywhere. Mom agreed to take me to the barn on Saturday.

When we got there, I didn't see Jeff's car. I started taking care of my horse, cleaning the stall and doing everything that had to be done. An hour went by, but no Jeff.

I climbed the ladder to the hayloft and I sat on a bale of hay by myself thinking of the good times I had with him here. Still, he didn't show up. I don't how much time went by, but I heard a car out front and I was sure it was him. I climbed down the ladder but when the door opened it was Mom coming to pick me up.

When I got in the car, she knew something was wrong. I guess she could see the sadness in my eyes. I was hurting and Mom knew it.

"He didn't show up?"

I looked over at her. I was surprised she asked me that. "No, he didn't."

"I didn't tell you, but your father told me Jeff lost his job at the filling station. They fired him."

"Why, what did he do?"

"He didn't show up for work. I'm not sure when, but I've got an idea what happened to him and you know why."

"How could I know?"

"It's when he spent two days with you." I was searching for words to answer her. I spoke angrily.

"Why did you wait until now to tell me this?"

"Princess, do you think you can fool me? Do you think you can lie to me, and that I'm not going to follow up and see where you are? You didn't stay with Michelle. I went by there. I didn't say anything, but I knew you were somewhere with Jeff Gray. I knew I couldn't stop you, and I didn't say anything to your father."

I cry so hard I couldn't talk. Mom stopped the car and was asking more questions, but I wouldn't answer so she took me home.

I shut the door of my room behind me. Mom didn't follow. I stayed there all afternoon and cried so hard it hurt, I'm crying all the damn time now, I didn't know where Jeff was or what he was doing. I was afraid. I was afraid I'd never see him again.

The next day at Sunday School, Michelle had a surprise for me. "Princess, I've got a message for you from Jeff."

"Where is he?"

"Tomorrow night, he wants you to meet him at his family cemetery. He said to wait until dark."

"How am I going to get there, I don't know how I'm going to get there!"

"Tony said we would pick you up. You can tell your mother that we're going bowling, the cemeteries just across the street on Gillespie Lane you've been there before"

"Please thank Tony for me. Surely Mom will let me go bowling with you two. Did Tony say anything was wrong with Jeff?"

She paused. "He lost his job at the filling station."

"Oh, Michelle, I'm in so much trouble."

"Tell your mother that we're going bowling. Call me tonight and let me know if you can go. Tony and I'll pick you up tomorrow night."

After dinner that night, I helped Mom wash the dishes. She knew something was up. We'd done this before. Only this time, I wanted to talk to her.

"What's up, Princess? Is there something you want to talk to me about?"

"Yes, Michelle asked me to go bowling with her and Tony tomorrow night. Can I go?"

She hesitated and she rinsed a few more dishes before she answered. "Tell me the truth, Princess. You're going to the bowling alley, but you're going to see Jeff, aren't you?"

"Mom, please let me go. He's leaving and it's over. It's been two weeks since I've seen him. He lost his job and I'm responsible, you know I am. So please let me go to the bowling alley. I'm going to say my goodbyes. Please let me go. All of this is going to be over soon and you know how I feel. Remember how you felt when my dad left and you never saw him again? Please, Mom, let me go."

She shuffled her feet, "Yes, I remember. I'll never forget it. It haunts me what happened to your father. Ok, Princess Against my better judgment, you can go, but, I say it over and over and you're not listening, you know this not going to end well. You know you've got a big heartbreak coming and it's going to be bad. Princess, it's going to hurt so bad you're not going to be able to handle it."

"I know, Mom. I know it is. Thank you for letting me go." We finished the dishes and I went to my room.

The next day after Dad left for work, I helped Mom do the housework. I patiently waited all day for Tony and Michelle to pick me up. I was going to get to see Jeff one more time, maybe the last time. I didn't tell my mother, but while in my room I wanted to die. I was already hurting. I wanted to die.

It seemed like it took forever, but finally, they got there. Mom watched me get in the car. She knew I was going straight to him. It was almost dark when we got to the bowling alley.

Tony took me across the street behind the church where Jeff was waiting. He was walking among the graves when we pulled in. A three-quarter moon lit up the sky, the night was warm. Tony said he'd be back in a little bit to pick me up. I opened the cemetery gate and ran to Jeff's arms.

"Where have you been? I thought you left me. Why did you wait so long to get in touch with me, knowing how worried I am about you?"

He held me so tight it almost hurt. He kissed me and said, "I'm leaving."

I pushed him back, "What do you mean you're leaving?"

He turned his back on me and took a step away. "I'm leaving, Princess. I can't take it anymore. I'm going to leave, and I'm not going to Richmond."

I screamed at him, and my body was trembling. "You're not leaving without me! You're not leaving without me!"

"Stop it! You can't go!"

When he said that, I tried to pull myself together before I said anything again. “Where are you going, and when?”

“I don’t know. I’m just going.”

“Please take me with you. Don’t leave me here; I’ll die.”

“You won’t die. There’s somebody, special for you.”

“I’m with somebody special.”

“I won’t let you give up everything to leave with me.”

“It’s too late, If I don’t have you, I don’t have anything.”

“That’s not true. You’ve got a bright future and you’ve got parents that love you. Princess, please listen to me. I’ve done you wrong, and I know it. I’m regretting it now, but we’re only teenagers and I can’t take you with me. I have no job. My life is going to be hard and I know it. Look at me, Princess. Look at me. I never thought I’d ever say this to you.” He paused. “I love you so much, I can’t let you do this. You can’t go with me. I’ve got nothing, no future, and no money. I’ll have to live in my car until I find a job, and when I do it’s not going to pay much. Princess, without money we can’t do anything.”

“I’ve got money.”

“I know you’ve got money. You’ve got everything, and that’s the reason you can’t leave. You cannot go with me.”

“Please take me with you. Don’t leave without me.”

We walked back to Jeff's car and got in. He put his arm around me and I put my head on his shoulder. We sat there without talking. The moon was shining through the car window, it had a lonely feeling. It felt like the last time, it was tormenting me, After this, he would be gone forever. I felt like I had to do something.

"When are you planning on leaving?" I asked.

"I'm not sure, but soon."

"Please don't leave right away. See me again. Promise?"

"It's not going to change anything, Princess."

"Please don't leave until we can figure something out."

"There's nothing to figure out. I'm leaving Wednesday night."

I could barely speak. It was over. "What time are you leaving Wednesday? Please meet me here so I can say goodbye. Make love one more time before you go, please."

"Ok. I'll meet you here about dusk Wednesday night just to say goodbye. It's over, baby. It's time that you moved on."

I didn't answer Jeff. I was thinking about what I was going to do. I didn't know what, but my mind was zipping back and forth. Then an idea came to me. I'd sneak away from home Wednesday night. I couldn't take anything with me, but when Jeff left, he would have to take me with him. I'd make him. All kinds of schemes and plans were going through my mind. He was not leaving without me.

Car lights came from around the church, and I was sure it was Tony. We asked him to bring me back Wednesday night. He reminded us they would be having Wednesday night church services so it might be better to meet in the bowling alley parking lot. If Jeff wanted to, he could drive away with me. That's what we decided to do.

I kissed Jeff before I got in Tony's car. "Promise me you won't leave until you see me," I begged him. "Promise me you won't leave without saying goodbye. Please, Jeff, promise me."

Jeff took me in his arms and after a minute finally said, "I promise you I won't leave until I say goodbye."

My world was falling apart and I couldn't stop it. On the way home none of us talked about what was going on, I was hurting. When I walked into the house, Mom looked at me but never said a word. I lay in bed and felt every beat of my heart. It was as if the whole bed was shaking, keeping rhythm with my pain. I was thinking about what Jeff and I did together this summer, how is coming to an end. All I could think about was the joy and the good times and how good the sex was. But none of that meant, it was all behind me. My future was bleak. I was having crazy thoughts. I didn't want to live. I couldn't imagine being without Jeff. To think, it all started with a kiss.

The next morning, breakfast was waiting on me when I walked in the kitchen, Mom was waiting for me to sit down at the table. I sat there running my fork through my eggs, not wanting to eat. She watched me closely. I could feel it. Finally, she said, “You’re not talking, Princess. How did it go last night?”

“I saw him, He’s leaving; he told me last night. He’s leaving, so you don’t have to worry anymore. It’s all over,” I told her.

“Are you sure it’s over? I’ve got some bad news for you, baby, it’s just started. You’re in for some lonely nights. You’re going to be thinking about all the memories you made this summer. I know, I still haven’t forgotten my memories. But time will ease the pain and the pain will fade away slowly. Now you’ve got to be concerned about your schoolwork. You’ve got to start getting busy. Stay busy; it will help you keep your mind off of what just happened to you.”

While sitting at the breakfast table I couldn’t understand why I was so numb. “If it’s all right with you Mom, I want to go with Michelle to the bowling alley. She and Tony are bowling now and made some friends there. I’d like to go and watch them, ok?”

“Yes, that’s ok with me. In a few weeks, school will start, and that would help you keep your mind off of what’s happening. Just keep busy at school, work and you find other things that will be your priority in life, not a little girl fantasy of first love.”

“Mom, you know it’s more than that? You told me about my father. You know it’s more.”

I tried to stay busy the rest of the day, but Mom was right; I could hear Jeff’s voice, I could feel his touch, I could imagine lying naked with him. But I could also hear Jeff saying you can't live off of love. I desperately wanted to.

I got through the day, but that night was sleepless. I was making a plan to surprise Jeff. I was leaving with him. I made up my mind. I leaving with him whether he liked it or not.

Wednesday morning, I put a show on for Mom and acted like everything was right in my world, that everything was behind me. I tried to deceive her.

After lunch, I got my savings account book and walked downtown to the bank. On the counter, I filled out a withdrawal slip. I was nervous. I didn't know what they would say. Everyone knew me here because Michelle's father was the president of this bank. I was afraid something could go wrong. I stood in front of the teller, Mrs. Jones, who knows everybody in town. I handed her the withdrawal slip. She looked at it and then back at me.

"Princess, why are you withdrawing this much money?" she asked. "Are you going to buy yourself a car?"

"I'm thinking about," I said. "I'll be sixteen soon, and my dad is going to help me look for one."

She looking at me suspiciously. I was sure she could sense I was nervous. "What kind of car are you looking for? Are you going to buy a new one?"

"I don't know yet. My dad's going to help me look."

"You know this is a lot of cash to be carrying around, so you better be very careful and not let anyone know that you've got this kind of money on you," Mrs. Jones said.

"I'm going straight home from here."

She counted out $5,000 in $100 bills. When she handed me the money, she said, "You be very careful. Why didn't your mom bring you down?"

I hesitated to answer. "She told me it was all right. She was very busy at the time. I'm going straight home."

As I turned to walk out, I saw her go to Michelle's father's office. I was sure I wouldn't get out the door before he said anything, but he didn't. On the walk back home, I wondered if Michelle's daddy had called my parents.

Mom didn't say anything when I walked in, so I took the money to my room and put it under my pillow. It would stay safe there until I got ready to leave that evening. I knew I couldn't take any clothes with me, but I had everything planned out and Jeff had to take me now. I had enough money for both of us to get started. I was sure I had figured it out, and I was going to leave regardless, and nobody could stop me.

Time seemed to stand still, and that afternoon took forever. As I was getting ready for Tony and Michelle to pick me up, Mom didn't seem suspicious. It was 6 o'clock and Tony and Michelle pulled up. Before I went out the door, I told Mom goodbye. My dad was in front of the TV. I walked over to say goodbye. I knew he wasn't my real father, I couldn't stop loving him just like that.

I didn't say a whole lot on the way to the bowling alley. It wasn't that far across town, but I knew Jeff wasn't there yet. He would wait until dark.

I watched Tony and Michelle bowl the first game. They didn't have a clue what I was getting ready to do. I looked out the door, but Jeff still wasn't there. I hoped the plans didn't get mixed up. I went to the door twice, but he wasn't there, and I wondered if he was going to leave without telling me goodbye.

Then somebody from behind the counter called my name out. "Princess Grant, someone on the phone wants to talk to you."

I was sure it was Jeff, but when I answered the phone it was my mother.

"Princess, I wanted to see if you were there?"

"Yes, Mom, I'm here. Are you checking up on me?"

"Yes, I am. I just found out you took money out of your savings account today. What are you doing?"

"Mama, I took some money out to buy some clothes for this coming school year."

"Princess, I know how much you took. Are you going to buy $5,000 worth of clothes?"

"Who told you? That's my business."

"Ok, control yourself and don't do anything stupid."

I hung up the phone. I had no idea what was going on in my house. I went to look out the door and saw Jeff had finally gotten there. I ran to his car and jumped in.

I looked in the back seat and it was full of Jeff's clothes.

"I didn't think you were going to come and see me," I said. "I was worried. I've got some good news, Jeff. I'm going with you."

Jeff looked up at me and said, "No, you can't. You can't go with me. I don't know where I'm going or what I'm going to do. I may have to live in my car for a while. Princess, you can't go. Now quit talking silly."

"Jeff, you don't have to worry about money. I've got some money. I took $5,000 out of my savings today so we will have enough to get started."

" I know that's a lot of money, but it's still not enough. Princess, we're teenagers. You can't give up everything to go with me. Now that's just the way it is. You can't go with me."

"Why are you saying this? You know I want to go."

"I know you do, and I want you to go, but you can't. I don't have any idea what I'm going to do or where I'm going. I'm just going!"

"Take this money then if you won't let me go with you. Take the money to help you get started, and maybe someday you'll come back to get me."

"No, I'm not going to take your money. I can't do that."

"Then take $500 of it, just enough to help you. Please take it. Make love to me right now before you go because I know I'm going to die when you go. I just know it."

Jeff reached over, took me in his arms, pulled up my blouse and kissed around my nipples. We lay down in the seat. I pulled my pants down on one leg and Jeff began to make love to me. The whole time I was crying because I knew this could be the last time I'd be with him.

All of a sudden, there was a knock on the window. "Jeff Gray! Get up get your clothes on and get out of the car. Young lady, get your clothes on and get out, too!"

It was the Galax Police. I got weak all over as I pulled my pants up and Jeff and I stepped out.

The officer grabbed Jeff, handcuffed him behind his back and asked me, "Young lady, how old are you?"

I answered him in a trembling voice. "I'm fifteen."

"Jeff, how old are you?"

"I'm sixteen."

"Jeff Gray, I'm arresting you for statutory rape."

"He didn't rape me! He didn't rape me! Please, officer, he didn't rape me!"

"It doesn't matter, you're underage. In the state of Virginia, you have to be eighteen years old to have consensual sex, and you are not the age of consent. Therefore, Mr. Gray's in trouble for statutory rape. Stand over here while we search your car."

Another officer held us while they searched Jeff's car. He had some beer in the cooler.

"Jeff, you've been drinking. Did you give this girl beer or alcohol?"

"No sir," Jeff answered.

I said, "He didn't rape me officer, and he didn't give me a beer. Please, let him go. He didn't do anything!"

"Young lady, we're going downtown to the station and calling your parents. Your father telephoned earlier to let us know that you were missing."

"I'm not missing. I'm right here at the bowling alley. Please officer, let Jeff go. He didn't do anything."

Then Jeff told me, "Be still, Princess. It's all over, baby, let it go."

I hung my head crying, and they put us in the back seat of a cop car. On the way to the Police Station, I said, "Promise me, promise me when you get out of jail in the morning, you'll come and get me. I'm going with you and you can't stop me. Please promise me, Jeff. Promise me you'll come and get me in the morning."

Jeff said calmly, "It's over for us. There are no more moments. Remember, baby, no yesterdays, no tomorrows. It's just right now, and for the first time, right now is not a good time. It's over, Princess. You've got to go on with your life. I've messed you up, and I didn't mean to. I drew you into my world. Princess, look at me."

With his hands cuffed behind him. He said, "You want me to make a promise to come and get you, it's over now. You've got to make me a promise."

I was choking back the tears. “What, Jeff? What do you want me to promise?”

“I want you to promise that you’ll go on with your life and that you’ll forget everything we did together. You’ve got a whole new life in front of you, baby. I’m done. My life stops tonight, but you've got to promise me you'll go on. Please, go to school and get your education and meet that right guy and put me away forever because I’m gone. This is the end of it. Princess, this is the end of it.”

“No! Please, don’t talk that way, Jeff. Your parents will get you out of jail in the morning. My parents are not going to press charges against you. I won’t let them. You didn’t rape me. You didn’t hurt me. No, Jeff. Promise me you’ll come and get me in the morning!”

Jeff turned his head from me. When we got to the police station, they separated us. I was screaming and out of control. Then my mother and father walked in.

The sheriff met my parents and I could hear my father tell him, “I want you to lock him up and keep him there so he will stay away from my daughter.”

“Mr. Grant, we can hold him until he sees the magistrate in the morning and sets bail. If he can be bonded out, a court date will be set. If he gets a lawyer then they’ll want to question your daughter, but this is state law, so he may go to jail for statutory rape. It may go to court if he gets a lawyer because there is a clause in the law, a Romeo and Juliet amendment because they're both underage, so your daughter may have to testify that she didn't consent to have sex with him."

"I'm her father, and I'm going to press these charges, whatever I can do to keep him away from my daughter!"

I screamed at him from the next room. "You're not my father! You're not my father!"

They shut the door to the office, and I couldn't hear them anymore. Finally, Mom and Dad came and took me to the car. I begged them to let me see Jeff before I left but they wouldn't. On the way home, Mom and dad got into an argument.

That's when Dad asked, "Did you tell her, Connie? Did you tell her I was not her father? How could you?"

My mother looked back at me, then turned to him and said, "I had to Doug; I had to. She was going in the wrong direction, and I didn't want her to make the mistakes I made. I had to tell her."

This is the first time I saw my dad angry at my mother. When we got home, they made me sit at the kitchen table. Dad wanted to talk to me.

"Princess, listen to me. I'm sorry your mother told you that I wasn't your father. I love you as though you're my own daughter and I always have. I didn't want to see you mess your life up with that boy. That's the reason I was so strong against it. Now I can't change things, you are my daughter."

My mom and I were crying. The man I thought was my father sat there, and deep down I couldn't stop loving him. He took care of me, but now I hated him. He took Jeff away from me.

"You didn't have to call the law on him. He didn't rape me. I gave myself to him because I love him. Don't push charges. Please don't. If you love me then please don't push the charges on Jeff; he didn't rape me."

"It's out of my hands, Princess," said Dad. "The Commonwealth of Virginia has charged him with statutory rape. When they found beer in his car, they charged him with contributing to the delinquency of a minor. Jeff is also underage. Where did he get the beer? Were you drinking beer with him? How long has this been going on, Princess? All the rumors I heard were true, I just knew they were."

I fell face down on the table, screaming and crying. Mom helped me to my room. I turned around at the door and looked at Dad. "I hate you! I hate you so much! You took everything away from me! Why?"

Then he answered me. "Because you're fifteen years old. We worked hard to see that you get a good education, to see that you're taken care of. That's why! We love you. Now what's done is done, and that's the end of it!"

"No, it'll never be the end of it for me. I'll never forgive you for this, never!"

Mom took me to my room and I asked her to leave me. I took my clothes off and fail into bed. I don't remember falling asleep.

When I woke up, I jumped in the shower. I decided I was going to run away. I couldn't stop shaking, my whole body. I was in a nervous wreck. I couldn't speak, and I gasped for breath. It was like the life was being drained out of me and I was weak.

Then Mom knocked on the door. I didn't answer it, but she came in any way. When she spoke to me, I acted as though she was not there.

"You need to come down and eat." I couldn't talk to her. I heard none of it.

"Princess, you've got to come down and eat."

I walked into my bathroom and locked the door behind me. Once I heard her leave, I got my suitcase out and I started packing clothes. I decided when Jeff came, I'd leave with him. I got dressed and sat on the side of the bed, trembling.

Mom came back to the room. It was already lunchtime and I had no idea. "Princess, it's past noon now; you've got to come out of this room. You've got to eat."

I sat there staring at the wall, not responding to her, I just couldn't. She left and I still sat there. The trembling, the shaking, was unbearable. I looked out the window. It was getting dark and Jeff had not come yet. I didn't know what happened. I waited on him, but he didn't show up. I sat there until I fell asleep.

A knock on the door woke me. It was mother again. The day and night had passed and I didn't realize it. When she came in, she saw my suitcase. "Where are you going, Princess?"

I was forced to answer in my shaking voice. "I'm leaving, Mom. When Jeff comes and gets me, I'm going to leave with him. I might as well tell you. I'm late. I think I'm pregnant. I'm carrying Jeff's baby, and you can't stop me from leaving."

She stared at me without saying a word. Until she asked, "How many days late are you?"

"I think five. Jeff doesn't know. I'm going to leave with him when he comes. You can't stop me. I'm leaving with him."

She got up in front of me and said. "I'm not going to try to stop you, but I've got some bad news for you. Jeff is not coming."

"Yes, he is, As soon as he gets out of jail"

"Princess, I wanted to tell you yesterday, but you wouldn't let me. Baby, it came on the radio yesterday that Jeff Gray..." her voice was cracking and she started crying. "Princess, the news on the local radio station WBOB said that Jeff hanged himself in the Galax City Jail that night they locked him up. I couldn't tell you yesterday. The rumor has it they didn't take his belt away from him and he climbed to the top of the steel bar, put his belt through it, slipped his neck in the belt and dropped. The weight of his body snapped his neck, he died instantly."

I froze in place, I stopped crying. I couldn't cry anymore. She was still talking, but her voice was fading from my hearing. I couldn't breathe, I couldn't move. All I could feel was a heavy thumping in my chest. I sat there, just staring at the wall. Mom was talking, but I couldn't hear her. She backed out of the room and shut the door. The next thing I remember my parents were picking me up out of the floor and laying me down in my bed. I still couldn't move.

I didn't know what happened. They were crying standing over top of me. I asked Mom to help me sit up on the edge of the bed and I told my father. "Daddy, I'm carrying Jeff's baby. I'm pretty sure I'm pregnant. What am I going to do now? I was leaving with Jeff. I was going to beg him to marry me. I was hoping you'd give him a job, but he's gone. What am I going to do, Daddy?"

Tears were running down my dad's face. They couldn't stop me from seeing Jeff and my mother kept warning me what could happen. It didn't make me stop loving Jeff although he was gone.

Then Dad answered me. " we're going to be here for you. Your mother and I are going to see you through this. We'll do what we have to do for you. If there's a new baby coming, then there's a new baby coming, and that's what we're going to do, Princess. We're going to see you through, whatever happens. We're going to be here for you. I don't care that you know that I'm not your father, but I want to tell you something, Princess. You are my daughter and now you're caring my grandchild, that's the way I look at it. We love you. Your mother couldn't stop you from what you were doing, and I was too busy thinking everything was all right with my family and it wasn't. I guess you know everything about your mother's past now? I love you like you're my own baby because you are my baby, don't you ever forget that." My father kissed me on my forehead, looked me in the eye and hugged me. "You're my daughter," he said over and over. "You're my daughter."

My mother stopped crying. She sat with me for the rest of the day until I asked her to leave. I needed to be alone. Jeff was gone and he wasn't coming back. I had his baby in me. I didn't know what was in front of me; I just knew I'd never forget what was behind me.

Chapter 15

A day passed, I was still numb I couldn't feel anything now. I still couldn't cry. I could barely breathe. Everything was shutting in on me, but with the help of my mother and father, I got through the second day. That evening they asked me to come down to sit at the kitchen table and talk about my future. I really wasn't ready to talk about anything, but I knew I had to.

Then Mom put the question to me. "Princess, I just want you to know that Dad and I are going to support you, whatever you decide to do. We don't know what you want to do. You know for sure that you're pregnant, do you?"

"Yes, Mom, I'm pregnant. I don't know how many days it's been since my last period, but I'm pregnant."

Mother asked, "Have you noticed any morning sickness. Are you feeling nauseated?

"Not yet. Am I supposed to?"

"If you're pregnant that could start anytime. Most women do have morning sickness, but not everyone."

Then my father said, "Princess, don't get me wrong, but I've got to ask you this question. Do you want to keep this baby?"

I wasn't ready for that question, it surprised me. "Don't you want this baby?"

"Don't get angry, Princess. I just want you to know what you're in for. You're only fifteen, and it's a lot of responsibility being a parent. This is the beginning of you making decisions. We told you from the beginning when you told us you were pregnant that we'd be here for you, but you've got to make decisions. This is not about what I want. This is about what you want to do."

Mom spoke up. "We don't know what you want, Princess. You've got all kinds of options. You can give the baby up for adoption if you choose to."

"Would you have given me up, Mom?"

"No, I would not."

"Dad, you said you're here for me. I want this baby. I know it's going to be hard and my whole world has changed. Being a teenager is over. I've got to be a mother now. I know I can't do it by myself. Mom, you said you wouldn't give me up. I can't give this baby up. It is the only thing that I've got left. Like you, Mom, it is the only thing he's left me, memories and a baby."

"Have you told anyone that you're pregnant? Did you tell Michelle?" Mother asked

"Nobody knows, I haven't told anyone, not even Michelle because I wasn't sure that I was. That's one of the reasons I got money out the bank and met Jeff at the bowling alley. I planned to run away with him, but he didn't want me to go. He didn't know I was going to try to go with him. He wouldn't even take the money, not even $500 to get started. I asked him to meet me there that night, Mama. It's my fault that Jeff killed himself. I asked him to make love to me one more time before he left. I knew it was over, but I didn't want it to be. Daddy, I was going to ask you to give Jeff a job. I could ask him to marry me. Instead, he got arrested, and it is my fault Jeff killed himself. I can't live with that, Mom. I killed him. I killed him with my love. He was hurting so bad."

I started crying again, and my parents cried with me. I was so thankful to have them as my parents. They didn't throw me out and didn't turn their backs on me. Mama tried to console me. Dad sat and listened.

"You cannot go through life blaming yourself," said Dad. "Jeff knew what he was doing, he knew he took advantage of you."

"Mom, he told me he loved me. He didn't want to love me. He started out hating me and he did everything out of spite because he thought I was a rich snob, and I was. He told me he fell in love with me even though he didn't want to. Mom, this is unbearable."

I got up from the table and left my parents there crying. I went to my room and fell on my bed, gasping for breath.

After a few minutes, Mom knocked on my door she had more words to say to me. " your father and I were talking, you and I are going to stay with your grandmother in Richmond. We'll find you a doctor down there and stay until you have this baby. After that, we will decide what to do."

"Mom, I want to stay and go to Jeff's funeral or at least go to the funeral home. I know Tony and

Michelle will probably go. Maybe they'll take me with them Jeff didn't want to go to Richmond now I have to go I want to see him before I go."

"I can take you if you want me to."

"No, Mom, I'm going to have to face his mother by myself. I don't know what I'm going to say to her. It's my fault that Jeff killed himself. It's my fault."

"That's not true. Jeff had problems way before he started seeing you. If it's anybody's fault, it's his parents'. You told me they were fighting all the time and drove Jeff crazy. Didn't he tell you he wasn't good enough for you?"

"Yes, he did, but he was good enough. He was more than good enough for me, Mama. I don't know what to ask you anymore. I don't know what to do. All I know for sure is that I hurt."

"Let me tell you what I did. There is one thing better for you than it was for me. At least you know what happened to him. To this day, I don't know what happened to your father. He's gone and I've never heard from again. Take it one day at a time because that's all you can do. Just one day at a time, Princess, one day at a time."

"Mom, Jeff kept telling me that he and I had no yesterday, that we had no tomorrow, we just had that moment together. Mama, the moments are gone; there's no more."

"One day at a time, baby, one day at a time." She got up and left me there wondering what was coming next.

It didn't take long for all the rumors to start in a small town like Galax. Some said that Jeff hanged himself, others said that the cops did it. But one thing's for sure, they never took Jeff's belt and that's what he hung himself with. I didn't know what his parents were going through.

I listened to the radio for the funeral announcements. I was going to his funeral or at least I'd go see his body at the viewing. One of my biggest fears was to confront his parents. I had a big decision to make, would I tell his parents I was carrying Jeff's baby? I didn't know what to do. I think my mom and dad wanted me to keep it a secret. People think it's shameful and a disgrace to have a baby out of wedlock and I kept forgetting I was only fifteen.

The next morning while having breakfast, Mom turned the radio on to listen for funeral announcements. Every morning on the local radio station, they reported the latest deaths in Galax and surrounding counties. They named the survivors of the family and told the time of the viewing and the funeral and where it would be held.

I called Michelle that afternoon and asked her to go with me. She said yes and offered to pick me up with Tony to see Jeff for the last time. But this time, I wasn't sneaking to see him.

About 5 o'clock, they came for me. On the way to the funeral home, Michelle asked, "Are you ok?"

I looked up at her, "No, I'm not ok."

Michelle was crying, and of course, there were tears running down my cheeks. Tony was listening and driving. We got to the funeral home where there were a lot of people there from high school that knew Jeff. We got in line to view his body. Jeff's mother was standing beside the coffin greeting people. Tony pointed out Jeff's father sitting in the corner. When we finally got to see Jeff, the three of us stood there looking at him. He almost had a smile on his face. As I stared at his pretty face, long hair, and his broad shoulders, I wanted to touch him, but I didn't. Then Tony introduced us to his mother.

"Mrs. Gray, I'm Tony.
Jeff and I were very good friends
on the football team.
This is Michelle, my girlfriend,
and this is Princess, a friend of Jeff's."
Then Jeff's mother shouted,
"I know who she is!
She's the one who was with Jeff that night!
She's the reason he killed himself!
I know who the snobby bitch is!"
The place got quiet.
"I loved Jeff," I said.
"I loved him more than you did!
He came to me because he had no peace!
He loved me!
He was leaving that night!
He loved me!"
Then his mother answered
"How could you love him
more than his own mother?"
Then I screamed out loud,

"Because I'm carrying his baby!"
There was total silence.
You could hear a pin drop.
I did it,
I told everybody I was carrying Jeff's baby
I said it out loud for everybody to hear,
and the silence was deafening.

Michelle grabbed me by the arm and walked me to the car. People were staring at us as we walked out. Tony drove us away and I asked him not to take me home. I wasn't ready to go there. I didn't know what I was going to tell Mom. I'm sure the word would get back to her that I told everybody. I couldn't help it. Michelle turned around in the seat and looked at me. She never said a word, but from the expression on her face, I could tell she was shocked.

We drove to the Dairy Bar and ordered a drink. Michelle finally asked. "You're pregnant? Why didn't you tell me?"

"I really wasn't sure what to do after Jeff killed himself. My time of the month didn't start. I'm pretty sure I'm pregnant."

Tony had his head down on the steering wheel, listening to me and Michelle. What else was he going to do?

Michelle asked him, "Take us to Fries to kill a little time."

Tony started the car and we drove towards Fries. I really didn't want to go there. I remembered that day up behind the dam and what a wonderful day

Jeff and I had together. It was that day Jeff told me he wasn't going back to school, he was leaving with his family to go to Richmond. We drove up above the cotton mill and parked on the side of the road. I could see behind the dam. I knew around the curve was a sandy bar where Jeff and I spent the day. We got out of the car. It was almost dark.

"What are you going to do, Princess? Are you going to quit school?"

"I think Mom and I going to go to Richmond to have this baby."

"Are you going to keep it?"

"Yes, I'm keeping Jeff's baby. It's my baby. Mother asked me if I wanted to put it up for adoption, but I don't. I'm going to keep it, Michelle, whatever happens. Mom and Dad said they would support me whatever I decided to do. I didn't realize what good parents I've got compared what Jeff lived with. I've got very good parents."

Michelle hugged me, and we cried together. "I'm sorry, Princess. I'm sorry all this happened. You were so happy with Jeff."

"We can see what kind of mother he had. Jeff was always fighting the world, always fighting. He told me once that I was his refuge, that I was his peace of mind. I love him so much, Michelle. I don't have a clue what I'm to do now. I'll go to Richmond to have his baby and try to get back in school somewhere. I don't know if I'll come back to Galax or not. I just have to go and see what happens. I wasn't going to say anything about me being pregnant, but it's too late. I told everybody in the funeral home tonight and now the whole town knows. Jeff Gray killed himself because of me, he got me pregnant."

Michelle wanted to blame Jeff. "He got you pregnant, and he couldn't take it!"

" Jeff didn't know I was pregnant. I didn't tell him because I really wasn't sure. If I hadn't asked him to meet me that night, he would still be alive, I killed him; I know I killed him."

Tony said, "You didn't, Princess. I knew all about Jeff's home life. We were close friends, and he would tell me about it. I'm going to tell you something that I haven't told you before. Jeff told me about a week ago that he wished he could take you with him, and that you're the first thing he's ever really loved that much. You're the first love that made him feel like he was a real man for a change. Princess, he didn't kill himself because of you, he killed himself because he lost hope, being with you, living in peace. Jeff was really a deeply caring person, but when you live in a place with no peace and you witness the things that his parents did in front of him you feel like you can't escape the pain. Princess, you were his peace and you were his hope, but he knew he couldn't live up to the standards he thought you deserved. It's not your fault, Princess. You got to believe that. Jeff had a lot of problems, and he told me you were helping him with those problems. You gave him confidence in himself. So, it wasn't because of you; he just lost hope. His family pushed him too far, and it drove him over the edge."

I smiled through watery eyes and said. “I want to thank you for giving me one of the best summers, I know I’ll never experience one like this again. I can’t because the one I experienced it with is gone and there’ll never be another like Jeff. Even with all of his problems, I loved him.”

Michelle asked Tony to take us home. I had no idea what I was going to tell Mom when I got there. I knew she’d find out so, I might as well tell the truth. As we drove up to my house, I knew I was in Tony’s car for the last time.

Mom was waiting on me, just like I knew she would. I asked her to come to my room and left Dad in the living room. He knew it was girl talk. I sat on the edge of my bed and she sat in a chair beside it. She asked how I handled going to the funeral home and seeing Jeff and his parents.

I went ahead and told her. “I’ve got something to tell you, Mom, and you’re not going to like it.”

“What happened? Is everything ok? How are his parents taking it?”

“Mom, when we were in line to view Jeff’s body, *Tony was introducing me and Michelle to his mother* when she stopped Tony and said she knew who I was. She said I was the reason he killed himself. It hurt me so bad. I told her I loved Jeff and then she asked how I could love him more than his own mother, out of nowhere I just blurted it out that I’m carrying Jeff’s baby. Mama, everybody in the funeral home heard me. Now the whole town knows.”

My mother is staring at me, and I could tell she didn't know what to say. "Princess, you may not be pregnant. It's too early to be sure. You're only a few days late. You don't know for sure. You could start your monthly cycle anytime. It's going to take at least, probably four weeks before you really know for sure. We haven't seen a doctor yet, so I know you think you are, but you may not be. We've got to go to Richmond and get you a doctor. I don't want to stay around here. I've talked with your father and in the next two weeks, we're going to Richmond."

"But, Mom, what am I going to do about school?"

"I haven't figured it out yet. Maybe when we get to Richmond we can get someone to come in and homeschool you, so you don't get behind. Whatever happens, Princess, we're not going to let you get behind in your education. If you're pregnant, we'll do what we have to do.

You say you want to keep Jeff's baby, and you don't want to put it up for adoption, then that's what we're going to do. But I'm going to make sure that you don't get behind. So, we're leaving in the next two weeks before school starts. We'll stay in Richmond with your grandmother. I haven't told her yet."

"Mom, I want to call Michelle. I want to ask her to come to see me to tell her what I'm doing."

"I guess you should, but I hope there's not too much talk in this town, but we can't help that now. Just wait a day or two. Let things calm down and wait until after they bury Jeff, then we will go to your grandmother in Richmond."

I gave Michelle a call and told her to come and see me. In my room with the door shut, we talked.

"Michelle, I'm going to tell you what I'm going to do. After they bury Jeff, Mom and I going to Richmond and stay with my grandmother. We're going to find me a doctor down there, but Mom told me something I didn't think about. I think I'm only a week late or more, I don't know. But Mom thinks there's a good chance I may not be pregnant, maybe it's too soon and my period could start anytime."

Michelle said, "Maybe you're not. Princess, let me ask you something, why did you blurt out at the funeral home that you are pregnant with Jeff's baby?"

"Because his mother hurt me. She didn't love him as much as I do. I know she didn't."

"I guess a mother's love is much different than between two lovers."

"Michelle, I only know that the more I was with Jeff, the more I loved him." Then I started crying. "Michelle it's my fault Jeff is dead it's my fault!"

"How can you say that. He was leaving!"

"Because I asked him to see me one more time. I asked him to make love to me one more time, Michelle. If I had not asked him, he wouldn't have been there that night. It's my fault! It's my fault! I cry all the time, it grieves me so much, and I'm the reason Jeff is dead. That's hard to live with."

She hugged me and told me it wasn't really my fault, but deep down I couldn't get that out of my heart. He was gone forever and I had to leave town.

Then I asked, "I was going to ask you and Tony to take me to Jeff's grave, but I guess I'll ask Mom to do it. After they bury him, I'm going to go in that graveyard by myself and I'm going to sit at the foot of Jeff's grave. Michelle, I'm going to talk to him. I've got some things I want to ask him. I know I won't get an answer, but I don't care, Michelle. I've got to talk to him before I leave Galax."

Michelle was crying with me. "You act like you're never coming back. We're not going to stop being friends."

"I'll have a baby to take care of. You'll be busy going to school another year. You'll graduate. Mom's talking about getting me a tutor to keep me up with my schoolwork, but I know trying to take care of a baby is going to be hard."

"I've got to go, Princess. I want to tell you something. We've had the best summer of our lives. Will you see me before you leave?"

"Yes, you know I will. You're my best friend ever."

We went downstairs and Michelle left. Then Mom wanted to talk to me. We sat at the kitchen table like we usually do for family talks. "Mama, will you take me to the Allen graveyard where Jeff is going to be buried? I want to talk to him."

"Yes, I'll take you when you want to go."

"I want to go at night, mama. I want you to leave me there after dark because, after dark, Jeff and I always met there. I want to talk to him, do you understand?"

"Yes, I understand, and I'll take you."

The day of Jeff's funeral, Michelle called when it was over and told me that Tony went and that he was surprised there were so few people there. The coach and some of the football players were there and family members were asked to be pallbearers. The next day, I asked Mom to take me that evening after dark.

On the way to the cemetery, Mom asked me if I was sure I wanted to do this. I made it clear to her that I did. We pulled behind the church. Since the grave was fresh, I could see it before I got out of the car. "Princess, I'm going to wait here for you. Take as much time as you need, but I'd feel better if I stayed with you. I'll let you be private with Jeff because I know that's what you want."

I got out of the car, walked to the foot of his grave and stood there. Then I asking him some questions.

"If you knew I was pregnant,
would you have killed yourself?"
Now my voice was cracking
"I don't know if you can hear me,
but I'm going to talk to you anyway.
I want to tell you how lonely I feel
knowing you're never coming back.
The summer we had together

I don't know how to describe it.
I read a book one time
where a couple had a magical summer.
Our summer was beyond magical.
Jeff, I miss you.
I want to let you know something before I leave,
I'm pretty sure I'm pregnant.
I'm going to Richmond in a few days
before school starts to get a doctor.
I promise you, Jeff,
I will take care of your baby
and it will never have to live the hell as you did.
I don't know if I'll ever get married.
You told me there's no yesterday, no tomorrow
It's just this moment we have together
I promise you, Jeff.
I plan to have a lifetime of moments with our baby."

I stayed there at the foot of Jeff's grave, standing in the moonlight. Out of the corner of my eye, I could see mother walking towards me. She came up beside me and put her arm around me. I laid my head on her shoulder, we both cried. I didn't want to leave, but Mom helped me back to the car, and we drove back home.

Chapter 16

Rumors spread with all kinds of lies about why Jeff killed himself. Most decided I was to blame, and I felt that way. If I hadn't called him that night, Jeff would have left. Dad was hurt by all the rumors he heard about me and Jeff, our secret rendezvous, he never stopped loving me. Whatever Mom and I decided to do, he was supportive.

The school would start in a few weeks, but not for me. I had to leave. I called Michelle to come over to say goodbye. We had been friends since childhood, and it was hard to leave her. She was there when it all happened. We shared everything together, even our first love. When she came, we sat on the front porch.

Michelle's emotions were obvious, and so were mine when she said, "I'm going to miss you. School won't be the same."

"I already miss you. What a wonderful summer we had. Why did he have to end it like this? It was my fault."

"You've got to stop blaming yourself. Jeff had a lot of problems way before he met you. Don't you think sooner or later this would happen to him?"

"No, Michelle, it's my fault. He told me that the first day he kissed me that he was sure that I would smack him. There was something in his kiss, I don't know how to explain it, but it's like a light bulb went on in my brain. I fell in love with him that day. I felt bad about making fun of him. I could feel the pain he had living with his family. Michelle, we have everything, and the best thing we've got is good parents. He had none of that. Mom and I are leaving in the morning, and I don't know when I'll be back. We're going to live with my grandmother. Mom is going to find a teacher to come in and keep me up to speed with my schoolwork. I've got to find a doctor. Michelle, I'm going to have a baby. I'm not sad about it. I'm not worried. I want Jeff's baby. I know I may change my mind when I have to get up and feed it and change its diaper. I know all that's coming, but Jeff is gone and he left me part of him. I know that sounds crazy. I'm too young to know how serious it is to be a mother, but I can't wait to hold Jeff's baby – my baby. Am I crazy, Michelle?"

"Yes, you're crazy, but Jeff was crazy too. You'll never be in love like that again, Princess. Now you have to be a grown-up before your time. I'm trying to keep it real between me and Tony I can't come out and say I love him. I love what we're doing together. This is high school, who knows what will happen when we graduate or where we'll end up. I don't know what college I want to attend. Tony and I are making memories, and I'm having a great time, but after this happened to you," she paused. "Princess, I never believed in a thousand years it would end like this."

We hugged each other and I told her, "I've had to mature really quick, and it's not easy."

We wiped away our tears, and I watched Michelle walk out of sight up the street. I had a new world in front of me and I had no idea how I was going to handle it, but I had to do it whether I liked it or not.

The next morning, we had breakfast with my father. I've never seen Dad cry before, but he lay down his fork, looked over at me and said, "Princess, you know I love you very much, and I'm sorry this happened to you, but I hope you see why I was so against you seeing Jeff Gray. I just want to let you know this doesn't stop me loving you, and I'm going to be there for you. So please go do what you have to do, and when you bring the baby home it will be my grandchild because it's part of you."

We all sat there crying. My father was a great man, and he never stopped loving me even though I disobeyed him. I was determined to see Jeff and nothing could stop me, I was paying the price.

We all hugged as a family. The car was packed the night before, we were ready to go. On the way out of town, I asked Mom to let me go by Jeff's grave one more time. I walked through the gate in the cemetery and stood at the foot of his grave. I never said anything, I just looked. I didn't take long before I got back in the car with Mom and we drove away.

She looked over at me and asked, "Are you ok, baby?"

"No, Mom. I know I have to be ok now. I'm going to be a mother, and I'm going to ask you all kinds of questions between here and Richmond about what I should expect. Will my breasts start filling up with milk?" I paused. "Mama, I'm scared."

"That's normal, You're experiencing new things. When your body starts changing and adapting to the baby inside you, your instincts will take over because you'll protective of the new human being that you are responsible for. You'll go to great lengths to protect your baby. If you're any kind of mother, your baby will come first in your life. I'll be here with you. I tell you what I experienced with you and how afraid I was. I was in the same situation, but I still don't know what became of your father."

"Mom, do you hate him?"

"Yes, I do, but let's not talk about it. Things can't be changed now. You've heard it all before."

I sat back in the seat and relaxed. We didn't speak a whole lot. Mom called Grandmother and told her we were coming, but she didn't tell her why. I guess she'd tell her what really happened when we got there. My grandmother was a good woman, but I was sure she was going to carry on about this, so I had to be prepared.

We pulled in front of her house. It was so hot and humid in Richmond, August, Sweat was running down my face. Grandmother came out, hugged me first thing. We went into the house and sat at her kitchen table. I can't remember all the conversations that we had that day, but she never disappointed me. She supported, looking at my mother, remember what she went through when she was pregnant with me.

I did overhear one morning before I got out of bed, the two of them were talking about when Jim left. I know I was hurting to hear them talk. My grandmother never got over my mom getting pregnant before she got married. That's just way it was back then, and it hadn't changed much in Southwest Virginia, you had your baby that's what was expected.

After we got settled in, Mom started calling doctors and finally made an appointment. I was unnerved, and scared. I had to leave my home and come down here where nobody knew me. When we got in the doctor's office, he shook his head at me because I was so young and pregnant.

He asked, "Miss Grant, how old are you?"

"fifteen."

"And you're late on your monthly cycle?"

"Yes, sir."

"How many days are you late?"

"If I timed it right, I'm probably about four weeks, I guess."

"You didn't go to your family doctor and get some testing done"

"No, sir, there was so much going on. You see, Doctor, my boyfriend committed suicide. He didn't know I was pregnant, in all the commotion and the fact that we were not married we came to Richmond to live with my grandmother, to be honest, we came here not to embarrass my family, I want this baby."

"Ok, then take this cup and give me a urine sample. Leave it in the restroom, a nurse will pick it up. Then come back in here, I would like to do a physical." I went to the bathroom and tried to pee in a cup. I was so nervous I could barely get the cup full. I put the top on it and came back into the doctor's examining room.

The nurse gave me a robe to put on so the doctor could examine me. He came back in, listened to my heart and looked in my ears and eyes. While we were in there the nurse knocked on the door and handed the doctor a piece of paper. Then he told the nurse to draw some blood. He looked at it and told me to get my clothes on while he went to the waiting room to ask my mom to come in with us.

And then he said, "Your urine has traces of blood. You told me you think it's only been four weeks?"

"Yes, about four weeks."

"Have you had any discomfort in urinating, have you been crapping?"

"No, sir."

"Have you been spotting blood in your panties?"

"No, sir."

"Young lady, go to the waiting room and wait for your mother. I want to speak to her."

"Is something wrong?"

"No, but you're so young, I hope there are no complications in your pregnancy. I just want to speak with your mother and tell her to keep a close eye on you in the next two weeks, then come back to see me."

I stepped out and listened at the door. I was wondering what was going on.

"Mrs. Grant," said the doctor. "Keep a close watch on your daughter. The next couple of weeks may be critical, her first pregnancy because of her youth. It's just a precautionary suggestion on my part."

"What makes you say that?"

"She's so young I just want to make sure that everything goes well, but be prepared just in case."

"Ok."

Before they could catch me listening, I hurried back to the waiting room. We stopped at the front desk and made another appointment.

On the way home, I asked, "What did the doctor say, Mom?"

"He wants me to keep a close watch on you because it's your first pregnancy and you're young. I'm going to call a couple of retired teachers to see if they want the job tutoring you at least four hours a day so you don't get behind in your schoolwork. Do you want to do anything the rest the day? Do you want to see Richmond? We can go to Byrd Park."

"Mom, don't get mad, but you know where I would like to go?"

"Where, why would I get mad?" Mom, please take me up Riverside and show me the big boulders in the middle of James River where you spent that magical summer with my real father."

She almost ran off the road. She pulled off to the side and looked at me and said, "No, Princess. I can't go back there. Don't ask me to."

I never asked her to do that again, but I could feel what she was feeling, and I know she knew what I was feeling. She could not relive those times, and I was trying so hard not to forget mine.

She hired a teacher to come in every day. I went to school in Grandmother's house. It was a good thing that my folks had money because it wasn't cheap to keep my schooling up to par. The summer in Richmond in August was unbearableble with the humidity. Their school started, and I missed going to my high school. I missed Galax.

By September, the evenings were cool, but the days were still hot. Before my doctor's appointment was due, I went to the bathroom to pee. When I pulled my panties down, there were blood spots in them and I freaked out. I didn't know what to think. I went straight to Mom when I got out of the bathroom.

"Mom, I've got blood in my panties."

"Is this the first time you noticed that?"

"Yes, just a few moments ago."

"I better call the doctor's office and take you to see what's going on." She made the appointment for the next day. I was anxious to find out what was wrong.

After the doctor examined me, he told us, "I don't think you can carry this baby to term. I'm not 100% sure, but it doesn't look good."

"What do you think wrong?" Mom asked.

"It's possible it's a false pregnancy. If it is, when you're not expecting it she may start cramping. If that happens, get her to the emergency room immediately and they'll call me."

It hurt me to think that I might not carry this baby to term. Thank God Grandmother and my mom loved and supported me. If Jeff only had that kind of love in his home, maybe this could've been different, but he didn't. Now it was a waiting game.

The next few days I felt ok; Mom gave me pads to put in my panties. I was still spotting, but there was no pain. I hadn't experienced morning sickness or anything not what I was told to expect.

Grandmother had a vegetable garden where she was picking green beans one afternoon. My teacher had just left for the day, and we all sat at the kitchen table stringing and snapping beans for supper. It was a sunny pleasant day until we heard a knock at the front door.

Mom went to the door to see who it was. When we didn't hear anyone, Grandmother decided to get up and look around the corner to see what was going on. There was still no one talking in the living room. I paid no attention at first. I thought maybe it was a door-to-door salesman.

Grandmother came back and sat down. She had a look on her face that I don't know how to describe. I had to speak up to get her attention. "Grandmother, who is it? Who is at the front door?"

She shook her head but didn't answer.

"Where is Mom?" I stood up to go to the door, but Grandmother put her hand on my shoulder and said, "You stay right here. Your mother's busy."

"Busy. What do you mean busy? I don't hear voices. Did she answer the front door?" We waited. I didn't understand what was going on and decided to see for myself.

When I went to get up again, Grandmother ordered me, "Stop, Princess!"

I didn't pay her any attention. I went into the living room where my mother was standing, looking at a man. "Mom, are you ok?"

She looked at me and told me, "Princess, go back in the kitchen."

"Mom, who is this man?"

Then he asked, "Connie, is this your daughter?"

In a stern voice, she answered, "Yes."

"Aren't you going to introduce me to her?"

"No, I'm not. I want you to leave here right now. Don't you ever come back!"

"But, Connie."

"You listen to me. Leave right now, or I'm calling the police. Get out of here, and don't you ever come back!"

He turned around, and walked back to the gate and drove off. Mom stood there watching him drive away. I couldn't understand what just happened.

"Mom, why did you talk to him that way? Who is he?"

She was trembling and breathing hard as she looked out the door. "Princess, go back and sit with your grandmother. I'll be in there in a moment."

I went back to sit down with my grandmother. Everyone was acting strange. My mother was angry. At least, I think she was. While I sat there, I asked grandmother, "Who was that man what's going on?"

Grandmother answered me "your mother will have to tell you."

"Why?"

Mother came back in and sat down. She was in a daze like she was somewhere else in her mind. I asked her. "Are you going to tell me who that man was what is going on?"

Grandmother spoke up. "Connie, you might as well tell her."

Mom shook her head and looked at me. "He's nobody, Princess. Nobody you need to be concerned about, just someone from the past."

My grandmother said, "Connie, get this over with now. She is not going to be satisfied after what just happened, and you are not either. So, it's time you told her the truth."

Mother sat for a moment and looked at me. "Princess, that man is your real father."

"What! Why didn't you! Why didn't you talk to him! Why didn't you tell him about me? That was my real father!"

"Because he doesn't deserve to know about you! He walked out on me over fifteen years ago and he walked right back in like nothing ever happened, hell no!"

Grandmother shook her head and asked, "Have you told her that Doug is not her real father?"

Mother looked up, "Yes, I had to tell her when she got involved with the boy who got her pregnant. I knew what she was headed for, and I had to tell her what happened to me." Grandmother shook her head and looked at me.

"Princess you're so young for all this to happen to you I'm sorry you had to find out about everything this way. I tried to tell your mother the same thing over fifteen years ago."

My mother jumped up from the table angry. "Ok mama, you'll never let me live it down! I know it's my fault! All of this is my fault because I wouldn't listen to you! Love blinded me, just like it blinded her, so it's my fault! Do you think I don't blame myself every day! That's the reason I had to tell her about Doug and how he took us in and took care of us. Go ahead mother just keep blaming me!" My grandmother got up and went into the next room.

I couldn't take it anymore and I shouted at both of them "Please! Please! Stop it! Stop it! Both of you, you're killing me trying to blame somebody for what I did. It's not your fault that I got pregnant; it's my fault! It's my fault that Jeff killed himself. Please both of you, please shut up!!" I had to shake myself to realize what I just said. It made me very angry with my grandmother blaming my mother and my mother blamed herself while I was the one sitting here pregnant. It was nobody's fault but mine. My Mom was right. Sometimes you think you're in love, but you're blind. And I was still blind in love with Jeff and all this was hurting me so bad I couldn't take it anymore!

The next morning while we were eating breakfast, everything seemed ok, but nobody was talking. I didn't dare ask any questions. It was just too much for my mother. She was right. I was pregnant and after fifteen years, her past knocked on the door. I knew what she was feeling.

After breakfast, I insisted on helping grandmother wash the dishes. I got ready for the teacher to show up and have my four-hour session with her until it was lunchtime. Grandmother and Mom both knew I wasn't going to let it rest now that I know my real father is alive. What was I supposed to do? I was so confused. I was fifteen and pregnant and the father that I was told was dead, now alive. I kept praying to God. I felt like this was all my fault just because I wouldn't listen to my mother. I loved Jeff and I went all the way with him and I would've gone even further if he would have gone with me.

The tutor showed up, and we went through my studies. I was supposed to be paying attention. I tried hard to concentrate until we got through it. Late afternoon was worse. My grandmother and my mom were not talking. I couldn't stop blaming myself for all of this. I waited till Mom went to the store, and while Grandmother was cooking supper, I had an opportunity to talk to her.

"Grandmother, let me ask you something?"

"Ok, What is it?"

"Is this my fault? If I listened to Mom in the beginning, none of this would have happened. It's all my fault!"

She took a moment, sat back, looked at me. "Princess, you're just like your mother. I'm sure I told your mother the same things that she was telling you not to do. Your grandfather and I never liked him from the beginning. I don't know why. He was a nice guy, but we just had that feeling as parents. I can't explain anything about that, but you can't blame yourself for this. And you can't blame your mother. It's just life.

I was so mad at your mother, but she was determined to be a good mother to you, and your grandfather and I were going to help her. She went to work, met Doug, he married your mother. Your mother gave birth to you, so that's the good that came out of all of it. I guess it took the pressure off of me and your grandfather. We couldn't have afforded to give you what Doug has given both of you. I am so grateful to him. So, don't blame yourself. We all make decisions and we're blinded because of the situation or the relationship we get ourselves in. You didn't give any thought to the consequences because we're in a world of fantasy, and fantasy worlds come with a big price. You've paid it, and your mother paid for it, so it's over.

You've got a good life, and if you have this baby, be the best mother that you can be because that's what your mother has done for you. Don't get mad at your mother and don't blame yourself. This is where we are and you've got to handle it, so, don't blame yourself."

Mom came back from the grocery store, Grandmother almost had supper ready. I tried to be pleasant while we were eating, no one brought up Jim again. We all three started talking among ourselves again, never bringing up the problems.

When the sun went down, we sat on the front porch. Grandmother lived in a nice neighborhood, and I never gave television a thought while I was there. There was just too much going on to watch television. I knew I was in a special time in my life, and I felt like this last year I had grown from a little girl into a woman.

I would be sixteen soon, but it didn't seem like that would make a difference. The stress of the last day and a half took some life out of me. I felt bad, and I kissed grandmother and Mom goodnight. I went to my room before I knew it, I was asleep.

I don't know what time it was, but I was awakened by a pain in my lower abdomen. I was cramping and the pain was getting worse. I went to the bathroom and sat on the commode. The pain got intense and I screamed out for Mom. "Mom, Mom! Please come here!"

Mom knocked on the bathroom door. "What's wrong, Princess? What's going on?"

"Mom, I'm cramping badly. It hurts. It hurts bad!!" "Ok, baby. As soon as you can, get some clothes on. I'll get the car started and we'll rush you to the emergency room. The nurses will call the doctor when we get there!"

On the way to the hospital, the pain was not letting up. Finally, we were in the emergency room and the staff took me to the back. Mom went with me, and Grandmother waited on us. They had my legs up in stirrups when the doctor got there. He opened me up and sucked everything out. I overheard him say to the nurses, "There's no development of a fetus and no early stage of a baby."

"Miss Grant, this is a false pregnancy. I want to keep you overnight. We'll do a D&C tomorrow and then your mother can take you home. There was no formation or any early stages of a baby here. There should be no more pain."

"When you sucked it all out, the pain went away," I told him.

The doctor left. I looked up at Mom and said, "I guess it's all over."

"Baby, your life is just starting. I'll be back in the morning. After the doctor does what he has to do, we'll go home."

I spent the night thinking about everything that happened, and how my summer ended up. I didn't know how I felt. I guess I was relieved. There was still a lot in front of me when I got back to Galax.

The doctor was there early the next morning, it didn't take long for him to examine me. Then, mother and grandmother came in. "How are you feeling?" Mom asked. "I feel better."

"You should be happy, Princess," Grandmother said. "You can go back to school now, back to Galax. You've only missed about a month. Hopefully, you can pick up where you left off."

"I'm not sure that I'm happy. I am relieved, I'm not going to be a mother, I'm going to have to face a lot of people when I get back to Galax. I don't know what to think."

Mother said, "I'm not going to care what people think anymore. I've kept a secret all of these years that Doug was not your father. I'm going to ask you to do one thing for me, Princess. Please, don't you ever tell anybody in Galax. I'm not going to tell Doug that we saw Jim."

"Yes, Princess. For all we're concerned, Jim is dead," Grandmother said. "Anyway, he shouldn't be brought back up to interfere in your life ever again. It wouldn't be fair to Doug. So, for all of us, never let anybody in Galax know that Doug is not your father."

"I've lived with thinking my real father was dead until now. Only a little while ago Mom told me that Doug wasn't my father. She didn't know if Jim was alive or not. Now that I know he's alive, I'm not going to say anything to anybody. Mom, I've embarrassed the family too much."

"Don't you ever say that again, Princess, don't you ever think that again. Let's get you better now and we'll take you home after you have this procedure done. Mom, why don't you come with us?" My mother asked my grandmother

"Lord no, Connie. Richmond is my home; I'm not leaving here till I absolutely have to. Then you put me in a nursing home. All of my friends are here, and it's the only place I know. Thank you for asking me, but no."

The nurses came and got me to take me to get the D&C done. It didn't take long till I was back in my room and they were doing the release papers so Mom could take me back to grandmother's house. When we got there, my mom called Doug and gave him the news that it was a false pregnancy and that we were coming home. I knew he would be happy to hear it.

That afternoon, I was back at Grandmothers. Soon, I'd be going home back to Galax. I didn't realize all the questions I would have to answer, like what happened to the baby. I didn't think about it; I was just glad to be going home. The pain of Jeff Gray was deep in my heart and my real father was alive, but I promised mother I never said anything about that. I loved Doug, and he was my father.

The four-hour trip from Richmond to Galax was nice. It was fall, and all the leaves were turning their brilliant colors. The closer to Galax, the more anxious I got. When we got to the town limits, I wanted to stop by Jeff's grave and tell him what happened. Gillespie Lane, across the street from the bowling alley. That's where it all happened, the last time Jeff made love to me, the last night I saw him. Mom agreed to stop to let me see Jeff's family graveyard. We drove in behind the church, I sat in the car looking at the gate until I finally got out.

Mom rolled down her window and asked,

"Are you sure you want to do this?"

"Yes, Mom, I do."
"Princess, you've got to let this go."
"How do I do that?"
"I don't know, baby. I really don't know."
I stepped through the gate
and walked to the foot of his grave.
"Jeff, I'm back home.
I wasn't really pregnant.
It was a false pregnancy, I'm sorry.
Now I have nothing of you but a memory.
Why did you do this Jeff?
We could've worked it out.
At least you would be alive!
Jeff, I am so damn guilty.
This is all my fault.
I'm the reason you're in the ground here.
I'm the reason.
I'm so lonely,
and you're never coming back."
I fell to my knees screaming.
"Jeff! Jeff! Oh God, why did you do this!"

Mom came running over and helped me up off the ground. "Princess, baby, you can't do this. You've got to stop blaming yourself."

"Mama, I remember that night we got caught at the bowling alley. The sheriff told Jeff that he was under arrest for statutory rape. Mama, he didn't rape me. I gave myself to him. Mama, does age of consent mean I was too young to know what I was doing? Does it mean I was too young to love Jeff?"

"Baby, it's not that. Love has no age limit, but it has a maturity about it. I had to tell you about your father your real father. I was so in love with him I would've done anything to be with him. That's the reason I was so afraid for you, Princess. I knew exactly what you were going through and it brought back so many painful memories to me, but always remember baby, there's a fine line between love and hate."

Mother helped me back to the car. We stopped by a filling station to wash my face. She didn't want Dad to see me with my face red from crying.

When we got home, the first thing Dad did was hug me tightly and kiss me on my forehead. "I'm glad you're home, baby. This house is so empty when you're not here."

We both cried and he whispered in my ear, "I'm sorry, Princess. I'm sorry you had to go through this, but we all need to settle down and be a tight family. From now on I'll do everything I can to make sure you're both happy."

I was glad to be home. All of this happened so quickly, and I was anxious to call Michelle to let her know I was back. I was going back to school as soon as Mom made the arrangements. I didn't know she had called Michelle's mother and told her we were coming, when I called Michelle, she was anticipating my call.

"Michelle, it's m I'm back!"

"I know. Mom told me you were coming home. I'm glad you're back; I missed you so."

"Can you come and see me?"

"Yes, give me a few minutes to get my things together. I'll be by a bit later. Are you going to be home all day?"

"Yes, I have no place to go. I'm anxious to talk to you and see what's happened since I've been gone." After I hung up, I told Mom that Michelle was coming.

When she showed up, I said, "Let's go up to my room so we can have some privacy and talk. What's been going on since I was out of town?"

"Not much. It's been the same routine."

"How's Tony?"

"He's ok"

"Are you still seeing each other?"

"Yes, but things are changing. I mean, Princess you and Jeff were different than Tony and me. I mean we have a great time together, but this is just high school. We're not going to get married, we're still just dating."

"I guess I was remembering the summer we had. Things seemed wonderful; I thought it was for you too."

"Things were wonderful, but what Jeff did change everything. It certainly changed you."

"Yes, it did change me."

"When are you coming back to school?"

"Just as soon as mother gets me registered, I guess."

"Football season is almost over, and Thanksgiving is coming up. Princess, I haven't asked you what happened to your baby?"

"It was a false pregnancy. I started spotting, and Mom rushed me to the emergency room. The doctor sucked everything out of me, he said there was no sign of a baby. They gave me a D&C the next morning, and Mom and I decided to come home."

"A false pregnancy! Is that good or bad?"

"I don't know. On one hand, I'm relieved, but on the other, I loved Jeff so much that –" I paused. "I just don't know, Michelle. I guess I'm too young to know anything. I'm confused, anxious. I have a lot of regrets and a lot of guilt. I don't know how I feel, I just don't know."

"I'm glad you're home," she said, and we talk some more. "You had a birthday while you were away."

"Yes, I hadn't thought about it, but I hope Mom and Dad will let me get my driver's license so I can get a car."

"That will be nice. I'd better go. Maybe we can go to a movie or something. Let me know when you're coming back to school."

"I'm nervous about coming back to school and facing all those people. I'm sure they've said a lot of things about me by now."

"Don't pay any attention to what people say. It will soon pass. Nobody will remember it by the end of the school year." Michelle hugged me and left.

I stayed in my room for a while, thinking about what I'd been through and how I'd changed. For some reason, I felt out of place. I'm not sure how to describe how I felt, but it was like I was somebody else.

A few days went by and mother made all the arrangements for me to go back to school the following Monday. Michelle walked in with me and on the stairs, I could feel everyone's eyes on my back. Some people started sniggering and I'm sure they were making fun of me. Michelle and I used to make fun of other people, now they were making fun of me.

Then a boy named Todd came up in front of everybody and said, "Hey, Princess. If you need help at the barn with your horse Saturday morning I can help you."

All the other boys laughed loudly. That hurt my feelings. Michelle turned around and told him to shut up. I went to the front office to check-in and get my class assignments. There were a couple of new teachers I hadn't met. I tried to act like nothing ever happened. I didn't expect to get all the jokes and laughing behind my back. It's like my mother told me, what goes around comes around and it came back to me the hard way. I realized how much harm I had done to other people by making fun of them. I felt like the whole school was laughing at me.

It took a while to get used to being back in school. Things had changed for sure; it took a while for my life to get back to being normal, whatever that was.

By the end of the school year, it came time for prom. After my relationship with Jeff, it was hard to talk to other guys. I could tell all they wanted was something I wasn't ready to give them. Nobody asked me to the prom, and I didn't want to go anyway.

Mom and Dad knew a lot of things were bothering me. I didn't complain about it. I had the reputation of being easy for anyone to take advantage of. After our junior year, Tony and Michelle split up, but on good terms, of course. Michelle moved on like she said she would.

That summer, I got my driver's license, Dad bought me a secondhand car. Michelle and I did a lot of things together that summer. There was still one thing I couldn't do. I couldn't drive across the Low Water Bridge, go to Fries, or look at the dam. I knew I had to let it go, but it wasn't something that would happen overnight. It's crazy, but I can still hear a song or look at the mountains and be reminded of the memories. At the time it was really painful. I longed for them again but knowing it was impossible.

For the first time, a guy asked me out on a date. I decided to go, but I didn't tell Mom and Dad. I didn't know what they would think, and I didn't let him come by the house to pick me up. I met him and we drove around some and talked. We even made out some, and I liked it. I went out with him on a second date. That time he put his hands on my leg. I liked that, too, but I was afraid Jeff had gotten me addicted to sex. I resisted that guy and never went out with him again.

That summer, Michelle and I were sitting in my car at the Dairy Bar getting a bite to eat and I had another big surprise. Another car pulled up beside us, and I heard a voice that got my attention.

"Miss Grant."

"Yes," I said, as I turned to look who it was. I couldn't believe it. It was Jim, my real father. It startled me, and I wondered why he was there. "I saw you in Richmond at my grandmother's house."

"Yes," he said.

"Could I have a minute or two of your time?"

"I don't know. What is this about? I know you're a friend of my mother, but why would you want to speak to me?"

"I'll be truthful with you, ma'am, a long time ago I dated your mother before she got married. As a matter of fact, I was going to ask her to marry me, but something happened and I couldn't get back to her. I found out that she was in Galax and was married and had a family. I know I'll never be able to get a chance to tell her what happened and the reason that I didn't come back."

I didn't dare tell him that he was my real father I thought it was best to leave it alone because Michelle was there listening to every word we were saying and I promised Mom I would never bring that up to anybody in Galax.

"I thought maybe you would give your mother a message for me because I know she's not going to talk to me, and I can understand that, given what happened."

"Let's go over to the picnic table and we can talk." We took our drinks and food and went to the picnic table. I was anxious to hear why he didn't come back. Then, he told me his story.

"As I said, I was in love with your mother, and I was going to ask her to marry me but I did something really stupid. I was trying to make some easy, quick money and I did the wrong thing.

I stopped him and asked, "What did you do, rob a bank?"

Jim lowered his head and answered, "It was worse than robbing a bank. I had a friend that knew a man who was going to Mexico, driving back loads of marijuana and taking it to the big cities. So, I had a chance to make some quick money, a lot of money, and I went to Mexico in his car and loaded it with marijuana. Before I crossed the border, I got caught. I spent the last fifteen years in a Mexican jail and had no way of contacting anybody, no way of letting your mother know what happened to me. I was stuck and I spent a miserable fifteen years of my life thinking about what your mother must think of me. She would probably think how stupid I was to spend that much time in a foreign prison. It was unbearable at times."

Then I asked him, "Let me get this right, you didn't run out on her, you just couldn't get back. Is that what you're telling me?"

"Yes, that's what happened. There's no way now that I can ever explain it to her. It's too late anyway, she's married and has a daughter. I'm not trying to cause trouble; I just won't let her know that I didn't run out on her. I couldn't get back, and there was no way to get in touch with her."

Looking at Jim, I almost told him he was my real father, but I decided not to. He should never know.

Doug was the only father I knew. I was glad Jim didn't run out on my mother, but I didn't know if I should tell her or not. "You want me to tell Mom what you just told me?"

"You're the only chance I've got. I wouldn't dare go to your house. I might make your father mad at me for trying to talk to his wife. I'm just somebody from her past, I loved her deeply, I really wanted to marry her. Talking to you, seeing you, I'd say she did really well for herself. I'm sure you have a great, loving family, and I don't want to cause any trouble. I just need to get this off my chest. Would you please tell her what I told you?"

"Yes, I'll tell her. I don't know how I'm going to tell her. She may get upset with me for even talking to you, but I'm glad I did. I'll tell her."

"Thank you so much. Did you know you look just like your mother? You're a very pretty girl, and your Mom's a good person. I'm leaving Galax today, I better go. I just took a chance when I saw you. I know your mother had to go on with her life, and I'm trying to do the same. It can't be brought back and things can't be changed. It's too late, but I tell you something, young lady. I loved your mother. I guess I still do, I wouldn't be here trying to tell her what happened, but I thank you for helping me."

"That's a sad story, Jim. It seems like I've been in the middle of sad stories for the last couple of years. I'll tell her."

Jim shook my hand, got in his car and drove away. I never saw him again. I didn't dare tell him that he was my real father. I thought at the time, it would make it worse. To tell you the truth, I didn't know how I was going to tell Mom about this but I knew she deserved to know after all these years.

After Jim left, Michelle said something that also surprised me. "Princess, are you related to that man? You have similar facial features."

"Why would you say that?"

"I was listening to you talk, and I was looking at him. For some reason, I think you are related."

"That's crazy!"

"I know. Are you going to tell your mother what happened?"

"I told him I would. I don't know how, but I'm going to do it."

I took Michelle home and tried to get to my house early so I could talk to Mom before my dad got home. I don't know why I didn't tell Jim I was his daughter. It just seemed like everybody was going through so much and I thought I would just leave well enough alone. It wasn't going to change anything in my life. Now that I knew he didn't run out on Mom, I wanted to tell her, but I didn't want to make it worse. When I got home I asked her to come to sit with me on the front porch.

"Mom, I've got something to tell you.
Hear me out before you say anything.
Jim just left Galax, and he talked to me before he left."
"What do you mean he spoke to you?
What did he have to say to you?"
"Don't get excited, Mom.

He wanted me to tell you what happened to him."
"I don't think I want to hear what happened to him!"
"It's not what you think, Mom.
He didn't run out on you."
"Princess! You weren't there.
You don't know what he did.
He left, and he never showed up again
until we saw him at your grandmother's fifteen years later.
Now, what kind of excuse does he have for that!"
"Mom, he was going to ask you to marry him,
but he did something stupid."
"I was the one who was stupid
by believing him to start with!"
"Mom, let me tell you what he told me,
I believe him.
He told me he was going to ask you to marry him,
and he was trying to make some quick, easy money.
He knew a guy that made him an offer to go to Mexico
and drive back a car full of marijuana.
He got caught, and he's been in a Mexican jail.
He had no way of getting in touch with you or anybody
no way of telling you what happened.
He told me he went through hell."

" Did you tell him he was your father?"
"No, I didn't.
I told you I wouldn't tell anybody.
I kept my word.
I didn't tell him."

"Thank God. I'm glad you didn't tell him."
"Mom, Doug is the only father I knew.
He always will be."
"I thank you for telling me this, Princess.
Now I know he really loved me
and that he wasn't just using me.
It's closure for me, Princess.
It's closure."

I'm glad I told Mom all about that. I kept my word that I wouldn't tell anybody Doug was not my real father. I was glad Mom had closure, but I wanted to know if I'd find closure for myself.

The next school year was my senior year, and I was asked to the prom. That time I went and enjoyed myself. The memory of Jeff would never leave me, but I was recovering, trying to have a normal life, put it all behind me.

Looking back now, I was glad I went through that. It was the most exciting, wonderful time in my life, and the saddest time in my life at the same time. I graduated high school and attended Duke University in North Carolina. I met a man there and we got married. It didn't last more than seven years. We never had any children. I moved back to Galax with Mom after Dad passed away and opened up an accounting office, doing people's taxes.

Sometimes I get lonely thinking about the past, but that's when I go to Fries and walk in a beautiful park by the side of New River. I can now stand to look up at the dam and remember that magical summer I had.

When we experience our first love,
we never think about the end,
or that love has a cruel, painful side.
In the beginning, love is so wonderful.
I occasionally go by Jeff's grave and speak to him
knowing he can't hear me. I tell him
I was sorry it ended that way.
"That night we got caught having sex,
the sheriff told you
that I was not of legal age to have consensual sex.
"The age of consent."
I guess that meant I was too young
to know what I was doing
I was too young ......to love you."

Acknowledgement Page

"I wish to thank God for allowing me to be a writer. It would not happen without him"

---Jiffy Day

Talent Team

Tutorial Editor: Corrine Watson
She is responsible for improving my writing and teaching me

Proof Reader: Meg Hibbert
She has been with me from the start

Manager & Graphics: Logo Hub, Merissa Sachs
Merissa's advice is priceless and she has also been with me from the start.

Artist: Catherine Gural-Sandoe, free-lance artist
Her art focuses on drawing, painting and printmaking.

I want to thank all the good people in Southwest Virginia who have supported my writing and my storytelling!

Catherine Gural-Sandoe

free-lance artist

Catherine's Focus is in:
Drawing
Painting
Printmaking

She earned her Bacherlor of Arts degree in Studio Art from Hollins University.

Following school she worked as an instructor and volunteer at the Chestnut Creek School of the Arts in Galax, Virginia.

There she was inspired to grow as an artist and as a teacher.

Catherine currently lives with her husband and car in Northern Virginia.

This book is dedicated to

Carty Phillips

Remem

bering a friend who came to
see me 3 days before he hung himself
in the Galax City Jail in the 1970s

Made in the USA
Columbia, SC
16 September 2019